The Affairs of Harriet Walters, Spinster

Cathy Spencer

Comely
Press

Published by Comely Press

www.comelypress.com

978-0-9917259-7-7

To Kate and Laura.

May all your dreams come true.

Chapter One

The day that Harriet had dreaded was here; her last day at Willoway, the only home that she had ever known. When she had learned four months ago that she and her mother were to be forced out, Harriet had been overwhelmed. Where were they to go, what possessions could they take, what would happen to the servants? Father should have dealt with this, but Father was gone and Mother was prostrate with grief. So, Harriet had buried her emotions and grappled with practicalities. She had worked like a slave to make all of the arrangements, and now she was exhausted. Looking for a moment's respite, she ducked into the sitting room and sank onto a sheet-draped chair. Gazing about the room, she thought how cold and unfamiliar it looked with the furniture pushed up against the walls and everything packed away in crates. She should have had the leisure to tour about the house and grounds to make a proper goodbye, but Mother was keeping her too busy for such an indulgence. Mrs. Walters was frantic that she and her daughter should depart before her nephew arrived to take possession of the estate.

Her mother was calling her again. "Harriet! Harriet! Where are you?"

"Tarnation," Harriet muttered under her breath as Mrs. Walters hurried into the room, her face flushed and agitated.

"There you are. Did you find my mourning brooch? And what about the silver? Has Jenkins loaded it onto the wagon? Don't be dilly-dallying when there is still so much to be done."

Harriet rose from the chair and took her mother's arm. "Mother, calm yourself. Yes, I found the brooch yesterday and put it in your jewellery chest. As for the silver, Jenkins has taken care of it. Everyone is following my packing list, and we will be leaving as soon as John has finished loading the wagon. Now, why not sit down and rest for a moment? I don't want you getting another one of your headaches." She whisked the sheet off the chair she had just vacated and helped her mother to sit. Mrs. Walters shook her head and reached for her daughter's hand.

"Forgive me, my dear, I am sure that you are managing everything beautifully. It's just that I cannot bear the thought of seeing that man take possession of our home. Your dear father has been gone but three months, God rest his soul. I had hoped never to see this terrible day." Mrs. Walters' shoulders began to shake, and Harriet sighed and rubbed her mother's back. Jenkins, the housekeeper, entered the room carrying a tea tray.

"Here you are. I thought you might enjoy a cup before I put these things away. John says that everything is loaded onto the wagon, and that the carriage is waiting for you." Jenkins placed the tray upon a side table, and Mrs. Walters reached for the housekeeper's hand.

"Oh, Jenkins, what would we have done without you? I only hope that your new employers will treat you well, and that you will be happy in your new home."

Jenkins patted Mrs. Walters' hand. "Thank you, ma'am. I've heard good things about the Mercer family from my Elsie, and it will be a treat to have her only half a mile away. Not that I won't miss you and Miss Harriet and Willoway. It's been a real home to me these past sixteen years. Never mind, here's a good strong cup of tea and one for Miss Harriet. Drink that. You'll feel better for having something hot." Harriet and her mother sipped their tea, keeping their eyes resolutely on the floor to avoid the view of the disfigured room.

Finally, Harriet straightened from where she had leaned against the wall and handed her cup to Jenkins. "Time to go, Mother," she said. "Helen will be wondering what's happened to us if we don't leave soon." She turned to Jenkins, who held out her arms to the young woman. Harriet walked into the embrace and clung to the servant.

"Goodbye, Jenkins, I'll miss you very much," she whispered in a gruff voice. She brushed away a hot tear that trailed down her cheek, struggling to keep her emotions in check. Giving way now would set a bad example for her mother.

The housekeeper stepped back, holding Harriet at arms' length. "I'll miss you, Miss Harriet. You've always been a good girl, steady and dependable. I know that you'll see your mother settled in comfortably at your sister's. God bless you, and good luck in your new life, Miss."

Harriet nodded and backed away, allowing her mother time to say goodbye. Then, taking a deep breath and one last look around the room, Harriet laid a supportive arm around her mother's shoulders and gave her a small squeeze.

Mrs. Walters gazed up at her daughter, pressing her trembling lips together. "I'm ready Harriet," she whispered. Together, mother and daughter walked through the front door and down the stairs to the waiting carriage, leaving Willoway behind forever.

Chapter Two

Mr. Walters had contracted a blood infection the previous spring that had quickly claimed his life. His unexpected death had left his wife and younger daughter homeless. Willoway had been entailed to a male heir, and Mrs. Walters had produced only two living children. Philip Walters, Mr. Walters' estranged nephew, was now the legal master of Willoway even though he had not set foot on the estate for six years. Philip had not attended his uncle's funeral, but had written to his aunt to express his condolences and to inform her of his intention to take possession of the estate at the beginning of September.

Helen, Mrs. Walters' elder daughter, was happily married and settled some eleven miles distant in a house already bursting with her copious family. There was not enough room to accommodate both Harriet and her mother, so Mrs. Walters had prevailed upon her sister, Mrs. Edna Slater, to provide a home for her youngest. Aunt Edna has taken a fortnight to consider the request before consenting. After all, Harriet was twenty-six years of age with no marriage prospects in sight, so her stay was likely to be indefinite. After leaving Willoway, Harriet was to deliver her mother to Helen's home and enjoy a short visit before journeying to her aunt's house in the village of Rexton.

As the carriage and wagon drove up the drive to her sister's home, Harriet saw the front door open and Helen emerged, babe in arms, to greet them. Helen was like her mother: pretty, petite, and fair. Harriet, who took after her father's side of the family, was tall and thin with a ruddy complexion and wiry hair that resisted her attempts to control it. Helen waved, and stepped up to the carriage as it rolled to a stop.

"Mother, Harriet, how are you? You poor dears, you must be tired." Jumping down from his seat, John helped Mrs. Walters to alight. Helen handed him the baby and embraced her mother, while Harriet climbed down without assistance.

"Welcome to your new home, Mother," Helen said. "I hope that you will be as comfortable here as you were at Willoway. The children are so excited to have their grandmother living with them. Sinclair is away at the moment, but he will be home very soon to welcome you himself."

"Oh Helen," was all an overwhelmed Mrs. Walters could say.

Helen had left the front door open, and a collection of young Watts erupted onto the front lawn. One of them came to stand by her mother's skirts, thumb in mouth, while the twins shepherded the other children away from the horses' hooves. The eldest boy picked up a handful of stones and hurtled them, one by one, at the nearest window. Fortunately, he did not possess the necessary skill or strength to reach his target.

"Harriet," Helen said, turning to her sister, "I'm so glad that you can visit with us for a few days. You must be worn out from arranging the move. You are to do nothing while you are here. Rest. I will take care of everything." Knowing better, Harriet smiled and pecked a light kiss on her sister's cheek.

"Helen, how lovely you look. Just like a painted madonna."

Her sister dimpled with pleasure. "Thank you, dear, you are always so kind. But let's not stand about in the drive. Come into the house and have some refreshments. Stay away from the horses, my darlings, and don't make any trouble for John." Smiling, Helen led her mother and sister into the house as the eldest boy turned to target the carriage.

Harriet spent the afternoon helping her mother to unpack. There was no spare bedchamber for Harriet, so mother and daughter were forced to share until her departure. It was crowded, especially with a steady stream of children dashing in and out to see what their grandmother and Aunty Harriet were doing. After rescuing some of her mother's delicate trinkets from their grubby little fingers, Harriet was relieved when Nanny came to collect the children for dinner. By the end of the afternoon, Mrs. Walters was reclining on the bed with a cool cloth draped over her eyes while Harriet rested on a chair beside her, her stockinged feet propped upon the mattress.

"I had forgotten how exhausting Helen's brood can be," Harriet muttered.

"It will take some time to get used to them myself," her mother replied. "Willoway was very quiet compared to Helen's house."

"Yes, it was definitely livelier when Helen was still at home. There was always a crowd of young gentlemen waiting on her."

Mrs. Walters rolled onto her side to peer up at her daughter. "Did you mind very much, Harriet?"

Harriet considered her response for a moment. What could she say; that it had hurt like blazes when she was a young girl with dreams of romantic love and no suitors? That she had cried herself to sleep after balls where Helen had danced every dance with a different young man while she had sat with her mother and the other matrons?

"No, Mother, not so very much. I may have been a little jealous of Helen's popularity when I was a girl, but I am resigned to my spinsterhood now."

"To your credit, your father and I never observed any jealousy in your behaviour."

Harriet smiled. "How could anyone abuse Helen, Mother? She is always so well-intentioned."

"Even so, it is good that she has Sinclair to watch over her and the children. She does not have your good sense or your strength of will, my dear."

Harriet did not respond; this was her mother's favourite refrain. "Don't worry, Harriet. God may not have blessed you with beauty, but He has more than recompensed you with other gifts, such as intelligence and fortitude." She would have preferred the scales tipped a little more heavily on the side of attractiveness, but God had not consulted her wishes.

Harriet gripped the arms of her chair and pushed herself to her feet. "It's time we dressed for dinner. Let me help you find something to wear, and then I will dress."

"Thank you, my dear. I cannot seem to find anything in this room."

An hour later, Mrs. Walters, Harriet, Helen, and her husband, Sinclair, were seated around the massive dining room table enjoying a little quiet conversation with their meal. Sinclair had welcomed his mother-in-law with a kiss on the cheek, and Harriet with a brotherly embrace. Harriet had once harboured a passion for Sinclair when he had been one of Helen's more dashing suitors, but now that they were both older and his waist had grown while his hairline had receded, her feelings for this kind man had subsided into a sisterly affection.

"So, Mother Walters, how is Aunt Edna these days? I do not recall seeing her for years now – really not since our wedding day," Sinclair said, passing the cheese.

"It has been a long time since she visited Willoway. She became something of a recluse after Mr. Slater's death. Her recent letters have been full of ailments."

"I have always thought that Aunt Edna's health was tied to her spirits," Harriet murmured.

Mrs. Walters shrugged. "You may be right, dear."

Sinclair turned to his sister-in-law. "I hope that you'll feel free to visit us whenever you please, Harriet. I only wish that we could offer you a permanent home."

"You are very kind, Sinclair, but I am sure that I will soon think of my aunt's house as a second home."

"I am sure that your presence will result in an improvement to Edna's health and spirits," her mother said. Sinclair and Helen exchanged a doubtful glance that did not escape Harriet's notice.

Chapter Three

The remainder of Harriet's visit passed in a whirlwind of activity. While her sister sat tranquilly nearby doing needlework or writing letters, Harriet read stories to her nieces and nephews, tossed balls, ran races, searched for toads, and gave needlework lessons to the twins. Although Helen seemed insensible of the demands her children placed upon Harriet, Sinclair was more observant, and invited his sister-in-law for solitary country walks whenever his schedule permitted. Harriet treasured these outings. She had hidden her grief over the twin losses of both father and home from her mother, but Sinclair was a sympathetic audience to whom she could pour out her heart. She did not go so far as to share her misgivings over her new home, however. Despite what she had told the others, Harriet was too well-acquainted with her aunt's disposition to be optimistic of their living contentedly together, but she thought it unfair to burden her brother-in-law with concerns that he could not remedy.

On the morning of Harriet's departure, Mrs. Walters did not come down to breakfast. Instead, mother and daughter said their goodbyes privately before Harriet took her leave of Helen and the children.

"I am so glad that you were able to enjoy a little respite with us before taking up your duties with Aunt Edna," Helen said. "Give my love to Aunty, and do not worry about Mother. I will do my best to see that she is cheerful and comfortable."

"Thank you, Helen. I know that you will."

"Come along, Harriet, we must take advantage of the fine weather while it lasts," Sinclair said, both driver and escort on this expedition. Sinclair handed her into the carriage, and soon they were on their way.

It was a beautiful, early autumn day. The morning air held a hint of coolness, but the landscape was still lush and green with wild flowers blooming in patches along the road. The pair of horses seemed glad of the exercise, their shoes beating a jaunty rhythm. The journey was some thirty miles. With frequent stops to rest the horses, Sinclair planned to be in Rexton by late afternoon. Harriet tried to prevent her apprehension over her new life from spoiling her enjoyment of the day. It was a treat just to be free of all responsibility for a few hours.

As the afternoon shadows began to lengthen, Sinclair guided the carriage into Rexton's main street. Harriet had visited Rexton for her uncle's funeral four years earlier and was able to direct him to the house. They passed shops and a little green before finally stopping before a handsome brick building. Two windows framed the front door, while five more adorned the second storey. An iron fence encompassed the lawn, with large, leafy oak trees standing on either side of a walkway bordered by curving flower beds. Neither a stray leaf nor a dead blossom disturbed the neatness and precision of the yard.

They studied the house in silence for a moment. Turning to her, Sinclair said, "Well, Harriet, are you ready?"

Harriet nodded, and together they stepped through the well-oiled gate and proceeded to the front door. A young maid wearing a ribboned cap and an apron over a plain grey dress responded to Sinclair's knock.

"Good afternoon. I am Sinclair Watts and this is my sister-in-law, Miss Walters. I believe that Mrs. Slater is expecting us?"

"Yes, sir," said the maid, bobbing a curtsy. "Come right this way." She led them down a carpeted hallway to the sitting room, announcing them to the room's single occupant.

Plush velvet drapes were drawn against the late afternoon sun, so it took a moment for Harriet's eyes to accustom themselves to the gloomy interior. The room was furnished with heavy wooden furniture belonging to an earlier age. A bronze eagle held pride of place on a side table beside a sofa. In the middle of that sofa sat a diminutive lady in dull black bombazine, a silver mourning brooch her sole ornament. Her small black eyes flitted from visitor to visitor.

"Good afternoon, Aunt Edna. I hope that you are well?" Harriet said, curtsying. "You remember my sister's husband, Mr. Sinclair Watts?"

"Yes, I remember you, sir. How d'you do?"

"Very well, Aunt Edna," he replied, stepping forward to bow. "I'm pleased to see you again. It has been some time since last we met. Perhaps it was at my wedding?"

"No, sir. Before he passed – God rest his soul – my husband and I attended your first child's christening," she responded. She eyed Sinclair for a moment. "You've grown stouter since then." Gesturing to chairs on either side of the sofa, she added, "Be seated, if you please."

"Thank you, Aunt," Harriet said as she and Sinclair took their seats. Harriet's eyes were drawn to the faded pattern in the Persian carpet at her feet. Looking up, she found the older woman watching her.

"Mother and Helen send their love," she said, attempting to make polite conversation.

"Yes, how is your mother, now that she has lost both house and husband? I was too unwell to attend the funeral myself. I had one of my terrible headaches. I am often plagued by them, and am forced to go to bed for days on end when I have one. Only a little chicken broth will do when I am so afflicted. I have a dull headache today, as a matter of fact. That is why the draperies are drawn."

"I'm sorry to hear that you are unwell, Aunt," Harriet said. "Mother misses Father very much, of course, but Helen and Sinclair have made her quite comfortable in their home."

"What foolishness, to be turned out of one's home at her age. Had your father provided better for you, you would not now have to rely upon the charity of your relations."

Harriet was angered by this slur upon her father, but held her tongue and stared stonily at the floor. She had to rely upon this woman for her living now, and it wouldn't do to begin with a fight. Sinclair coughed, and Aunt Edna turned to him.

"I trust that you are well, sir? I am too prone to respiratory infections to risk entertaining a contagion."

"No indeed, I am quite fit, Aunt. Just a little dryness in the throat. Travelling thirty miles can be thirsty work."

"Humph. Niece, pull the cord for the maid."

Harriet rose and did as she was bid, and the neat little maid returned.

"Grace, where is the tea? It's late," her employer said.

"Cook was just adding the teapot to the tray when you rang, ma'am."

"Well, run and fetch it, girl. Don't keep us waiting." Grace scurried out of the room and returned minutes later laden with a heavy silver tea service and a plate of sandwiches.

"You might as well pour, Niece – it will be your duty from now on. What are you waiting for, Grace, get back to work."

"Yes, ma'am."

Harriet looked questioningly at her aunt. "I like my tea undiluted, but sweet. Put in three spoonfuls of sugar, if you please."

"Yes, Aunt." Harriet poured and stirred in the sugar before passing the cup to the lady.

"What kind of sandwiches did Cook make today?" Aunt Edna asked, eying the plate.

"They appear to be chicken."

"Good, I can stomach a little chicken. Pass the plate, if you please."

Harriet obliged, and then poured tea for Sinclair and for herself. The trio lapsed into silence as Aunt Edna chewed her sandwich. When the widow showed no sign of offering food to her guests, Harriet reached for the plate and offered it to Sinclair before taking a sandwich for herself.

Aunt Edna said, "Dinner is served at six o' clock here. I do not tolerate people coming in late to meals. I have a delicate stomach and I must eat regularly. Plain food – none of your rich sauces for me. I retire early and I rise early, unless I am unwell and obliged to spend the day in bed. You will run errands for me, Niece. It will save the servants trouble, and provide you with some exercise. You can start by going to the milliner tomorrow. The hat she sent was not at all what I had ordered. She trimmed it with beads instead of feathers, and it looks shoddy. You will return the hat and have her fix it to my specifications. I also told Reverend Simons that you will be stopping by tomorrow to discuss parish visits. The reverend is a good, solid man, but he needs more support from the parish. Some of the female members are shockingly lax in their duties, and I expect you to set an example for them.

"Yes, Aunt Edna," Harriet said, shrinking before this sudden onslaught.

"I also want you to watch for those ruffians from the boys' grammar school. My gardener, Brown, has caught them climbing into my orchard more times than I care to remember. Climbing over the wall and stealing my apples, can you believe their impudence? I complained to the headmaster once, but he is ineffectual." Aunt Edna scowled.

"But what can Harriet do about the boys?" Sinclair asked.

"Why, I expect her to keep her eyes open and a stout stick handy. Send those boys back over the wall with a good smack. I truly wonder at the way young people are raised these days, with no respect for other people's property. Boys need to have respect knocked into them, in my mind. You just look sharp when you're in the garden, Harriet."

"Yes, ma'am." Harriet glanced at Sinclair out of the corner of her eye. He was staring at the carpet, one corner of his mouth twitching dangerously.

"Well, that's all I have to say about your duties for the moment. I'm sure that I will remember more when the occasion presents itself. Summon Grace, and have her show you and Mr. Watts upstairs to your rooms. The groomsman will bring up your trunks. I'm going to lie down for a little rest before dinner. I will meet you in the dining room at six o' clock sharp."

Sinclair and Harriet stood as Aunt Edna rose and left the room. Harriet sank back into her chair with a sigh, while Sinclair patted her shoulder.

Chapter Four

Sinclair gave his sister-in-law an affectionate kiss before leaving after breakfast the next morning. Aunt Edna gave him a curt nod, and sent Harriet to the milliner's shop. Harriet was forced to make a second visit before the hat's decoration satisfied her aunt, and was then dispatched to wait upon Reverend Simons at the manse. The manse was situated at the end of a side street next to the church and the solitary graveyard. A sober-faced, sturdy female of indeterminate age admitted Harriet, escorting her to the reverend's study and announcing, "A Miss Walters to see you, Reverend."

"How do you do, Miss Walters," said the gentleman in a deep, rumbling voice, rising from behind his desk. Middle-aged and angular with silver streaks threading through his black hair, Reverend Simons' reserved manner was as welcoming as the graveyard's next door.

"Very well, thank you, sir. Pleased to make your acquaintance," Harriet said with a curtsy. "I've come on my aunt's bidding. She thought that I might help with the parish visits."

"Ah, yes, I remember discussing it with her. So, you have arrived at last, Miss Walters. I hope that you will be a credit to your aunt's fine name in this community. Please sit while I make up a list."

The good man sat back down behind his desk while Harriet passed the time looking about the drab room. The only decoration was an oil painting of Christ in agony upon the cross. His wounds were particularly sensational, and Harriet looked away in dismay. Privately, she had misgivings about the success of these visits, although her sense of obligation goaded her into trying. Harriet had accompanied her mother on charitable visits back at Willoway, but she had never known what to say to the elderly and infirm, and had left all of the talking to her mother.

When the reverend finished writing and handed her the folded paper, she rose and promised to visit the name at the top of the list that very day.

"Ah, yes, that would be Mrs. Higgins," Reverend Simons said, walking Harriet to the study door. "She is somewhat deaf, although she would never admit to it. Enunciate clearly, speak slowly, and you should do well, Miss Walters."

"Yes, Reverend Simons. I shall try my best."

He nodded. "That is all God asks of you, child. Neglect your Christian duty at the peril of your soul."

"Indeed, sir, I shall do my best," Harriet promised, backing into the hallway before turning to escape the manse as quickly as she could. Standing outside on the sidewalk, Harriet unfolded the list and studied the seven names written there. None of them meant anything to her. "Heaven help me, why must the first one be deaf?" she muttered.

Harriet tucked the paper into her reticule and followed the reverend's directions to Mrs. Higgins' home on the outskirts of the village. She was pleasantly surprised to find a pretty thatched cottage with roses blooming in the front garden, but the path leading up to the door was overgrown, and Harriet surmised that the widow had to rely upon others for the property's upkeep. Squaring her shoulders, she strode up to the front door and rapped hard with the iron knocker. When there was no response, she rapped even harder.

"Coming, I'm coming, wait for me," a reedy voice called from within. The door creaked open to reveal a round, elderly female with white hair knotted on top of her head, her wrinkled face wreathed in a welcoming smile. Her sleeves were pushed up to the elbows and her forearms were dusted with flour. The widow wiped her hands on her apron.

"Yes, my dear, what can I do for you?" she asked.

"Good day, ma'am. Are you Mrs. Higgins?"

"Yes, my love."

"How do you do? My name is Harriet Walters. I am Mrs. Slater's niece, recently arrived in Rexton. Reverend Simons suggested that you might enjoy a visit.

"Reverend Simons?" Mrs. Higgins queried.

"That's right, Reverend Simons sent me."

"You must be new to the parish. I haven't seen you before. Come in, my dear, come in. Why don't you follow me back to the kitchen? I was just having a cup of tea. I didn't catch your name, my love?"

"My name is Harriet Walters."

"Harriet Waters?"

"No, Harriet Walters," she shouted.

"Oh, Walters," Mrs. Higgins said with a nod while leading the way to a well-scrubbed kitchen. A lump of pastry and a rolling pin sat on top of a floured wooden table in the middle of the room. "I was just making a pie for my supper. Why don't you sit in that chair by the back door where there's a bit of a breeze blowing while I pour you a cup of tea. It's a might hot in here with the oven heating. What do you take, dear?"

"Just a little sugar, please."

"Just the way I like it," Mrs. Higgins said, pouring milk into the cup before the tea and handing it to Harriet. "I made some shortbread this morning. Would you like some?"

"Please don't go to any trouble."

"Oh, no trouble, no trouble."

Harriet sipped her tea as Mrs. Higgins limped to the pantry and reached down a tin. "Here you are," she said, placing it before Harriet. "Help yourself while I finish rolling out my crust. The oven will be just right soon, and I want to get my pie baking."

Harriet noticed a bowl of peeled apples sitting on the table next to Mrs. Higgins' elbow.

"Can I cut those up for you, Mrs. Higgins?" she asked.

"What was that, dear?"

Harriet picked up the knife from beside the bowl and waved it over the apples. "May I slice the apples for your pie?"

"That's right, I grow the apples right here in my own back garden. My neighbour's youngest comes over evenings to gather them for me."

Harriet plucked an apple from the bowl and began slicing it.

"Why, that's right kind of you," the widow said. She rolled out the pastry and fit it into a pie plate, telling Harriet all about her children and grandchildren as she worked. "And then there's my second son's wife by the name of Ellie. She's not from around here, you know. Her people live about ten miles down the road from Rexton."

Mrs. Higgins rattled on while Harriet watched her mix sugar, flour, and spices together, tossing them with the apples before dumping the coated fruit into the crust. She cut some scraps of butter to pat over the fruit before rolling out a second crust to top the pie. Crimping the edges and cutting some slots into the pastry, Mrs. Higgins finished the pie and popped it into the oven.

"Well, that's done. Can I invite you to stop and have some supper with me, Miss Waters? I have a nice piece of cold tongue left over from yesterday, and I was about to fix some potatoes and beans to go with it."

"You are very kind, Mrs. Higgins, but I must be getting home to my aunt. She is expecting me for dinner. Thank you all the same for the delicious shortbread and tea, though. I hope that I may drop in to visit you again sometime."

"Another visit? Well, of course you can, my dear, of course. There's nothing I'd like better. I'm always at home or around back, working in my garden. Why don't we just step out the front door and I'll cut some roses for your aunt. They're doing very well with this fine weather. Just right down the hallway and through the door, my love. It will only take a minute."

Harriet returned to her aunt's house with a lovely nosegay wrapped in a spare piece of brown paper that Mrs. Higgins had found stuffed in a kitchen drawer. Harriet handed Grace the flowers before bolting up the stairs to change her dress. She was late for dinner, and her aunt would be expecting her.

Harriet found her aunt in the sitting room with a pot of tea, but she was not alone; a mature woman with silvery hair sat on the sofa beside her. The lady was dressed in a fine muslin gown and a straw hat decorated with a profusion of autumnal fruits and flowers. She smiled widely as Harriet stopped short and curtsied.

"I beg your pardon, Aunt. I did not realize that you had company."

"Come and sit down, Harriet. Where have you been all afternoon? Mabel, let me present my niece, Miss Harriet Walters. She's my sister's youngest. Remember me telling you that my sister's husband died and the estate was entailed away to the nephew? Harriet, this is Mrs. Evans, a neighbour and a life-long friend."

"How do you do, Miss Walters? You look very well with your cheeks all pink from being out-of-doors. It is a fine afternoon, isn't it?" the lady said.

"Yes, lovely. I am pleased to make your acquaintance, Mrs. Evans." Turning to her aunt, Harriet said, "I visited Reverend Simons at the manse, and he gave me a list of parishioners to visit. I have just come back from seeing Mrs. Higgins."

"Visiting the parishioners already, Miss Walters? How kind of you," Mrs. Evans said as Harriet sat down. "You can't have been in Rexton very long yourself."

"She arrived yesterday, Mabel."

Mrs. Evans' eyebrows rose in surprise. "Just yesterday? And how did your visit with Mrs. Higgins go?"

"Quite well, I think. Mrs. Higgins told me all about her family and gave me tea and shortbread. So I fear that I do not have much appetite for dinner, Aunt."

"Well, pour yourself a cup anyway. It's a thirsty walk from Mrs. Higgins' house. I was just telling Mabel about my new hat and the trouble the milliner gave me with it. I swear that I will take my business elsewhere if she doesn't follow my instructions in the future."

Harriet was tired from her exertions and sat back in her chair, allowing the conversation to wash over her. Mrs. Evans smiled at her from time to time and directed an occasional comment her way. Harriet thought that she had a pleasant voice and a kindly face, while the lively gleam in her eyes bespoke intelligence.

After half an hour, Mrs. Evans said, "Look at the time! I have to return a book of poetry to the lending library, and it's half an hour before closing. But, before I go, I am curious to see who else is on your visiting list, if I may, Miss Walters?"

"Certainly," Harriet said, passing it to the lady.

"Reverend Simons will have you making a tour of the village with these far-flung addresses! I hope that you are athletic, Miss Walters, or perhaps your aunt will lend you her carriage to visit some of the country addresses?"

"Oh, the carriage is unnecessary. I am quite a walker, Mrs. Evans."

"How tireless youth is. Well, the rest of your shut-ins are all old dears like Mrs. Higgins, so you should have no difficulty in getting to know them."

"Yes, Mrs. Higgins did most of the talking today. All I had to do was listen, which was more than agreeable to me."

"Edna, we must think of some young people for Miss Walters to meet now that she is here. I would introduce you to my daughter, Miss Walters, but Diane lives in London with her husband, and only comes to visit once or twice a year. Rexton is a pretty spot, but it lacks society."

"Well, what can one expect when our houses and the manse are the only decent homes in the village, Mabel? I'm sure that my niece did not expect to find society here in Rexton."

"No, Aunt, I assure you that I did not have any such expectations."

"Of course not, Edna. I did not mean to suggest that," Mrs. Evans said. "All the same, it's too bad that there are so few young people in the village."

"What with my Henry doctoring in Jamaica, and Lucy and Caroline with their own families, Harriet cannot expect young people to be visiting me every day. Of course, when I pass over, Henry will inherit my property and return to England. He writes of how much he misses our climate and civilized society, but a young doctor must take what opportunities he can to establish himself."

"Of course, Edna," Mrs. Evans said, patting her friend's hand and glancing at Harriet. "Well, the least I can do is to invite you both to dinner. How would Wednesday suit?"

"Don't worry about Harriet. She is sure not to have any prior engagements," Aunt Edna said with a snort. "Wednesday evening will suit us just fine."

"Wonderful," said Mrs. Evans, rising from the couch. "I look forward to your visit." Aunt Edna walked her friend to the front door, leaving Harriet in happy anticipation of at least one evening that week not spent entirely in her aunt's company.

Chapter Five

The next day was unseasonably cool, and rain lashed against the windows all day long. Aunt Edna complained of joint pain and headache and kept to her room. She still managed to keep Harriet busy, however, with mending and reading aloud from religious tracts until Harriet thought she would go mad. Fortunately, the rain ended overnight, and the sun broke through the clouds the following morning. Harriet decided to escape outside before her aunt could assign her any new chores.

Donning an old pair of sturdy shoes before venturing out, Harriet crunched along the gravel path that led from the house into the formal garden. A gentle breeze whispered through the shrubberies' freshly-washed leaves. Harriet trailed her fingers through the droplets spattered atop a box hedge and paused to inhale the scent of pine.

Rounding a corner, she came upon a charming scene: the path led up a hill to a dainty bridge with a miniature Grecian temple perched on top. Harriet strolled over the bridge, pausing to watch the crystalline water tumbling over the stones, before climbing the slope to the temple. She passed through the portico and found an iron bench to rest upon.

"The garden is certainly pleasant," she thought. "My aunt must have employed an architect to do this – I do not see her sour hand in its design. It's comforting to know that all of this awaits outside if I can but escape the house."

Abandoning the temple, Harriet followed the path until it ended in an apple grove, enclosed on three sides by an ivy-covered, stone wall. She lingered among the dripping trees, relishing the air's earthy scent. The boughs were heavy with fruit and Harriet plucked a ripe-looking specimen. Munching as she picked her way through the trees, she eventually came to the wall. She could hear children's voices outside in the street and laughed, wondering if these were some of the "ruffians" from the grammar school that her aunt had warned her against. Their chattering drew closer, and then stopped. Harriet was about to stroll away again when she heard a scrabbling sound on the far side of the wall. She froze; it sounded as if someone were scaling it.

As she watched, a hand fumbled for the top, and a leg was flung over the wall. Harriet was of two minds; should she stay to repel the intruder, or should she hurry back to the house and let the gardener worry about it? She decided to see what would develop, and darted into the shadows behind a tree to hide.

All was still, and then she heard a thud. Peering from behind her tree, Harriet saw a diminutive boy of perhaps seven or eight crouched in the sunlight next to the wall. With his blond curls and rosy cheeks, he looked more like a cherub than the devil his behaviour suggested. He was dressed in the short pants, white shirt, and grey jacket of the boys' grammar school.

The child surveyed his surroundings before straightening from his crouch. "I'm in the orchard," he called to his confederates on the other side of the wall.

"Just don't let the old lady catch you, Oliver. She said she'd have the constable on anyone who trespassed in her orchard again." A chorus of jeers followed this remark.

Oliver's eyes grew large, and he swallowed. "Right," he said to himself. Leaving the relative safety of the wall, he ventured into the trees. He passed close to Harriet, his eyes on the ground, searching for apples. The rain had driven some of the riper fruit from their branches, and he picked up one after another and stuffed them into his pockets.

Branches creaked overhead, and his eyes rose to consider them. The closest branch was too high for Oliver's reach, but he ran to the base of the tree anyway. Grasping the trunk with his hands and knees, he pulled himself up. The coarse bark scraped his skin as he climbed to just below the branch, his small fingers straining to grasp it. Harriet snuck closer until she stood beside the tree, concerned that the fragile-looking child might fall. He seemed to give up, hanging by both hands for a moment, until suddenly launching himself at the branch. Harriet gasped, Oliver's startled eyes met hers, and he missed the branch and fell crashing to the ground.

Harriet dropped to her knees beside the child. His eyes were closed and his chest was still. She touched his face, and his eyes popped open in terror.

"Don't call the constable, lady! I'll give the apples back. I only took the spoiled ones," he said.

As the boy scrambled to rise, Harriet noticed a trickle of blood dripping onto the back of his collar. He teetered, and she caught him as he fell. Oliver screamed and struggled in her arms.

"Help! Help! The old lady's got me!" he cried.

"No, it's all right. I'm not going to hurt you," Harriet said, trying to hold him still until she could determine the extent of his injuries. The other boys heard, however, and screamed his name in the street.

A man's voice abruptly shouted, "I'm coming, Oliver!"

Panicking, Harriet released the child and jumped to her feet. She stared as a man scrambled over the wall, lowering himself by his arms and jumping the last feet to the ground. He was tall, spare, and young, dressed in a scholarly black gown atop a tweed suit. Spotting Harriet with the boy at her feet, he ran pell-mell toward them.

"Hey, what do you think you're doing there!" he shouted. Harriet shrank back as he reached them, shooting one furious glance at her before crouching beside the child.

"What happened, Oliver? Are you hurt?" He caught sight of the blood on the boy's collar and said, "You *are* hurt." Pulling a handkerchief from his pocket, he shook it out and pressed it against the wound.

"I'm fine, sir," Oliver said, struggling to sit up. The young man helped him into a sitting position while Harriet hovered beside them.

"Did you hit him?" the man demanded, glaring at her before gently parting the boy's hair. Oliver winced.

"What? No, of course not. He hurt himself falling out of the tree," Harriet sputtered.

The man spared her a withering glance before turning back to the boy. "Does your head hurt, Oliver?"

"No, sir."

"Can you stand?"

"I think so."

The man stood and helped Oliver to his feet. He ran his hands up and down the boy's limbs, searching for other injuries.

"Shall we take him back to the house? I can fetch a doctor," Harriet suggested.

"No, I don't think that's necessary, Miss . . ?"

"Walters."

"The cut on his neck is superficial. You've got some scrapes on your knees, though, Oliver. How did you come by them?"

The child hung his head. "Climbing up the tree, sir. I was climbing it when the lady screamed, and I fell."

"I see." The young man turned to Harriet. "It seems that you were telling the truth."

"Of course I was telling the truth, Mr. . . ?" Harriet retorted.

"Ash. I'm the history master at the boys' school."

"Well, Mr. Ash, that's exactly what happened. How dare you think that I would strike a child?"

"I apologize, Miss Walters. Only, the way that the other boys were screaming, I thought that Oliver was being attacked."

"When in fact he was in the orchard to steal apples," Harriet said with a stony face.

"I know, and I'm sorry. The headmaster has warned the boys against trespassing on Mrs. Slater's property, but young Oliver can't seem to resist a dare, no matter how foolish it is. Mrs. Slater is quite a tartar, so I hope that you will find it in your heart not to report this to your employer. I will see that Oliver is suitably punished for his transgression."

"To my employer?" Harriet said, scowling. "Who do you take me for? To my aunt, you mean." She crossed her arms over her chest and glared at the schoolmaster, who stared back at her in confusion until understanding dawned upon his face. Oliver looked from one adult to the other.

"I beg your pardon. I did not know that Mrs. Slater had a niece visiting."

"Living with her, sir. I am living with Mrs. Slater."

"It would seem that I am behind in the village gossip. My apologies again, Miss . . ?"

"Walters!" Harriet snapped. "I'm in mourning. And my dress is perfectly adequate."

Ash hesitated, fearful of putting his foot wrong again. "I beg your pardon?"

"Yes, the shoes are old, but it's been raining, and I didn't want to spoil my other pair."

"No, of course not. Your shoes look perfectly serviceable. And my condolences on your loss."

"Hmm," she said, pushing the hair out of her face.

"Perhaps Oliver and I should be going?"

"Yes, I really think that you should."

"But before we do, let me apologize again for Oliver's trespass and for anything I might have said in the heat of the moment that offended you."

"I'm very sorry, Miss. I promise I shall never do it again," Oliver added in a pleading tone.

Harriet glanced down at his small, anxious face, and half-smiled. "I'm sure that you won't, Oliver, and I'm glad that you didn't hurt yourself too badly by falling out of the tree."

"Oh, that was nothing. My ma says I've got more lives than a cat."

"Really," she said with a larger smile. "I'm glad to hear that."

"Yes, she said that all her children put together don't get in as much trouble as I do. She said that . . ."

"That's enough, Oliver. We've taken up enough of Miss Walters' time," the schoolmaster said, taking the boy by the arm and turning to Harriet. "I wish that we could have met under more pleasant circumstances, Miss Walters, and I hope that you will forgive my churlishness when you consider this incident, and not report it to your aunt." He smiled hopefully, and Harriet noticed that he had fine hazel eyes that crinkled quite attractively when he smiled.

"Well, no harm has been done, and Oliver has learned his lesson, I should think, so I see no point in bothering my aunt with this matter."

Oliver beamed and Ash nodded gratefully. "Thank you. We will leave you now so that you can get on with your day. This way, Oliver." Ash took the boy's hand and hurried toward the wall, only to hesitate and return again. Harriet sighed in exasperation, wishing them gone.

"What now?" she asked.

"We'll just be leaving the other way – through the gate, if you don't mind," Ash said with a rueful smile.

"Yes. Fine. Good day to you, sir," Harriet said, turning her back on them and heading for the house.

Chapter Six

That evening, Harriet and her aunt drove the few blocks to Mrs. Evans' home. Situated at the top of the main street, it was the grandest house in Rexton, a three-storey, honey-coloured stone edifice with an iron gate surrounding the property. The carriage passed through the gates and round the circular drive to the front entrance. A footman hastened to assist them from the carriage, and a butler responded to their knock at the front door.

"Good evening, Mrs. Slater," he said with a bow.

"Good evening, Rogers. I believe that Mrs. Evans is expecting us?"

"Yes, madam. Please follow me." Harriet and Aunt Edna followed him down a spacious hallway and into the drawing room, where Mrs. Evans rose to greet them. The room was too comfortable to be considered elegant; the furniture was over-stuffed and scattered in casual groupings with cheerful bouquets of garden flowers displayed on every table. A great slate fireplace with a crackling fire gave the room a handsome focal point.

"How are you this evening Edna, Miss Walters? Please sit down and be comfortable," their hostess said. "Dinner will be ready shortly. Can I offer you a glass of Madeira?"

"I will take a glass," Aunt Edna responded, settling herself on a sofa in close proximity to the fire. Rogers returned with a wine decanter and three crystal glasses, and served the ladies.

"Have you managed to go outdoors much over the past two days, Miss Walters?" Mrs. Evans inquired as she accepted a glass from the butler. "It has been disagreeably wet and cool."

"She went for a long walk in the garden today," Aunt Edna said, taking a generous sip from her glass. "The hem of her gown was disgraceful when she returned. I do not understand why anyone would want to go out walking after a rain before the puddles had dried up."

"No doubt an energetic nature like yours grows impatient with confinement, Miss Walters?"

"Yes. It was a beautiful morning, and I wished to explore my aunt's garden. It's been years since I've seen it."

"I can understand that. Did the garden meet your expectations?"

"Yes, both it and the apple grove. The air was delicious after the rain, and the trees are so fine and sturdy. There will be an abundant crop this year."

"You're right about that, Harriet. Mabel, there will be plenty of apples to press into cider if you wish to keep to our usual terms?" Aunt Edna said.

"That will suit me fine, Edna. You see, Miss Walters, Edna and I exchange apples for hazelnuts when the crops are too abundant for our own needs."

"That sounds like a beneficial arrangement."

"Yes, it works out well. I believe that Cook has made a hazelnut torte for dessert tonight. She has a variety of ingenious ways to use up the nuts, including a particularly delicious hazelnut praline candy."

"I look forward to dessert then, Mrs. Evans."

The lady bent toward Harriet. "Yes, it's a shame we have to bother with the soup and the other courses when I would rather begin with the torte," she said, her eyes twinkling.

Rogers arrived to announce that dinner was ready. "Shall we go in?" asked Mrs. Evans, shepherding her guests into the dining room.

The rest of the week passed quietly for Harriet. She occupied herself with exploring the village and calling upon the widows remaining on her list. She always carried a homemade offering from her aunt's pantry on these calls, and came away with vegetables or flowers from her hostesses' gardens. Harriet still felt awkward on these visits, but the elderly women seemed glad of her company, and she was satisfied that her efforts were appreciated.

Sunday arrived, and Harriet accompanied her aunt to church. She had been looking forward to seeing the church interior since first setting eyes on it. One of Harriet's great pleasures was to tour old churches and tumbled-down ruins, her mind imagining what life had been like in the days when these structures had been new.

St. Michael's was a fourteenth century stone church of middling size with stone gargoyles grimacing down from the bell tower on passersby beneath. Entering the nave's dim interior, Harriet estimated that there was room for some two hundred people inside. She admired the beautifully carved wooden pews and the pulpit with its plump, painted cherubs. A jewel-toned, stained-glass window situated above the altar depicted the triumph of the Archangel Michael over the serpent.

As Harriet's eyes rose toward the vaulted ceiling, Aunt Edna whispered, "Watch where you're going, Niece. Don't be gawking all about." Harriet lowered her eyes and obediently followed her aunt into the Slater family stall. Mrs. Evans was already seated in the next stall, and gave Harriet a cheery little wave as Aunt Edna bowed her head in prayer. Harriet smiled and nodded back before glancing at the congregation. Occasionally, she caught the eye of someone she knew, and was rewarded with a welcoming nod or smile.

Harriet opened the hymnal to the first song and was humming it under her breath when a commotion broke out at the rear of the church. A group of some fifty schoolboys of assorted sizes and ages, overseen by five male adults, came trooping inside. Mr. Ash, dressed in a dark brown suit and carrying his hat, was part of their company. His hair was combed and his face solemn, giving him a very different appearance from the tousle-haired, chagrined young man Harriet had last seen leaving the orchard.

He led his charges into a pew and, taking his place amongst them, bowed his head in prayer. Harriet watched as he turned to shush some whispering boys, and caught his eye as he faced forward again. She acknowledged him with a cool nod and averted her gaze. Then the minister and his attendants processed up the aisle, and Harriet focused her attention on the liturgy.

It was a lively service, punctuated with shuffling feet, sniffles, and "hushes" from the grammar school pews. Aunt Edna glared over her shoulder at one particularly loud sneeze, and Harriet hid a smile behind her prayer book. When the school party came forward at communion, Harriet watched for Mr. Ash out of the corner of her eye. His head was bowed in prayer as he went by, and she made certain to be engrossed in her hymnal when he headed back to his pew.

Aunt Edna leaned over to whisper, "I mean to speak to the headmaster before he gets away after service, so we must leave as soon as the last hymn is finished. Don't take too long greeting Reverend Simons at the church door."

"Yes, Aunt."

Before the echoes of the final hymn had dyed away, Aunt Edna was on her feet and marching down the aisle. She dodged around the slower-moving parishioners, forcing Harriet to trot to keep up with her. She said a perfunctory, "Good morning, Reverend," before hurrying through the door, the minister still rising from his bow as she breezed past him.

"Mr. Harris, Mr. Harris, a word with you!" Aunt Edna cried as she pushed through the crowd of milling boys who had spilled out of the church the moment they were released. A slight, white-haired man turned in answer to her hail. He fixed a smile upon his face and came forward to greet her. Harriet noticed that Mr. Ash paused to watch as the headmaster and her aunt drew together. His eyes sought Harriet, but he looked away when he saw her watching him.

The headmaster bowed deeply, removing his hat and raising good-natured eyes to Aunt Edna's face. "Good morning, Mrs. Slater. What a fine day. I trust that you are in good health?"

"I am well, thank you, sir. Let me introduce you to my niece, Miss Harriet Walters. Miss Walters lives with me now."

Harriet curtsied as Mr. Harris bowed again. "Very happy to make your acquaintance, Miss Walters," he said before returning his attention to her aunt. "Is there anything that I can do for you today? I trust that there has been no further interaction between my boys and your apple trees?"

"None that I know of, Mr. Harris. On the contrary, I have a little proposition for you that would be of benefit to us both."

"Indeed? How very interesting."

"Yes. You see, it's time to harvest my apples, but we are short-staffed this year and the crop is particularly large. Normally, my gardener's daughter and her husband would assist us, but the young man fell and broke his leg, so they cannot come. Since your boys are so good at scaling my trees, I thought that some of the older ones might harvest the crop under my gardener's supervision. In return, I will pay for their labour in cider. What do you say to that, Mr. Harris?"

"It's a tempting proposition, Mrs. Slater, very tempting. Of course, the boys must not miss any of their lessons, but they could come by mid-afternoon and work until early evening."

Aunt Edna sniffed. "The harvest will take longer if they cannot work full days, but I suppose that it will have to do. I can provide refreshments for them."

"I will need one of the masters to accompany and supervise the boys. We take full responsibility for their safety while they are away from home, as you can no doubt appreciate. Perhaps our youngest and most athletic master, Mr. Ash, would be the best choice." Mr. Harris pointed toward the schoolmaster, and Aunt Edna turned to consider him. "He is very good with the boys. Of course, I would have to obtain his approval to the scheme."

"Hmm – I suppose another pair of adult hands would be useful. The harvest will be finished all the sooner. That would be agreeable, Mr. Harris."

"Let me put it to Mr. Ash then," the headmaster said, turning away and beckoning to the young man. Mr. Harris and Mr. Ash consulted while Harriet and her aunt waited. The history master nodded, and Mr. Harris patted him on the shoulder before returning.

"Mr. Ash has generously consented to your plan, Mrs. Slater. They can start tomorrow afternoon, if that would suit?"

"That would suit me excellently. Have them call at the kitchen door, and Brown, my gardener, will escort them to the grove. A pleasure doing business with you, sir."

"And with you, Mrs. Slater. Miss Walters, it was delightful meeting you," he added, bowing with a smile. "Good day, ladies."

The headmaster returned to his flock, and the grammar school company set off for home. Harriet looked over her shoulder and intercepted a glare from Mr. Ash as he turned to go.

"Poor man, I imagine he felt coerced into today's scheme," she thought, accompanying her aunt to the carriage.

Chapter Seven

Mr. Ash and a crew of eight boys arrived promptly the following afternoon. Harriet caught sight of them from her aunt's bedroom, where she was helping the elderly woman to unpack and air her winter clothing. She stared down wistfully at the little troop, wishing that she could join them rather than remaining shut up in her aunt's stuffy chamber.

"Harriet, have you seen my muff? I'm sure that I packed it in the trunk with my fox tippet. Where can it be?" Aunt Edna asked.

"Coming," Harriet replied, tearing herself away from the window.

An hour later there was a rap at the door, and Grace entered the room. "Excuse me, ma'am, but Cook was wondering about sending the buttermilk down to the gentleman and the boys from the school?"

"I already instructed her to send Sara down to the orchard with the buttermilk," Aunt Edna said.

"Only, Cook was wondering if she should wait until they come in for refreshments? There are ten of them with Mr. Brown, and Sara would have to make two trips to carry enough buttermilk. Cook doesn't want to part with her for so long."

"I could carry the second bucket if you like," Harriet offered. "Then Sara could return sooner to help with the refreshments."

Aunt Edna considered her suggestion for a moment. "You make sense, Niece. Hurry down to Cook and tell her that you will help Sara. Grace, you stay here and help me finish unpacking my clothes."

Harriet fairly burst from the room, delighted to make her escape. She ran down the back stairs to the kitchen to inform Cook of the change in plan. Cook filled a second bucket with buttermilk, and the two women left the house together, swinging the buckets by their rope handles. Sara seemed as happy to escape Cook as Harriet did her from aunt, and chatted all the way about the difficulties of making "proper" pastry.

By the time they had reached the orchard, Harriet's arm ached from carrying her load. She rested the bucket on the ground and looked around to see what the harvesters were doing. Mr. Brown knew how to work his crew efficiently. He had Ash and the four largest boys, wearing leather aprons with pockets, propped up in the trees picking apples while the younger boys collected and sorted the apples into baskets on a low wagon.

Brown smiled at the young women. "Ah, Miss Walters, I didn't expect to see you here. It's good of you to come along with the buttermilk and young Sara. We were getting fair parched. Here, boys, come and sit down on the grass, and Sara will pour you a drink. Miss Walters, would you mind serving our workers on the ladders?"

"Not at all, Mr. Brown."

The larger boys scurried down their ladders on Harriet's arrival, and pressed around her. She passed a wooden cup between them, and they took turns drinking. They thanked her when they had finished and sat down on the grass to rest. Ash did not leave his labours to join them, however, so Harriet walked over to his ladder.

"Mr. Ash, may I offer you a cup of buttermilk?" she called up to him. He glanced at her, and climbed down. Taking the cup she offered, he said, "Thank you, Miss Walters." He drank deeply before returning the cup and turning to climb up the ladder again.

Harriet was surprised by his eagerness to return to work. "Will you not rest for a moment?" she asked. "Mr. Brown and the boys are."

Ash looked around at the others before taking a seat upon the grass. He stared into the distance and did not say a word to her, causing Harriet to wonder at his silence.

"The boys are doing a fine job, Mr. Ash. The baskets are already half full," she said in a conversational tone.

"Yes, they are good workers."

"It is very generous of you to help with the harvest. I know that my aunt would have been hard-pressed to get the apples in this year without the school's assistance."

"Generous, Miss Walters? Are you being ironic?" he said, his eyes cool and his manner aloof.

"Excuse me, sir?"

"My punishment is appropriate, do you not think?"

"Punishment? For what?"

"For trespassing on your aunt's property last week."

"Why would you be punished for trespassing, sir?" Ash was silent, staring steadily at the ground. Suddenly, Harriet understood. "Do you think I told my aunt about catching you and Oliver in her orchard last week? You assumed wrongly, sir!"

"Then what were your aunt and Mr. Harris discussing after service last Sunday? Why else was I chosen to supervise the boys?"

"They were discussing my aunt's lack of harvesters this year, and Mr. Harris suggested you as an overseer because you are the youngest and most fit of the masters."

Ash's eyes grew large. "Really? Then this had nothing to do with our trespassing?" he asked.

"Of course not. I told you that I would not tell my aunt." Harriet bent to pick up the bucket as Ash scrambled to his feet.

"Miss Walters, I do apologize. I was wrong to assume that you had gone against your word and, once again, my behaviour was churlish. My only defence is that I do not know you well enough to recognize that such behaviour is beneath you."

"No, sir, you do not know me at all," Harriet retorted, stalking away. She strode over to Sara, who was sitting on the wagon talking with Brown. "Come, Sara, we are finished here."

"Yes, Miss Walters," the girl said, scrambling after her. Harriet marched through the garden and into the kitchen, where she returned her bucket with a curt nod to Cook. When Brown brought his workers to the kitchen later that day, Ash looked for Harriet, but she was nowhere to be found.

Harriet's temper had cooled sufficiently the following afternoon to accompany Sara again with the buttermilk. As she had done the day before, Harriet took refreshments to the boys on the ladders before taking her time to visit Ash's tree. This time, however, the history master was waiting for her at the foot of his ladder.

"Here you are, sir," Harriet said, proffering the cup without meeting his eyes.

"Thank you," he said, taking it from her hand. "I wonder, Miss Walters, if you are aware that we have a lending library here in Rexton?"

"I was aware of it, but I have not visited it yet," Harriet said in a frosty tone.

"I frequent it regularly myself. Reading is one of my great pleasures." Ash reached into his pocket and withdrew a slender book. "I borrowed this yesterday. It's a history of the local churches, including St. Michael's. I thought that you might enjoy reading it." He offered it to Harriet, who hesitated before taking it from his hand. "Are you interested in church histories, Miss Walters?"

"Yes I am," she admitted.

"Have you visited Wells Cathedral yet? It's well worth seeing – centuries old, and not very far from Rexton."

"Yes, I visited there once with my parents. But I preferred the ruins of Glastonbury Abbey and the Tor," she said, casting him a sidelong glance.

"Ah, the seat of the legends concerning old King Arthur."

Harriet turned to face him. "I know that it is probably just folklore, Mr. Ash, but when one sees the mist shrouding the Tor, it is easy to imagine it surrounded by water."

"The location of the island of Avalon, you mean? King Arthur, Queen Guinevere, and the Holy Grail?"

"Yes, and do not forget the legend surrounding Joseph of Arimathea and the Glastonbury Thorn," Harriet said, her eyes shining at the romance of the tales.

"Poetic legends surrounding a venerable site," he said with a smile. "Of course I am aware of the tales, but my professional interest lies in a very different direction, in the Roman occupation of England. That is one of the reasons I sought a teaching position here in Rexton – for its proximity to Bath. The Romans used Bath as a spa town, you know."

"Yes, I had heard of that. I have not yet had the opportunity to visit Bath."

"I hope to spend some time there this summer to research the Roman occupation."

"That sounds fascinating, Mr. Ash." Harriet looked down at the book in her hand. "Thank you for the loan of this. I will read it tonight and return it to you tomorrow."

"There is no hurry. I don't have to return it for another week."

"Well, if you really do not mind, I'll hold onto it until the end of the week."

Harriet tucked the book into her pocket and bent to pick up the bucket. "I must get back to the house now. My aunt has an errand for me to run. If the weather continues fine and you and the boys return tomorrow, perhaps we can talk again."

"I would enjoy that," Ash said. He watched Harriet walk away and smiled as he remounted his ladder.

Harriet was leafing through the church history in the sitting room that evening, her aunt at a nearby table writing a letter, when Mrs. Evans arrived.

"Please do not get up," she said, seeing that Harriet was about to stand. "Cook made some praline hazelnut candy today and, as it was such a pleasant evening, I decided to deliver it myself." She sat down beside Harriet and drew a round tin from her bag. Opening it, she offered her some candy.

Harriet drew out a slab of the hazelnut-studded, buttery confection, and tasted it. "Mmm, this is delicious," she said, the butter and sugar melting in her mouth.

Mrs. Evans smiled and passed the tin to Aunt Edna, who helped herself to a generous slab. "Thank you, Mabel," she said. "I'll steal your cook away from you if ever she grows tired of catering to you and your guests. My cook has a deft hand with pies and pastries, but I would hire your cook just to make me candy."

"That is why I always bring you a supply, Edna – to keep my servants safe from your poaching." The two friends smiled at each other.

"Here, Harriet, ring for Grace and order us some coffee. I need something strong and hot to go with this candy."

Mrs. Evans settled herself for a visit. "What are you reading, Miss Walters?" she asked.

"A history of St. Michael's and the local churches, Mrs. Evans."

"Really? I've never heard of such a book," Aunt Edna said. "Where did it come from? Did Reverend Simons give it to you?"

"No, it's from the lending library. Mr. Ash gave it to me."

"Mr. Ash? Do you mean the man who has been harvesting my apples, Miss?"

"Yes, Aunt, the history master from the grammar school."

"How did the two of you come to be on such friendly terms, that he would lend you a book?"

"He noticed me at service last Sunday, and thought that I might be interested in learning something of St. Michael's history since I am new to Rexton. We discussed it when I helped to bring the buttermilk this afternoon."

Aunt Edna leaned back in her chair, clearly not pleased. "Your mother will not thank me for encouraging an acquaintance between you and a grammar school teacher, Harriet," she said.

"I do not think that Mother would have any objection to such an acquaintance, Aunt. Mr. Ash is a respectable person. Obviously, the headmaster thinks well of him."

"That's not much of a recommendation," her aunt snorted.

"Come now, Edna, Mr. Ash is a history master at a reputable grammar school, not a chimney sweep. You owe him some gratitude for his willingness to help you with your harvest. He also shows a high moral sensibility in loaning Miss Walters a book on church histories," Mrs. Evans said, smiling encouragingly at Harriet.

"Just see that you do not converse with Mr. Ash too regularly, or show him too much attention. I would not like him to become overly-familiar with you."

"Of course not," Harriet replied. But her aunt's admonition did not prevent Harriet from discussing other sites of historical interest with the schoolmaster over the next three days. Talks about local history led to talks about family history, and Harriet learned that Mr. Ash's father had also been a school teacher. Now retired, Ash's father and mother were living in Bristol so as to be closer to their daughter and her young family.

"Was it your father who instilled a love of history in you, sir?" Harriet inquired.

"Indirectly. My father studied literature, including the Greek and Roman classics, and I grew enamoured with stories of ancient times while listening to him read aloud. Hence my interest in the Roman Empire."

"I see. How fortunate that the Romans visited England. Otherwise, you would have to travel all the way to Italy to indulge your passion. How convenient." Harriet was rewarded with a laugh that made her insides glow.

"I never considered it from that vantage point before, Miss Walters. You are quite right."

The harvest was completed by week's end, and Harriet missed her talks with the schoolmaster. Meetings were infrequent after that. Sometimes she caught a glimpse of him walking with his pupils during the week, and she was usually able to exchange a nod or a greeting with him at Sunday services.

"I wish that I had been born a man and could be a grammar school teacher like Mr. Ash," Harriet reflected. "Teaching history would be a fascinating occupation, and I would enjoy the companionship of the other schoolmasters. My conversational partners are mostly limited to elderly widows, and their scope of interest is so narrow."

Harriet did enjoy Mrs. Evans' company, however, and pursued an acquaintance with her aunt's friend. Mrs. Evans was comfortable and empathetic, possessing a lively curiosity about most things that Harriet found stimulating. Although the lady had resided in Rexton for many years, she had also lived in London with her husband and had made a grand tour of the continent. Mrs. Evans also subscribed to a London newspaper and kept herself informed of politics and world events with a masculine voracity. One day, as she dropped by Mrs. Evans' house to deliver a dress pattern, Harriet confessed that she would like to live in London and travel to the continent, too.

"I can understand your wish to travel, Miss Walters," the lady said, "but what attracts you to London? It's such a big city, and you have lived mostly in the country."

"London has so many attractions. Cathedrals, the British Museum, royal homes, theatre, concerts, shops . . . . I have lived in the country for most of my life, it is true, and I do love it, but I long to experience the culture and variety of life in a big city."

"I understand. I had lived in Rexton all of my life before Mr. Evans married me and whisked me away to London. I was not a young woman when I married – did Edna not tell you?" she asked, noting Harriet's surprise. "Oh, yes, I was twenty-nine when I married. I was engaged to another man when I was younger, but my intended died of influenza. I remained at home with Mother after that, and then she died and Mr. Evans married me. He was my cousin, you see, and twelve years my senior. His family was impatient for him to marry and produce an heir. They were dismayed when we were betrothed, however. They wanted him to marry someone younger, I believe, not an old spinster like me. And, as it turned out, his family was right. I had difficulty bearing children, and Diane was the only child to survive to adulthood. Those were hard years for us, but Mr. Evans always stood by me, no matter what difficulties we encountered. He was a good man, Miss Walters, and practical too." The lady laughed. "Do you know, he always maintained that a woman should keep a few good pieces of jewellery at hand in case of financial disaster, and he did buy me some beautiful things. I don't wear them very often – they are too grand for me – but I will pass his advice along to you."

"It is unlikely that I will have the opportunity to take advantage of your advice, Mrs. Evans," Harriet replied.

"I would not be so certain of that if I were you. Your life is much like mine was, Miss Walters. You live a quiet life dependent upon your aunt, as I once did with my mother, but see what happened to me! You never know what hand might be dealt to you. Readiness is all."

"I have no cousin to rescue me."

"Perhaps not, but there is an interesting schoolmaster in town." Harriet blushed. "How is Mr. Ash, by the way?"

"He was well when I saw him at church last Sunday, but I did not have the opportunity to speak with him. As you know, my aunt does not encourage our friendship."

"Yes, I fear that Edna's idea of a suitable husband is rather limited. I doubt that Mr. Ash's income is very large, but other people have married on a schoolmaster's salary and been happy. And you never know what opportunities may come along to an energetic and intelligent young couple. So tell me, Miss Walters, what do you know of Mr. Ash?"

As Harriet spoke of the schoolmaster's interest in the Roman occupation of England, Mrs. Evans looked thoughtful. "Do you know, Harriet, this time of year can be very dull with the weather so dreary and Christmas preparations not yet begun. It would be nice to have some little event to look forward to – perhaps of an educational nature? I am sure that the St. Michael's Women's Association would be delighted to hear Mr. Ash speak on the Roman occupation of England. It wasn't long ago that the remains of a Roman temple were discovered in Bath. I wonder if Mr. Ash could be induced to give a little lecture on the subject, perhaps followed by a small reception? Do you think that he would have the time, given his duties at the school? I should think that Mr. Harris would be happy to share his school's resources with the rest of the village."

Mrs. Evans paused, noticing Harriet's worried expression. Harriet was afraid that Mrs. Evans would want her to approach Mr. Ash herself, and she felt bashful about asking for a favour.

Mrs. Evans patted her hand. "Don't worry about a thing, Miss Walters. Leave it to me. I will write to Mr. Ash tomorrow to see if he's interested, and acquaint you with his response as soon as I hear back. Will that do?"

"That sounds wonderful. I would be happy to assist in any way that I can. Perhaps Aunt Edna could be persuaded to provide sandwiches and pastries for the reception?"

Happily, Ash wrote that he would be honoured to speak to the Women's Association, and Mr. Harris gave his permission. Mrs. Evans convinced Reverend Simons of the worthiness of an educational lecture for the ladies of the church, and the minister encouraged them to attend. After service the following Sunday, Ash was waiting for Harriet as she, Aunt Edna, and Mrs. Evans emerged from the church. Harriet introduced the schoolmaster to her aunt and to Mrs. Evans.

Mrs. Evans said, "We so look forward to your lecture next Sunday. The Women's Association is abuzz with anticipation."

"Thank you, Mrs. Evans. I am happy to lecture upon one of my favourite subjects. I did wonder, however, if there were any particular topics that the ladies would wish me to address?"

"That is a very important consideration," she replied. "Unfortunately, Mrs. Slater and I have a luncheon engagement which requires our immediate departure. However, Miss Walters and I have discussed the lecture at length, and have come up with one or two points that you might care to include. If Miss Walters does not mind, perhaps she would share these thoughts with you on the walk home from church?"

"I would have no objection, if it is convenient for Mr. Ash," Harriet immediately responded.

"That is most generous of you, Miss Walters," Ash said. Let me just mention the plan to Mr. Harris, and I will be back directly." He rushed away to find his employer.

"What luncheon engagement do we have, Mabel?" Aunt Edna asked as Ash hurried over to the headmaster.

"Our luncheon engagement, Edna. Don't tell me that I forgot to invite you? How forgetful of me. Please do come. I'd like to show you the gown I had made from your pattern. I had it cut from blue silk."

"Do not believe for a second that I don't know what you're up to, Mabel Evans." Aunt Edna turned to Harriet. "You have my permission to walk home with Mr. Ash, Harriet, but come straight home. I don't want the whole parish to see you dawdling around the village with a strange young man."

"Of course not, Aunt Edna. Besides, Mr. Ash is not a 'strange young man,' and now that Reverend Simons has announced the upcoming lecture, everyone will know who he is."

"Humph," Aunt Edna said, "we'll see. Just behave yourself, Harriet. Look, he's coming back."

"Come, Edna, you can ride in my carriage and send your driver home," Mrs. Evans said as she drew Aunt Edna away.

"All settled, Miss Walters. May I escort you home?" Ash asked, offering her his arm. As they walked, the history master outlined his ideas for the lecture. Harriet thought them excellent, but suggested that Ash also discuss the lives of the Roman soldiers who remained behind on British soil. When they had exhausted the topic, Ash changed the subject.

"By the way, Miss Walters, I understand that you are making parish visits to a relative of one of my charges."

"I am? To whom?"

"To Mrs. Higgins. She is the great-aunt of Oliver Jones."

"Truly? Mrs. Higgins mentioned that she had a great-nephew at the school, but I did not imagine that it was Oliver. How is he?"

"Managing to stay out of trouble, for the present. I think that his adventure in your orchard had a profound effect upon him," he said with a wry smile.

Harriet laughed. "I'm glad to hear it. Does Oliver ever visit his aunt?"

"Only once, that I know of. Of course, the walk to the school is too far for Mrs. Higgins to manage."

"Well, the next time I see her, I'll tell Mrs. Higgins that I'm acquainted with one of her nephew's teachers. How is he doing with his studies, by the way?"

"Better now. He is forced to board at the school because his family lives too far away to make the daily journey. It was difficult for him to be away from home at first, but he has made friends with two or three of the boys and is beginning to take an interest in his lessons. He's also an enthusiastic participant in the athletic events Mr. Harris stages for the boys. And Mrs. Harris is very good with the younger boys."

"Mr. Harris has a wife? I didn't know that."

"Yes, he and his wife have a cottage on the school grounds. She is constantly at the school – no doubt that is why you have not met her. She stays with the youngest boys when the rest of us go to church on Sundays. They have prayers and bible instruction with her in the chapel."

Before long, the couple arrived at Aunt Edna's house; Harriet couldn't believe how quickly the time had flown. As he held the gate open for her, Ash paused. "I've enjoyed our talk very much, Miss Walters," he said.

"As have I, sir. I would invite you in for some refreshments, but my aunt is not at home."

"Perfectly understandable," he said. "And thank you for your advice concerning my lecture. I hope that the ladies will not find it too dull."

"Of course not. You speak with such authority and enthusiasm on the subject, I'm sure that the ladies will be enthralled."

"I fervently hope so. You know, I've only lectured to schoolboys before." Leaning closer, he said, "Perhaps if things are going poorly, you could contrive to faint?"

Harriet laughed. "I doubt that that will be necessary, sir. But if you require anything else, I would be pleased to assist you."

"Thank you, Miss Walters, I will remember that." Releasing her arm, Ash bowed and departed. Harriet was so pleased with their encounter that she skipped into the house and began planning her post-lecture compliments for next week.

Chapter Eight

The following Sunday, Harriet rose earlier than usual to make a special effort with her hair and dress. She had finished with mourning clothes and was wearing her best white muslin gown. Harriet was the first one down to breakfast, and was eating a piece of toast when her aunt came into the morning room.

"You're up early, Niece," Aunt Edna said. Suddenly noticing Harriet, she stopped to stare at her. "Good heavens, girl, what have you done to your hair? I've never seen you in ringlets before."

Harriet patted her head nervously. "My hair is always difficult, Aunt, but I so wanted it to look attractive today. Do you like it?"

"I'm not sure. The ringlets are so very large. They remind me of fat sausages."

Harriet's face fell and she stared down at her plate. Aunt Edna eyed her grimly. "Don't look so glum, child. I had a great mane of hair like yours, too, when I was a girl. My mother finally hired a maid who knew how to cut and dress it to its best advantage. The maid also showed me how to make a pomade which did wonders for controlling it. Grace is quite clever with hair. I'll have her give you a lesson or two on how to dress yours. For today, I suggest that you wear your larger bonnet with the high crown. You are going to need extra hat to cover those ringlets."

Harriet jumped up. "What a good idea. Thank you, Aunt." She hugged the old lady impulsively before rushing from the room.

"Silly girl," Aunt Edna grumbled before sitting down and helping herself to food.

After service, Aunt Edna, Harriet, and Mrs. Evans descended to the church hall to see if the caretaker had arranged the tables and chairs as instructed. A podium had been placed at the front of the room, a large vase of late-blooming flowers and grasses resting on a stand beside it.

"Very attractive," Mrs. Evans said, "although the food tables look rather plain. I'll bring some linens from home to cover them. I should be back by one o' clock. Will you be here by then, Edna?"

"Yes, Harriet and I will return with Sara to set up the refreshments."

"Very well. I'll see you then."

The ladies and their servants returned at the appointed hour to complete their preparations. By the time Ash arrived forty-five minutes later, the hall was already filled with chattering women who visited with one another and admired the plated food for the reception. The schoolmaster gazed around the hall with trepidation as Harriet bustled over to greet him.

"How do you do, Miss Walters? I had no idea that the church had such a large female congregation," he said.

"Actually, Mr. Ash, not all of the ladies you see here today are members. Some of the Women's Association invited friends and relatives to hear you speak today. It has become quite the social event. I'm glad that the publican's wife brought two roasts with her. We'll need the extra food." Harriet stopped surveying the room to study her friend. "You're not nervous, are you? You look a little pale."

"Nervous? To be truthful, I am a little. Such a large company of adults, particularly ladies, is a bit unnerving."

"I do apologize, sir. The gathering is definitely larger than we had anticipated, but the ladies are all so welcoming and so eager to hear you speak. Will you have a glass of apple cider before you begin? Aunt Edna's cider is not only delicious, but has a calming effect on the nerves."

Ash groaned as a new arrival was noisily greeted by her friends. "Lead the way, Miss Walters. I will definitely have a glass," he said.

Harriet and the schoolmaster wove their way through the crowd to a table bearing jugs of cider and glasses. She uncorked a jug, poured a glassful, and handed it to Ash. Mrs. Evans joined them just as the schoolmaster finished gulping it down.

"How are you this afternoon, Mr. Ash? Such a fine turnout. You must be pleased," she said.

"Oh, I am, Mrs. Evans. It's gratifying to know that so many ladies are interested in English history." Harriet glanced at him, wondering if he was being ironic.

"Yes, indeed. Ah, I see that you're having some of Edna's cider," Mrs. Evans said. "Excellent idea. You don't want a dry throat for your speech."

Harriet took Mrs. Evans aside as the schoolmaster poured a second glass. "I'm afraid that Mr. Ash is a little overwhelmed by the size of today's audience, Mrs. Evans. I suggested a glass of cider to calm his nerves."

"Poor man – I can understand his trepidation. We have assembled rather a mob, haven't we? Perhaps I can do a little better for him than cider, however." She reached into her reticule and pulled out a silver flask, masking it with her body.

"You carry a flask?" Harriet whispered, scarcely believing her eyes. Only gentlemen carried flasks, not ladies.

"Certainly. You never know when a little brandy will be required." Turning to the young man, she said, "Here is something better than cider for your nerves, sir. Why not try a drop of brandy?"

Having already finished a second glass of cider, Ash accepted the flask. "I don't usually imbibe outside of festive occasions, Mrs. Evans, but I am grateful for it today," he said, downing a few swallows of the liquor. He paused, taking hold of the table. "What a curious sensation I have in my throat – the warmth of the brandy following the chill of the cider."

"Don't be shy, sir. Have another drink," Mrs. Evans said, raising his arm. Obediently, Ash swallowed another generous dram or two.

Aunt Edna came to inform them that the ladies were ready for the lecture to begin. She contemplated Ash's flushed face as he straightened his jacket and ran a hand through his hair.

"Of course, Mrs. Slater, I shall begin straight away," he said, wobbling on his feet a little. "Wish me luck, ladies."

"Good luck, Mr. Ash," the three women chorused.

As he walked purposefully to the podium and withdrew some notes from his pocket, Aunt Edna inquired, "Is he quite well?"

"Shh," Mrs. Evans responded.

Raising his head and looking out over his audience, Ash bowed and began speaking. "Good afternoon, members of St. Michael's Women's Association and guests. I am pleased to speak to you today about a fascinating era in our country's history, the Roman occupation of England. I want to take you on a journey back through centuries of time to fifty-five years before the birth of our Lord when the general who was to become the great dictator of the Roman Empire, Julius Caesar, first stood upon English soil."

A hush fell over the audience as the schoolmaster told his tale, helping the ladies to imagine what their ancestors must have endured as the mighty Roman army swept across their land. The ladies were aghast as he described Roman warfare and the suffering inflicted upon those who resisted the invaders. After speaking at length about battle strategies and politics, he switched to a homelier topic, the lives of the Roman soldiers who settled upon English soil with their families. As he described the towns they built and the customs they brought with them from their homeland, the ladies hung upon his words. When he had finished lecturing, the schoolmaster welcomed questions from the audience, and answered them all adroitly. As he concluded his talk, Ash thanked them for their indulgence and bowed. The ladies applauded him most enthusiastically.

Harriet and Mrs. Evans exchanged delighted glances and hastened to congratulate the schoolmaster as the audience swarmed toward the refreshment tables. Aunt Edna rushed over to supervise the food.

"Well done, Mr. Ash!" Mrs. Evans said in a ringing voice as he withdrew a handkerchief from his jacket and wiped his damp face.

"The ladies were just spellbound," Harriet added.

"Thank you. It did seem well-received, didn't it?" he said with a wan smile.

"Why not take a seat with Harriet while I get you a plate of food and something to drink?" Mrs. Evans asked. "You must be parched after all that talking." She left, and Harriet guided the young man to a quiet spot at the front of the room. Ash sat down heavily and mopped his face again. Harriet gazed at him with concern.

"Are you feeling all right, sir? You look a little unwell," she said. In fact, the young man's face was clammy and his complexion had a decidedly greenish tint.

"Actually, Miss Walters, I am feeling a little dizzy," he said, grasping the arm of his chair and closing his eyes. "Breakfast was some hours ago and it may have been unwise to drink alcohol on an empty stomach. It seems a little warm in here to me. Does it seem so to you?" He opened his eyes to peer at her.

Mrs. Evans returned with a plate of food and a glass of fruit punch. "Here you are," she said, waving the plate under his nose. But instead of taking the food, the schoolmaster moaned and closed his eyes.

"Mr. Ash is not feeling well," Harriet whispered. "Perhaps we could help him outside for some fresh air?"

"Of course," Mrs. Evans said, looking concerned. With the support of a lady at each elbow, Ash climbed the stairs and staggered out onto the back lawn, where he sank onto a bench and cupped his head in his hands.

"Here, have something to eat," Harriet said, taking the plate from Mrs. Evans and offering him some beef and bread. The schoolmaster did not bother to raise his head. "Mr. Ash has not eaten for a few hours," she explained to her friend.

Mrs. Evans' eyes widened in comprehension. "That's right, Mr. Ash, do eat something," she urged. "What a lovely cool breeze is blowing after that stuffy hall. I'm sure that you will feel better soon." When he was still unresponsive, Mrs. Evans turned to her friend. "Harriet," she said, "I'm leaving you to find my driver and have him bring the carriage around back. Perhaps you could escort Mr. Ash home? Your aunt and I will remain behind to help with the ladies and supervise the clean-up until your return."

"Thank you, that is an excellent plan," Harriet replied. She looked down at the young man, who was beginning to list to one side. "I'll get him home safely."

"Good girl," Mrs. Evans said, patting her shoulder. Turning back to Ash, she added, "I'm leaving now. Thank you for the delightful talk today, sir. No, do not bother to rise," she added hastily as he attempted to stand. "Just sit and rest." She nodded at Harriet and hurried away.

"What a nice lady," Ash said, sitting back down again. "May I have some of that punch, please? I'm quite thirsty."

"Of course," she replied, taking a quick sip to ensure that it did not contain alcohol. Satisfied, she handed him the glass and he drank it down in large gulps.

"That's better," he said. "D'you know, I'm feeling so sleepy. If I could just lie down on the grass for a few minutes, I would feel better straight away."

Harriet panicked. She didn't know what she would do if Mr. Ash lay down on the grass before Mrs. Evans returned with the carriage. He tried to rise, but she shoved him back down again.

"No, why not lie down on the bench instead?" she said in a strained voice. "You don't want grass stains on your clothes."

"What a good idea," he said, collapsing onto the bench and resting his head in her lap before Harriet had a chance to move away. With eyes closed, Ash murmured, "You're a very amiable young lady."

Harriet was horrified. It would be a catastrophe if anyone caught them on the bench like that. She peered around to see if anyone witnessed her predicament, but she and the schoolmaster were perfectly alone. She looked down again. Ash's eyes were closed, and he began to snore.

"Drat," Harriet whispered, feeling terribly exposed. After a few anxious moments, however, she began to calm down. Likely the ladies would be eating and gossiping for a while longer, and Mrs. Evans would be back with the carriage any moment. She even began to feel hungry; it had been hours since she had eaten breakfast, too.

Harriet studied the plate of food on the bench beside her and selected an apple tart. She had just finishing eating it when Mrs. Evans rounded the side of the church. Her friend took one look at them and burst out laughing, covering her mouth with one hand lest she disturb the slumbering schoolmaster.

"I'm sorry for laughing, dear Miss Walters, but the two of you look so perfectly ridiculous," she whispered. Mrs. Evans drew closer and smiled down at Ash. "He looks so peaceful lying there. It would be a shame to disturb him."

"Yes, but we had better get him away from here before the ladies begin leaving the church," Harriet said.

"Yes, you are right," Mrs. Evans said, sobering instantly. She bent over Ash and prodded his shoulder. "Mr. Ash, it's time to wake up." When there was no reaction, the lady gave him a small shake. "Wake up, please." The young man snorted and continued snoring.

Harriet gently patted his cheek. "Mr. Ash, you must wake up. It's time to go home now. Please wake up, sir." His eyes fluttered opened and fixed upon her face.

"Hello, Miss Walters, how are you?" he asked.

"I'm very well, and glad to see you looking better," she said. "Now, Mrs. Evans and I are going to help to you stand and walk to her carriage. I'm going to take you home."

"Why, aren't you sweet," he said, smiling at her.

They pulled him to his feet and dragged him stumbling to the carriage. When they arrived at the vehicle, Mrs. Evans' driver jumped down to assist the history master to his seat. Harriet sat down beside Ash and slipped a hand under his arm to steady him. As the carriage started down the street, Ash's chin dropped to his chest, and he promptly fell asleep again.

The driver chose his route carefully, driving through the deserted back streets. When the carriage arrived at the school entrance, the gatekeeper, an elderly man in vest and slippers, shuffled out to meet them. He made a half-bow to Harriet and removed his cap.

"Good afternoon, sir," she said. "I've brought Mr. Ash home. He became ill after the lecture and will need some assistance in getting to his room. Can you help him?"

The gatekeeper stared at the snoring schoolmaster and smiled. "Aye, Miss, I can help the young gentleman to his room and see that he gets to bed." He winked, and Harriet stiffened in embarrassment.

"Thank you, you are most kind. The driver will help you get him down," she replied.

The driver shook Ash awake, and the two men lifted him onto the drive. Ash grinned at Harriet and waved before stumbling away with the gatekeeper.

"Back to St. Michael's now, Miss?" inquired the driver, his face a perfect blank.

"Yes, please," Harriet said, shaking her head over the afternoon's shenanigans.

Chapter Nine

Harriet had mixed feelings when she heard nothing from Ash in the ensuing week. She missed him, but feared that their next meeting would be very awkward. In the end, she determined to treat his drunkenness as if it had never happened.

"If Mr. Ash does not mention it, then neither shall I," she decided. "Perhaps he will not even remember anything untoward in his behaviour, given his condition."

After service the following Sunday, the schoolmaster was surrounded by a crowd of admiring women who wished to compliment him again on his lecture. He happened to look up just as Harriet and Aunt Edna descended the church stairs. Harriet raised her hand in a small wave of welcome, and the young man flushed scarlet.

"Oh dear, he does remember," she thought, ducking behind her aunt. The headmaster chose that unfortunate moment to approach the two ladies.

"It would appear that Mr. Ash's lecture was very well received, judging by his fair crowd of admirers," Mr. Harris said with a bow.

"Yes, he did not do too badly," Aunt Edna said. "Perhaps more of your masters will give lectures now."

Mr. Harris continued, "It was a shame, however, that Ash took ill directly afterward and had to go straight home. He stayed in bed for the remainder of the afternoon and evening, and still felt peaked the following day. But it was very kind of you, Miss Walters, to ensure his safe return." He smiled at the young woman.

"It was no trouble at all, Mr. Harris," Harriet said, blushing. "I'm sorry to hear that Mr. Ash was indisposed for so long."

"Perhaps it was brought on by nerves. However, I feel certain that he will not suffer a relapse should his services be required again.

Ladies," he said, nodding and taking their leave with a twinkle in his eyes.

Mrs. Evans joined Harriet and her aunt after the headmaster's departure. "It's good to see such well-deserved appreciation of Mr. Ash. He's a very fine young man, Edna. Not only was he generous in helping with your harvest, but he's an intellectual, and a fine speaker, too."

Aunt Edna looked at him appraisingly. "I suppose he is a useful sort."

Mrs. Evans winked at Harriet. "Harriet, will you add your compliments to those of his devotées?"

"I really do not think it necessary, ma'am. We already expressed our appreciation last Sunday."

"Come now, you don't want Mr. Ash to think that you're snubbing him, do you? And Edna, you really must pay him your compliments. After all, you want to stay in his good graces should you ever be short-staffed at harvest time again."

"You have a point, Mabel," Aunt Edna said. "The crowd is dispersing. Let us go greet him." Aunt Edna strode directly up to the schoolmaster with Mrs. Evans right behind her and Harriet trailing after them.

"Mr. Ash, I did not have the opportunity to compliment you on your lecture last Sunday, you left so abruptly. You did well, young man," Aunt Edna said, peering up into his face.

"Thank you, Mrs. Slater," Ash replied, taking an involuntary step back.

"You should be flattered, sir. That is high praise indeed coming from Mrs. Slater," Mrs. Evans said with a smile.

Bowing, Ash turned to include Harriet in their conversation. "I trust that you are well, Miss Walters?"

She met his eyes and quickly glanced away again. "I'm very well, sir. You are certainly looking better today." Harriet's voice trailed away as she realized how Mr. Ash would interpret that remark.

With a blank face, the young man replied, "I have another matter to discuss with you, Miss Walters, an invitation from your friend, Mrs. Higgins. She would like to ask you to a small gathering this afternoon that will include her nephew. I am invited, too, since I will be bringing the boy. Knowing that we both attend Sunday service, she thought that I might deliver the message to you. Will you come, Miss Walters?"

Before Harriet could respond, Aunt Edna said, "Seeing that Mrs. Higgins is part of your parish work, Harriet, you have my permission to go. I have no need of you this afternoon."

"Edna," said Mrs. Evans, "why not come to me this afternoon? Cook is trying out a new cake recipe, and I know that she would be delighted to have your opinion of it."

"Thank you, Mabel. Tell your cook that I'd be happy to try her cake. I'll drop Harriet at Mrs. Higgins' cottage along the way." She turned to the schoolmaster. "Perhaps you would be good enough to see my niece safely home afterward, sir? It will be dark by then."

"Of course. I would be happy to escort Miss Walters home." Smiling at Harriet, Ash repeated his question. "Will you come, Miss Walters?"

"Thank you, Mr. Ash, I would be delighted to," she replied with a shy smile. Mrs. Evans beamed as the schoolmaster nodded.

Chapter Ten

"Harriet, did you hear what I just said to you? Honestly, I don't know what's wrong with you this afternoon, you're so distracted," her aunt complained as they rode to Mrs. Higgins' cottage. Harriet carried a present for her hostess on her knee: a ripe, round cheese wrapped in a clean cloth.

"I'm sorry, Aunt," she replied automatically.

Aunt Edna studied her. "You have feelings for the schoolmaster, don't you, girl?" Harriet looked up, surprised that her aunt had noticed, but did not answer. "I'm not blind, Miss. I've raised two daughters. I recognize the signs."

"To be truthful, I'm not sure. I like Mr. Ash, but . . . ."

"You must think this through carefully, Harriet. Mr. Ash is your inferior socially. Besides, what would you have to live on? Your mother doesn't have enough to keep herself, let alone you, and you cannot expect anything from me. You know that, don't you, Harriet? I'm not a wealthy woman, and my son will get everything once I'm gone."

"Yes, I know."

"Very well, then, consider this a warning. Love is fine when the couple are suitably matched, but they cannot eat it." Harriet was silent, focusing on the view outside the carriage. Aunt Edna frowned and did not speak again until they reached Mrs. Higgins' house.

"Looks pretty tumble-down. You wouldn't catch me living there. The silly old woman should sell up and go live with her people before the property becomes worthless."

Harriet paused before opening the carriage door. "Mrs. Higgins came here as a young bride fifty years ago. She has many happy memories of this house and would not willingly part with it."

"Happy memories will not do her any good if she falls and breaks a leg." Harriet shook her head and descended from the carriage.

"Now, be sure to come home in good time tonight," Aunt Edna called after her.

Harriet followed the path to the front door and rapped more smartly upon it than she would have ordinarily, irritated by her aunt's comments. "Mrs. Higgins, it's Miss Walters!" she shouted. Moments later, the door swung open and Harriet stumbled inside. Catching herself, she turned and saw Oliver holding the door and staring at her. "Excuse me," she said. "I didn't expect the door to open so rapidly. Your great-aunt usually takes a few minutes to reach the front of the house."

Oliver smiled. "Auntie told me that you were coming. Auntie and Mr. Ash are both in the parlour."

"Is that Miss Walters, Oliver? Bring her in here, my love," Mrs. Higgins called. Harriet followed him into the parlour, where Mrs. Higgins sat on the sofa beside Mr. Ash. The schoolmaster stood as she entered the room.

"How are you, Mrs. Higgins?" Harriet asked, kissing her cheek. "This is for you," she added, handing her hostess the package.

"Oh, I know what this is. This is one of those cheddars your aunt's daughter sends, I'm sure. How generous of Mrs. Slater," she said, beaming with pleasure.

"You're right. My aunt heard how fond you are of cheese and insisted that I bring it today. And thank you for inviting me. What an unexpected treat."

Mrs. Higgins struggled to rise from the couch, and Ash hurried to help her. "You're very welcome, my pet. Thank you, Mr. Ash. These old knees don't get up so quickly anymore."

"It's good to see you again, sir," Harriet said with a curtsy.

"Yes, twice in one day. I am unusually privileged," he replied. The compliment brought a warm glow to Harriet's face.

Mrs. Higgins brought one hand to her ear. "I'm sorry to hear that you're ill, sir. My, you seemed well enough just a moment ago. Let me get you some of my tonic – it's a powerful restorative."

"Thank you, Mrs. Higgins, but I am quite well," the young man replied, looking perplexed.

Mrs. Higgins shrugged and turned to Harriet. "Miss Walters, before you sit down, would you lend me a hand in the kitchen? I have the kettle simmering on the stove and the teapot warming. Mr. Ash, you and Oliver look after yourselves for a moment while Miss Walters and I fetch the food."

Harriet smiled at the schoolmaster and followed Mrs. Higgins to the kitchen. She paused on the threshold, sniffing the warm, fragrant air appreciatively while the widow busied herself with steeping the tea. A large layer cake with a heavy fondant icing sat on a pedestal plate with a tray of jam tarts beside it. Another dish was wrapped in a white towel. Mrs. Higgins removed it, revealing a plate of scones studded with fat currants. Then the elderly woman limped to the oven and removed a rosy sliced ham, the scent of the meat making Harriet's mouth water.

"Now, Miss Walters, if you would take the tray with the plates and cutlery, I will carry out the tea pot. We'll come back for the food." Harriet insisted, however, that Mrs. Higgins let her fetch and carry while their hostess arranged the feast on a low table before the sofa. Oliver's eyes bulged as Harriet carried in the rich food. When all was ready, the elderly widow settled back upon the couch with a sigh of satisfaction.

"It all looks wonderful, Mrs. Higgins," Ash said, enunciating clearly and carefully. Oliver winked at Harriet from the other side of his aunt.

Mrs. Higgins nodded and smiled. "I'll serve up the cake if Miss Walters will pour out the tea. Oliver, why not tell us what you're reading in school this term while we pass around the plates?"

The young boy launched into a description of his school subjects and masters, but was more interested in describing an upcoming sporting event. "We're going to have 'Race Day' next week, Miss. I'll be running in the sprinters, of course. I'm very fast for my size. Even the bigger boys in my year can't catch me. I hope to win a blue ribbon, unless Johnny Randolph beats me. He's the only one anywhere near as fast as me, isn't he, Mr. Ash?"

"You outran him last week during practice, Oliver. I wager that you'll beat him again."

"I hope so, sir," the boy said with his mouth full of tart. "And when we're done the regular races, Mr. Harris is going to borrow two piglets from the farm next door so we can have pig races. You should come, Miss. It will be great fun."

"It sounds like it will, Oliver, but I doubt that I would be any good at catching a pig."

Oliver studied her for a moment, his head to one side. "You're probably right. It's best to be small and quick like me for catching pigs, but you're ever so tall. You would probably be better at the long-distance races. I bet your legs are really long under your skirts. I'm glad I'm not a girl and have to wear dresses."

The adults laughed, and Mrs. Higgins said, "You're growing so fast, Oliver, it's that hard to keep you in trousers. You can come and catch my hens if they ever get out again. My legs don't go so fast anymore."

"That's all right, Auntie, you're a wonderful cook," Oliver said. "May I have a slice of cake now, please?"

"Of course you can, my love." Mrs. Higgins patted his shoulder and gave him a generous slice. "Now, Mr. Ash, how about a piece of cake? I don't think the folks at the school are feeding you enough. You're too thin, sir."

"Yes, please, Mrs. Higgins," he said, extending his plate. "Actually, the staff looks after us very well. It's much better than bacheloring in private rooms." He took the cake and forked a piece into his mouth, his eyes closing in pleasure. "This is wonderful. Our cook is good with roasts and vegetables, but she can't touch you for the lightness of your pastry and cakes, Mrs. Higgins."

"Thank you, young man. I've been making that recipe for the past thirty years, so I ought to have it right by now. You come by any time you like with our Oliver, and I'd be happy to make you a cake or anything else you'd like."

"We have an agreement, Mrs. Higgins," he said, shaking her hand and smiling.

The little group chatted and stuffed themselves with good things while the sun's rays sank lower through the parlour windows. Noticing that it was growing late, Harriet jumped up to carry the dirty dishes and leftover food into the kitchen, where Mrs. Higgins refused any further assistance.

"You just leave everything lying where it is, Miss Walters," she said, tying two tarts and a slice of cake into a clean cloth for Oliver. "I have all evening to take care of the dishes. You three should be going before it's too dark to see the road."

Back in the parlour, Oliver and Ash were donning their outer things when the women returned. Ash helped Harriet into her coat while Oliver tied a scarf around his neck.

"Thank you for coming, my dears, and I hope that you can come again soon," Mrs. Higgins said, kissing her nephew and walking her guests to the front door. "Good night, and be careful not to catch a chill."

"Good night and thank you," her guests responded as they paused to shake hands or embrace her before venturing into the evening air. Harriet wrapped a shawl around her shoulders and followed the schoolmaster and his charge down the walk.

Ash waited on the road for her and said, "If you don't mind, there's a short-cut through the woods that will take us directly back to the school. We'll leave Oliver there, and I'll escort you to your aunt's home." Glancing out of the corner of her eye, Harriet observed Oliver jump into a pile of leaves before kneeling to pick up a pale stone that caught his fancy.

"That would be fine, Mr. Ash," Harriet said. They turned and watched the boy dart toward a scolding squirrel that brandished its tail at him from the safety of its branch overhead. Ash and Harriet laughed, and followed Oliver down a well-worn path that crossed through the woods, emerging next to a farmer's field. A cow had just poked its head through the fence to reach a mouthful of grass, and shook it at them as they passed. Coming to a stile, Ash mounted it first and bent to give Oliver his hand, but the boy jumped up beside him and clambered down the other side.

Harriet picked up her skirts and took Ash's proffered hand, climbing up beside him. "Allow me," he said. Grasping her waist, he lifted her off her feet and lowered her to the ground.

"Thank you, Mr. Ash," she said with a nod, enjoying the sensation of his hands around her waist.

Oliver grew tired from all of his running and held the schoolmaster's hand for the remainder of the walk. Harriet and Ash passed the time by discussing a travel book that she had just finished from the lending library, and they made up a list of all of the sights they would like to see if they ever visited the continent. Nearing the gate, the stars began to pop out in the night sky, and Harriet could smell wood smoke trailing out of the school chimneys.

"Good evening, Hubbard," Ash said as the gatekeeper emerged. "Here is Oliver Jones, home from a jolly party at his aunt's house."

"Aye, did you have good things to eat, young Oliver?" the elderly man inquired.

"Very good," the child replied with a yawn, "but I'm glad to be home now. I'm tired."

"I'm going to escort Miss Walters home before I turn in, Hubbard," Ash said. Would you please see Oliver to the dormitory?"

"It would be my pleasure," Hubbard said. "Come along, young Oliver. Let's get you out of the cold night air. Goodnight, Miss," he said, touching his cap.

"Goodnight, Miss," Oliver echoed, glancing over his shoulder as Hubbard led him away.

"Goodnight, Oliver, and good luck with the races next week," Harriet called after him. She smiled and turned to Ash.

"Shall we?" he said, proffering her his arm. Taking it, they ambled back down the drive together and out into the lane.

"He's a good boy. You can see that his great-aunt dotes upon him," Harriet said.

"Yes, and he's also very plucky. It's hard on Oliver, being so small for his age, but he makes up for it in spirit. No one and nothing gets Oliver Jones down for very long." Ash smiled. "When Oliver first came to the school, I was afraid that he might be bullied by some of the larger boys. You know the kind of thing that happens – allowances get taken or books thrown into puddles. The first boy that tried it on Oliver got a sharp kick in the shin for his trouble, and Oliver soon put a great distance between him and his tormentor. His speed and agility are his best defences for now, but the sports master says that he will tutor Oliver in boxing when the boy grows a little bigger."

"I'm glad to hear it," Harriet said. "Perhaps Oliver's diminutive size will spur him on to great successes. I like to see determination rewarded, even though people do not always get what they deserve."

"Yes, unfortunately that is true."

"Of course, I've never had the problem of being small for my age. Just the opposite, in fact. My sister is three years older than I, but I was never able to wear her hand-me-downs. I've towered over her for most of my life."

"Really, Miss Walters?" Ash said, stopping beside her. "Everyone in my family is tall, and you don't seem that tall to me." He held his hand level with the top of her head; he was a good five inches taller than Harriet. The young lady smiled, glad that she was dwarfed for a change.

They continued their walk in companionable silence until turning in at the end of Harriet's street. Their proximity to her home seemed to goad the schoolmaster into speech.

"Miss Walters, there is something that I must say before I leave you tonight," he said, gazing down into her eyes. "I have avoided a particular subject out of cowardice, but I really must address it now." He looked away. "I am referring, of course, to my behaviour after the lecture last Sunday. I'm embarrassed by the way I acted, and I feel that I owe you an apology."

"That is unnecessary, sir," Harriet said, fervently wishing that he hadn't brought up the topic.

"Unfortunately, I cannot agree with you, although I do not wish to dredge up unpleasant memories for either one of us." He turned to face her. "However, I wish to apologize if anything I said or did made you uncomfortable. I assure you that my behaviour was abnormal." Harriet nodded and looked away. He smiled ruefully. "It would appear that the alcohol I drank before the lecture to keep my nerves under control had a perverse effect upon me afterward."

Writhing with embarrassment, Harriet interrupted him. "Please do not apologize any longer, Mr. Ash. It was obvious that you are not a habitual imbiber." Ash nodded, and they continued on the short walk to Harriet's gate.

"Thank you, Miss Walters. I was correct – you are perfectly amiable," Ash said, breaking into a grin.

"And you are very entertaining, Mr. Ash," she said, emboldened by his levity.

"Touché," he responded, escorting her to the door.

Chapter Eleven

The next day Harriet was contemplating some muslin in the draper's shop window when Mrs. Evans caught up with her. "Miss Walters, I have exciting news," she said, panting. "My daughter, Diane, is coming for a fortnight's visit before Christmas."

"How nice for you, Mrs. Evans. Will her husband be accompanying her?"

"No, he's unable to get away until the parliamentary break. He's sponsoring a road bill in his riding that keeps him much occupied. Diane writes that Edward will probably not even notice her absence while she's away. But I'm so glad that you two will finally have the opportunity to meet. I've written to her about you, and she is very much looking forward to knowing you."

"I will be delighted to meet her as well. When does she come?"

"This Thursday. I plan to hold a dinner party for her the following evening. I hope that you and Edna will be able to attend?"

"Of course, Mrs. Evans."

"Good. I'm also inviting the Campbells and the Thompsons. I don't think that you have met them yet, but they've known Diane since she was a baby, and will be pleased to see her again. But, I must go. I have so many preparations to make. Give my regards to Edna." Mrs. Evans hurried away, as did Harriet to tell her aunt the news.

"So, Diane is back for a visit, is she? I'm glad that we had those new clothes made for you, Harriet," was her aunt's response.

The previous month, Harriet had caught her aunt studying her over the breakfast table. "Is something amiss, Aunt?" she asked. "Why are you looking at me so?"

"It's your dress, Harriet. I've never seen it before," Aunt Edna said with a frown. Harriet looked down at her gown, a plain dress cut from brown serge. It was sturdy and comfortable, and had received much wear in her former life.

"What are you doing today, Harriet? Are you planning on going out?"

"Yes, I've got a parish visit to make."

"In that dress?" her aunt asked, raising her voice.

"Well, yes. I often wore this when I went on charitable visits with Mother."

Aunt Edna looked at her askance. "That dress may have done while you were living in the country, but it won't do in Rexton. Don't forget, my girl, that what you wear reflects upon me. When you walk down the street, people will think, 'There goes Edna Slater's niece. Poor thing, she hasn't anything better to wear.' Well, it won't do, Harriet. I won't have my niece dressing like a pauper. After breakfast, we're going upstairs to examine your gowns, now that you've put off mourning."

"But, Aunt, I don't have the money to buy new clothes."

"Of course you don't. I'll pay for them. My dressmaker is both reasonable and clever. She can squeeze the value out of every penny, plus she knows a thing or two about dressing a woman to her advantage. You'll be in good hands with Mrs. Hensley. Now, finish that toast and let's go upstairs."

As it turned out, Aunt Edna rejected the majority of Harriet's gowns, saying that they weren't fit to be seen outside of the house. She ordered the carriage and carried Harriet off to the dress-maker's shop. Mrs. Hensley was a middle-aged woman of comfortable proportions who dressed to impress the village. That is, she did not wear the latest London fashions, but her clothes were well-cut, stylish, and functional. Before she knew it, Harriet was standing in her shift in the back room while Mrs. Hensley and Aunt Edna scrutinized her. The shop owner circled Harriet slowly, while Aunt Edna perched on a nearby stool.

"Well, what do you think?" her aunt asked.

Mrs. Hensley pursed her lips. "Not bad. She's very tall, that's true, and thin, but that's not a bad thing, considering today's high-waisted fashions. The bust isn't much, but we can add to it with pleats and tucks. We'll add a little fullness to the hips with a padded petticoat, too. Don't worry, Miss Walters. I've given many a girl a shapelier figure than nature provided, believe me. Her colouring is not too bad. Her hair's a nice rich brown, but her skin is a little ruddy. We'll stay away from colours that heat up the complexion. Perhaps a little powder on those cheeks? Altogether, I think that we can make something of her. Now, how many gowns were you thinking of ordering, Mrs. Slater?"

On the night of the dinner party, Harriet met her aunt in the sitting room wearing a new pelisse cut from a handsome dark green velvet and embellished with black braid. Beneath it, her white muslin gown was trimmed with pearl cord and had long, sheer sleeves. Grace had dressed her hair with pearl rope to complement the dress, and the added fullness made Harriet's face appear less angular. Aunt Edna wore a stylish black satin gown with a fox tippet and a black satin cap trimmed with feathers. Harriet had never seen her aunt dressed so fashionably before, and said as much.

"We must look our best tonight, Harriet. Diane always wears the latest fashions and looks very elegant. We do not want to look like paupers by comparison."

"No, Aunt, I'm sure we do not." Indeed, Harriet thought that she looked rather well that evening.

When Rogers greeted them at Mrs. Evans' door, Harriet noted that he was dressed in formal livery. He preceded them to the drawing room and announced them to its occupants. The other guests had already arrived, and were gathered around Mrs. Evans and a lady seated beside her on the couch. Harriet thought that the lady was the most beautiful creature she had ever seen. Her hair was golden blond, her complexion a creamy ivory with softly-tinged pink cheeks, and her eyes a sparkling green. She wore a white satin frock gathered over a matching petticoat, the hem and capped sleeves trimmed with pleated tulle, and white kid gloves drawn up over her elbows. Wisps of bang and little side curls peeked out from beneath a turban trimmed with matching white tulle and ostrich feathers. The lady turned to note the new arrivals and smiled graciously at Harriet and her aunt. Mrs. Evans rose to welcome them.

"Edna, Miss Walters, do come in. Miss Walters, this is my daughter, Mrs. Fitzwilliam." Harriet curtsied as the exquisite young woman nodded and extended a graceful hand.

"Do come and sit beside me, Miss Walters," Diane said. "I've so been looking forward to meeting you. Mother has written about what a darling you are. You have certainly livened up Rexton for her." Harriet, who felt like a giant towering over Diane, was happy to take Mrs. Evans' place on the sofa.

Mrs. Evans added, "Miss Walters, let me introduce you to our other guests. Mr. and Mrs. Campbell, this is Miss Walters, Mrs. Slater's niece. Mr. Campbell is a retired Member of Parliament." Harriet nodded while the gentleman made a short bow, but did not smile. His lady watched her with gimlet eyes.

"And this is Colonel Thompson and Mrs. Thompson." A trim, grey-haired man with a kindly smile bowed to her, while his wife smiled.

"Edna, I was just telling Mrs. Thompson how much you enjoyed the new cake Cook made," Mrs. Evans said, drawing Harriet's aunt into conversation.

Once the gentlemen had retaken their seats, Diane turned to Harriet. "Miss Walters, how are you enjoying Rexton? I understand that you've been here for three months already."

"Very much, Mrs. Fitzwilliam. It has a pretty prospect."

"I agree. Rexton is a lovely village, and very restful. I enjoy escaping the crowds and grime of London to visit mother here once or twice a year. London is such a lively place, but one must be at one's best there, which can be a strain. Unfortunately, I have only a fortnight free before my husband is released from the House and my son returns home from university for the Christmas holidays."

Harriet was amazed. "Pardon me. Your mother told me that you had a son, but she didn't say that he was in university. I can hardly believe you have a son that age."

Diane dimpled and placed her hand upon Harriet's. "You are a darling! Yes, I have a grown son, although I did marry quite young. But tell me, Miss Walters, have you ever visited London?"

"Not yet, Mrs. Fitzwilliam, although I do hope to go someday. There is so much to appreciate in London."

"True, although I find that once one has visited the attractions, one hardly ever goes again. The crowds can be so tiring. No," she said, looking around the room, "I find life in the country much more to my taste."

"I often find that the opinion of people who are not obliged to live in the country," Harriet said with a smile to soften her words.

"Perhaps you are right. It is easy to say one prefers life in the country when one has a life full of variety back in the city. When you do visit London, Miss Walters, you must promise to stay with me. I would enjoy showing you some of London's treasures. I can enjoy them all over again through the eyes of a newcomer."

"Thank you, that would be wonderful," Harriet said with a wistful smile.

"Of course," Diane said, patting her hand. "Now, please catch me up on the latest gossip. Is your aunt still terrorizing the boys from the grammar school?"

Harriet was comfortable talking with Diane, who spoke as easily as if they were old friends, and they chatted until dinner was announced. Once in the dining room, Harriet found herself seated beside the intimidating Mr. Campbell. Fortunately, Diane was seated across the table from her, since Aunt Edna and Mrs. Evans took places at the opposite end. Harriet struggled to converse with Mr. Campbell, but conversation faltered during the fish course when the gentleman began to lecture her on Scottish independence. Fortunately, Diane joined in with an amusing anecdote about a fishing holiday that soon had the fierce gentleman laughing.

"Diane, do you expect me to believe that you were standing in the middle of a cold stream at seven o' clock in the morning, the mist heavy upon the water, trying to catch a fish? Faith, girl, your servant would not have rolled you out of bed by then."

"Normally that would be true, Mr. Campbell, but in this instance, I hadn't gone to bed yet. I borrowed a pair of wading boots from Fitzwilliam, and we all went out to catch our breakfast. *And* I caught the biggest trout of all, I'll have you know!"

"Ah, I know a fish tale when I hear it," he replied, slapping his knee with laughter. Harriet gazed admiringly at Diane. Not only was she beautiful and charming, but kind as well. Harriet was grateful to be acquainted with such an exceptional woman.

The evening was over before Harriet knew it. On the carriage ride home, she rested her head on the back of her seat and gazed up at the starry night sky. "What a wonderful evening, Aunt. I had such a splendid time."

"Yes, you seemed to be enjoying yourself. What did you think of Diane, I wonder?"

"She is marvellous – beautiful, engaging, and witty."

"Yes, she is that."

Something in her aunt's tone made Harriet gaze at her. "You speak as if you do not approve of Mrs. Fitzwilliam, Aunt."

Aunt Edna shook her head. "Don't forget that I've known Diane since she was a baby. She grew up to be a beguiling creature that everyone admires, but it would take more than that to impress me."

"She was very kind to me tonight."

"Yes, but it cost her nothing. That's not to say that I don't enjoy Diane's company, and you should, too, while it lasts. You'll not find anyone more amusing than Diane, and she is the apple of her mother's eye. But I'm always glad when her visits end, and I can see Mabel alone again."

Harriet held her tongue and said nothing more in Diane's defence, but she wished that her aunt would be more generous in her opinions.

Before they left that evening, Aunt Edna and Harriet made an agreement to meet Diane and her mother at church the following Sunday, followed by refreshments back at Aunt Edna's house. When Sunday came, Harriet and her aunt arrived at the church first. From her vantage point near the front, Harriet could see how faces brightened as Diane walked by or stopped to chat with people. Even the sober Reverend Simons beamed down at Diane from the pulpit, and was most solicitous in greeting her on the church stairs after service.

Harriet was waiting her turn to greet the reverend when Ash approached, hat-in-hand, to wish her a good morning. Harriet had not seen him since Mrs. Higgins' party the previous Sunday, and so much had happened since then.

"I had to go back to our pew to retrieve one of the boy's jackets, or I might have missed you this morning, Miss Walters," he said.

"I'm glad that you did. Tell me, how did Oliver fare in the races last week?"

"You would have been proud of him. Not only did he win a blue ribbon in his race, but he caught a pig."

"Good for him. I'm so glad. Please pass along my congratulations, Mr. Ash. Now that he is covered in glory, his aunt will repeat his successes for months to come, I am sure."

Ash laughed. "That is probably too true. I hope that you will not suffer from their repetition, Miss Walters."

"Not at all. His great-aunt is justifiably proud of the boy."

The schoolmaster glanced down the stairs and saw Harriet's party waiting. The wind tore at their clothes, and scurrying clouds darkened the sky. "But I fear that I'm keeping your aunt and her friends, and it threatens rain."

Harriet clutched at her hat before the wind could snatch it away. "Please, do come and say hello, Mr. Ash. I'd be happy to introduce you to Mrs. Evans' daughter. I'm sure that Mrs. Evans would wonder if I did not bring you over, too."

Mr. Ash stared down at Mrs. Fitzwilliam. "Yes, I believe that I saw her when she visited last year. I would be happy to know her."

Harriet led the schoolmaster to her party and made the introduction. "Mr. Ash is a historian and an excellent lecturer, Diane," her mother added. Mrs. Evans went on to describe the schoolmaster's recent lecture and the praise he had received from the parish ladies.

"I am sorry that I missed your talk, sir. It sounded like a fascinating topic," Diane said. Ash flushed a little at their compliments, and bowed.

"Young man, we're going back to my house to have a bite to eat. Why not join us, if Mr. Harris can spare you? There's room for you in our carriage," Aunt Edna said. Harriet's eyes widened in surprise; she had never expected any encouragement from her aunt in this direction.

"Thank you for your invitation," he stammered, obviously surprised as well. Ash saw that Mr. Harris was near and beckoned for him to join them.

"Mrs. Slater has kindly invited me for some luncheon, if you do not require my services this afternoon, sir?"

"I've nothing pressing for you, Joseph. Go and enjoy yourself. Just don't let the ladies lead you down the path of over-indulgence, eh?" The headmaster patted Ash kindly on the shoulder and nodded to the ladies before departing.

"Very well, come along with us, sir. Mabel and Diane, we'll see you back at the house." Aunt Edna marched toward her carriage with Harriet and Ash following more slowly.

"What an unexpected kindness, Miss Walters," the young man said.

"Yes, I wonder what she means by it?" Harriet replied with raised eyebrows.

Cook had left a cold lunch for Aunt Edna and her guests, which they fully enjoyed. Ash permitted himself one glass of wine with his meal, and Mrs. Evans teased him about not taking more.

"Even Mrs. Slater and I are indulging in a second glass," she said. "Or perhaps you would prefer cider?"

Ash grinned and shook his head. "No thank you, Mrs. Evans. Mrs. Slater's cider is deceptively potent."

"Humph, I don't know what you're talking about, young man," Aunt Edna remarked, drawing laughter from Mrs. Evans and a quizzical look from Diane, who changed the subject by inquiring into Ash's interest in the Roman occupation. The schoolmaster warmed to his subject, talking passionately about the new science of archaeological investigation and his intention of applying these techniques to the Roman ruins in Bath.

"How very fascinating," Diane said. "I've heard of the work that Napoleon and his scientists did during the Egyptian campaign. So, you're interested in doing the same in Bath? Tell me, Mr. Ash, have you ever visited Italy to study the Roman remains in situ?"

"No, although that would be a dream come true. Unfortunately, I do not have the resources for such an expedition."

"How frustrating for a scholar such as yourself. Well, maybe someday you will realize your dream. Meanwhile, you have your duties at the school," Diane said, leaning back in her chair to observe him.

"Yes, which I really must be getting back to. Thank you very much for your company, ladies, and for your hospitality, Mrs. Slater. It was a pleasant change from my usual Sunday routine."

"You are welcome, sir. We enjoyed your company as well, didn't we, ladies?"

"Yes, indeed," they responded.

Ash stood. Harriet half-rose, intending to escort him to the front door, but he exited too quickly to afford her the chance. Aunt Edna watched as Harriet slid back into her chair.

"Tell me, what did you think of our visitor, Diane?" Aunt Edna asked, turning to the lady.

"He seemed interesting. Some of the ladies of my London acquaintance also share a fascination with ancient civilizations. For instance, I attended a party at Lady Sloane's house last summer. The foolish woman had transformed her bedroom in the style of an Egyptian queen's. What a lot of money she spent on the project, plus the result was an atrocity." She laughed, Aunt Edna exclaimed over the absurdity of such an extravagance, and the conversation turned to other topics.

At the end of the afternoon, Diane extracted a promise from Harriet to go for a walk the following morning. "Mother is getting so lazy these days. I cannot entice her to walk for more than a mile or two. I'm sure that you must share my affinity for walking, Miss Walters. Will you come with me tomorrow?"

"I would enjoy that very much," Harriet said, delighted that Diane sought her company.

"Excellent. I'll call for you at ten o'clock."

The morning was clear and dry when the two women embarked upon their outing. They were dressed for the cold December weather and enjoyed the exercise. Harriet begged Diane to describe some of London's wonders to her as they rambled, and the lady was happy to oblige. After a time, however, the conversation turned to Harriet and to her life in Rexton.

"I understand from Mother that Mr. Ash is a particular friend of yours, Miss Walters," Diane said.

"I would not go so far as to say a 'particular' friend, Mrs. Fitzwilliam. He is an amiable and intelligent man, and I enjoy our conversations about history and old ruins."

"Do call me 'Diane,'" the lady said. "'Mrs. Fitzwilliam' sounds so stuffy. And may I call you 'Harriet'?"

"Please do," Harriet said, glowing. "But I fear your mother flatters me about Mr. Ash. He and I have some interests in common, it is true, but I think that he simply enjoys talking to someone who shares his interests.

"Please do not speak so slightingly of yourself, Harriet. I'm sure that many gentlemen find you appealing."

Harriet looked away and half-smiled. "Men do not take any particular notice of me, Diane. I've come to accept that fact. I am plain and unappealing."

"Nonsense, Harriet. You're willowy and graceful, with a fresh complexion and sympathetic eyes. I know fascinating, successful women who are not nearly as attractive as you. Perhaps you lack the confidence to shine in society, but confidence is the secret to any woman's appeal. That, and being a good listener. Gentlemen find it especially flattering when ladies hang upon their every word. Why, with a little practice, men will be clamouring for your attention."

Harriet smiled doubtfully. "Really?"

"Definitely," Diane said, sliding her arm into Harriet's. "That is why it's so important to beware of men who seek you out because of your fortune. I had to be vigilant against such scoundrels before Mr. Fitzwilliam claimed my hand. So, you must be cautious with your Mr. Ash."

"But I don't know what you mean. I have no fortune to tempt a man. If people think that I will inherit money from my aunt, they're mistaken."

"You may not be an heiress, my dear, but you're obviously a lady, and your aunt is a woman of means. Someone seeking financial gain, such as Mr. Ash, might assume that Mrs. Slater will leave you her property after she is gone."

"Such a person would be very much mistaken!" Harriet said with a frown.

"Exactly. Now, I know the situation between you and your aunt, but Mr. Ash may not be so well-informed. Just be careful not to encourage him too much, if you do not mind my saying so. How tragic it would be to tie yourself to a schoolmaster, only to live the life of a pauper. You must save yourself for someone who can look after you properly, Harriet. You deserve that." Diane squeezed Harriet's arm in a friendly manner.

As they strolled together in silence, Harriet pondered Diane's words. She did not like to think of the schoolmaster as a fortune hunter, but perhaps that explained his interest in her?

"Do you really think that Mr. Ash believes I will inherit my aunt's estate?" she finally said.

"Just be careful, Harriet. I do not wish to see you unhappily married. I have seen that happen too frequently among my circle to wish to see it happen to you."

Harriet nodded and took Diane's words to heart. She would not let her enjoyment of Mr. Ash's friendship affect her good judgement. Diane was a much more experienced and worldly woman than she, and Harriet did not want to appear foolish by falling prey to a fortune hunter.

The rest of Diane's visit passed very pleasantly. With Mrs. Evans' encouragement, Diane and Harriet were constantly in each other's company. Harriet saw nothing to change her initial opinion of her new friend, despite what her aunt had said.

When Diane finally returned to London, Harriet felt bereft, as if a bright star had passed from her orbit. Her sole consolation was that Diane had promised to correspond with her, and to pay another visit the following spring. Meanwhile, the Christmas festivities were approaching, and there was a visit with her mother and Helen and her family to anticipate.

Mrs. Evans dropped by to see Harriet and her aunt the morning after her daughter's departure. She settled into a comfortable chair before the fire, and propped her feet upon a stool.

"With you leaving for the Christmas holidays soon, Miss Walters, I thought a party might be pleasant before you go. Perhaps a card party or a musical evening? You have a pretty voice and you're accomplished on the pianoforte. What would you say to performing before a small circle of our friends?

Harriet shook her head. "I would not mind accompanying someone else, but I would not feel comfortable singing alone."

"Well, we can discuss that later. Would you like me to invite Mr. Ash to the gathering?" Aunt Edna stiffened on the couch beside Harriet.

"Will Mr. Ash still be in Rexton then? I should think that he would be going home to his own family for Christmas," Harriet said.

"He may be, Miss Walters, but I plan to have my party within the week. I'm sure that the school term will continue at least until then."

Harriet looked away. "Of course, you can invite whomever you choose, Mrs. Evans, but please do not invite Mr. Ash for my sake."

Mrs. Evans frowned. "I don't understand. I thought that Mr. Ash was your friend?"

"I suspect that he enjoys talking to me merely because I am a willing listener."

The lady was about to say more when Aunt Edna interrupted. "Harriet, my rose-coloured thread is missing. I must have left it upstairs with my embroidery bag."

"I'll get it for you," Harriet replied, glad to avoid any further discussion of her friendship with Mr. Ash.

When she was safely out of earshot, Aunt Edna said, "Mabel, I wish that you would not encourage Harriet to see Mr. Ash. I do not approve of their friendship."

"I know your opinion of the young man, but I am sure that Miss Walters likes him, and there are so few eligible young men in Rexton. You must not crush her one chance for happiness."

"It's Harriet's happiness I'm thinking of. Would you have her living in squalor on a school teacher's salary instead of being looked after comfortably by her own family?"

"Would you prefer that she never have a home of her own, and be forced to live as a dependent all of her life? Would you deprive her of the possibility of a husband and children?"

"Nonsense, you and I live quite contentedly without a husband and children. Helen has so many children – one of them will always provide a home for Harriet. Her needs will be met and, surrounded by family, she will be less alone than we are."

Mrs. Evans sat down on the couch beside her friend. "Really, Edna, I do not understand you. Do you regret having had a husband, children, and a home of your own? Would you take that chance away from your niece?"

Harriet's aunt put down her needlepoint to face her friend. "Of course not. How dare you say such a thing to me, Mabel! Mr. Slater was a fine man and a good provider, and my children and grandchildren mean the world to me. They are just not *all* the world to me, nor is your daughter and her family to you. And that's how it should be. Husbands die, children grow up and move away, and old women like us find things to do while we await our eternal reward.

"Oh, Edna, how dreary a picture you paint. What about love? What about the joy of holding your own baby in your arms? Miss Walters is still a young woman with her whole life before her. She has had such a little life, Edna. Don't ruin her one chance to be more than just a dependent."

The two women heard footsteps approaching down the hallway. By the time Harriet entered the room, Aunt Edna was placidly sewing while Mrs. Evans gazed into the fire.

"Here you are," Harriet said, delivering the thread prior to reseating herself.

"Thank you," her aunt said.

Harriet hesitated for a moment before saying, "There is something I wish to speak to you about, Aunt. Mrs. Higgins invited me to a Christmas gathering at her home this week, an early dinner on Friday. Shall I go, do you think? I did not wish to disappoint her."

"Will you be her only guest?" Aunt Edna asked, glancing up from her work.

"No, she'll be inviting her great-nephew as well. I suppose that Mr. Ash will be bringing Oliver." Mrs. Evans shot a sharp glance at her friend, who glowered back at her. Harriet's head was bent toward the carpet, so she did not see their exchange.

"It will be dark earlier and much colder than the last time you attended a party of Mrs. Higgins, Harriet. I suppose that I will have to send you in the carriage and have it fetch you afterward."

Harriet was relieved that her aunt was offering her the carriage; she did not want Mr. Ash to walk her home again. "If you do not mind, Aunt? I would not have to stay for very long. Perhaps an hour would be sufficient."

"Well, I suppose that you should go. I'm sure that Reverend Simons would expect as much."

"Yes. Thank you, Aunt Edna," Harriet said, bending her head over her own needlework.

Mrs. Evans cast a worried look in her direction. Pondering for a moment, the lady suddenly stood. "Well, I have some correspondence to finish before the afternoon post, so I must be leaving," she said. "Miss Walters, would you mind accompanying me on a little errand? I have finished knitting the scarf I was making for you, but I forgot to bring it with me. It promises to be cold this week, and you will be glad of it. Will you come with me to pick it up?"

Harriet put down her needlepoint, glad to be released from the tense room; she had heard raised voices from the second floor. "Certainly, Mrs. Evans. You're very kind to have knitted the scarf. I'm quite ready to go whenever you are."

"Excellent. Goodbye, Edna, and thank you for the coffee and cake," Mrs. Evans said, stepping around the lady.

"You're welcome," Edna said, giving her friend a quick pinch on the arm when Harriet wasn't looking. Mrs. Evans batted her hand away and followed Harriet from the room.

When they arrived at Mrs. Evans' house, the widow invited Harriet up to her room to fetch the scarf. Harriet had never visited her friend's bedroom before, and was charmed by the cheerful clutter. Embroidered pillows lay piled upon the bed, the dressing table was crowded with perfume bottles and pretty trinkets, and a comfortable chair, low stool, and table were placed before a fire burning in the hearth. An oil painting of a young girl leaning against a seated woman hung over the mantle. Harriet moved closer to study it while Mrs. Evans fetched the scarf from her bureau.

"That portrait was painted of Diane and me when she was eight years old," Mrs. Evans said, joining Harriet beneath the picture.

"I can see where Diane gets her beauty, Mrs. Evans. She looks just like you in that portrait."

"Thank you. My hair used to be that same shade of gold, but it has been grey for many years now." The two women stood before the hearth, Harriet admiring the picture while Mrs. Evans studied her young friend. "Diane lives too far away to visit very frequently, so I'm glad of your company, Miss Walters. You've made a sizable difference in Edna's life, too. She was isolated before you came, but now she takes an interest in the world again. Your coming has eased away all the little complaints she used to have."

"Thank you, I'm glad to hear it. I'm also grateful for your company, Mrs. Evans, and for your friendship with my aunt. Without you, she would not have any real friends in town."

"Well, we've been friends for a long time. It's ironic that we were girls together, and now we are together at the end."

Harriet seized her hand. "Don't say that. You're both in good health, and have many years before you, I'm sure."

Mrs. Evans patted her hand. "One never knows, and that is why old women like your aunt and I want to see our children happily settled before we pass. That includes you, my dear. I may not be your mother or even your aunt, but it would please me to see you happily married with a home of your own before I go." Harriet said nothing, and Mrs. Evans added, "I was surprised by what you said concerning Mr. Ash this afternoon. You two haven't quarrelled, have you?"

"No, nothing like that," Harriet said, her head drooping.

Mrs. Evans watched her. "I'm glad," she said. "You seemed to be getting along so well. I have hopes for the two of you."

"Perhaps you should not, Mrs. Evans. Perhaps any interest Mr. Ash has shown in me is due to a false impression of my expectations," Harriet said quickly, lifting her face to look at her friend.

Mrs. Evans' eyebrows rose. "In what way is he mistaken?"

"He may believe that I will inherit Aunt Edna's estate after she passes. Of course, that is not true."

"Do you mean to tell me that you think Mr. Ash is a fortune hunter? I've never had that impression of him. Why would you think that? Has he said anything to make you believe so?"

"No, not really, but Diane warned me that Mr. Ash's friendship may be based upon false hopes, and. . . ."

"Diane said that to you?"

"Yes, when we went for our walk in the country. I had not suspected him of being a fortune hunter before, but it seems likely to me now."

Mrs. Evans drew Harriet over to the stool and sat down in the chair beside her. Holding her hand and looking directly into her eyes, Mrs. Evans said, "Dear Miss Walters, please listen to me very carefully. I know something about men, so you may take my words to heart. I do not believe that Mr. Ash is interested in you because he thinks that you will be an heiress someday. I've seen how his eyes light up when you enter the room. I am sure that he likes you for yourself, and that he treasures your friendship. Do not so belittle what you have to offer, Miss Walters."

Harriet stared back at her. "I suppose that a lack of confidence is a failing of mine, but how can I be sure of Mr. Ash? No other man has ever shown an interest in me. I have no experience to judge by."

"Miss Walters, there is no hurry. Mr. Ash may not be the man for you in the end, but do not condemn him because of some false fear that Diane has instilled in you. I really do not believe that he is a fortune hunter."

Harriet shook her head. "Truthfully, I had not suspected him until Diane suggested it, and she doesn't really know him, does she?" She paused, and smiled. "Thank you for your advice. I promise that I will get to know Mr. Ash better before judging him. I do feel better for having talked with you, Mrs. Evans."

"I'm glad of it, my dear." The older woman leaned over to kiss Harriet's cheek. "Now, here's the scarf I promised you. I knit it in green and cream to set off your green pelisse. You will look very smart in it."

Harriet took the scarf and wound it jauntily around her neck. "It is lovely. Thank you so much for everything. Now, I had better be going before Aunt Edna misses me. I promised to help her pin up the hem of her dress this afternoon."

"Of course. Off you go, then. And give my regards to Mr. Ash when you see him at Mrs. Higgins' party."

Harriet smiled and gave the lady a quick hug before leaving the room with a new bounce to her step.

Chapter Twelve

Harriet brought one of Cook's excellent plum puddings to Mrs. Higgins' party. She climbed down from the carriage, clutching it closely in her arms, and dashed up the front walk through the rain, rapping briskly upon the cottage door. Mrs. Higgins opened it herself and pulled Harriet inside.

"There you are, my love. Oliver told me that he heard a horse outside in the lane. Welcome, and Happy Christmas."

"Happy Christmas, Mrs. Higgins," Harriet replied, hugging her friend with one arm. "And this is for you, from Aunt Edna and Cook. It's a plum pudding."

Mrs. Higgins drew back a corner of the cloth and sniffed. "Ooh, that does smell good. Your Mrs. Dale knows her way around a kitchen, to be sure. Please send my thanks to her and to your aunt.

"What have you been cooking?" Harriet asked. "Your house smells wonderful."

"Two of my favourites. Come along. Oliver and Mr. Ash are keeping warm in the parlour."

Harriet followed Mrs. Higgins down the chilly hallway and into the parlour. There she saw the mantle trimmed with pine boughs woven with ivy and holly berries. Oliver sat on the hearth rug toasting bread over the fire, the light reflecting in his fair hair. Ash sat at a nearby table, buttering Oliver's efforts. He stood when Harriet entered, and stepped forward to greet her.

"How are you, Miss Walters? Happy Christmas to you," he said, shaking her hand with a broad smile.

"Happy Christmas to you too, Mr. Ash," she replied. The expression on his honest face dispelled any niggling doubts still in her mind, and Harriet beamed back at him. Watching from the doorway, Mrs. Higgins smiled at them.

Harriet turned to the child. "Oliver, I didn't mean to overlook you. Happy Christmas to you, too."

"Happy Christmas, Miss. I'm making the toast for Auntie. She's going to give us rabbit on toast."

Mrs. Higgins laughed. "Not real rabbit, Oliver. Welsh rabbit. That's a mix of cheeses and other good things. We'll have enough toast when you're done that last piece." She took Harriet's hand. "Come over here and have a seat, love. There's Christmas punch on the table. Let me pour you a glass."

Harriet followed her to the linen-draped table. A heavy, cut-glass bowl filled to the brim sat amidst the nutmeats and sweets festooning the table.

"What a pretty punch bowl, Mrs. Higgins," she said as the widow poured her a glass.

"Yes, I'm very proud of this set. It was a wedding present. We brought it out every Christmas that Mr. Higgins was alive, and for our wedding anniversaries, too. I still bring it out at Christmas. Come here, you two," she said, beckoning to the schoolmaster and Oliver. "Take a bowl of punch, and let's have a toast." The guests complied, their glasses raised.

"Happy Christmas to us all, my loves, and a prosperous New Year," Mrs. Higgins said. They raised their glasses and echoed, "Happy Christmas and a prosperous New Year."

"Absolutely delicious, Mrs. Higgins," Harriet said.

"Now, sit down and don't budge an inch," their hostess said to Harriet. "Oliver is going to help me bring out the Welsh rabbit. Give me a hand, my love," she said, leaving the room with the boy. Harriet gazed up at Ash, who still stood.

"Please be seated, sir, and tell me of your plans for Christmas, if you will."

He sat beside her on the couch. "The term finishes on Saturday with a party for the boys that afternoon. Come Monday, I'll be taking the Bristol coach home to my family. It's been months since I've seen them – not since the summer – so I'm very much looking forward to seeing everyone again. What about you, Miss Walters? Will you be spending Christmas with your aunt?"

"No," she said with a shake of her head. "I'm going to my sister's home to visit with my family. I've not seen them since September, and I'm particularly looking forward to seeing my mother again. We've never been separated for so long before."

"And how will you get there?"

"My brother-in-law, Mr. Sinclair Watts, will be coming to fetch me in his carriage."

"Excellent. I'm glad that someone will be looking after you on the journey. But will Mrs. Slater be spending Christmas alone?"

"No, indeed. Her daughters and their families take turns visiting Aunt Edna each year. This year, Mr. and Mrs. Springer and their four children will be coming. They arrive next Wednesday. I'll be leaving the day after."

"What about Mrs. Evans? Will she be visiting her daughter in London?"

"No, not this year. They just saw each other, and Mrs. Fitzwilliam likes to entertain at Christmas. Mrs. Evans says that she prefers to have a quiet Christmas at home, but she will be spending Christmas day with my aunt. I'm sure that she will be in and out of the house as if it were her own over the holidays."

"Good," Ash said with a smile. "We shall all be enjoying a jolly Christmas. Oliver's father will be coming to get Mrs. Higgins and the boy next Sunday."

"Here we are, my dears," Mrs. Higgins said from the parlour door. Behind her, Oliver bore a plate with golden triangles of toast, while Mrs. Higgins carried a covered china dish. Harriet hurried to clear a place for them on the crowded table. When Mrs. Higgins lifted the lid, a cloud of steam rose from the dish.

"Mmm, that smells wonderful," Harriet said, inhaling deeply. She helped Mrs. Higgins prepare plates of toast covered with the delicious cheesy sauce, and passed them to the others. Soon the three adults were eating side-by-side on the couch while Oliver sat on the floor, his plate wedged amongst the dishes on the low table.

"Mrs. Higgins, will you marry me and make this for me every day?" asked the young schoolmaster.

"Bless you, Mr. Ash," the old woman said with a chuckle. "I would, except that I would soon grow tired of cooking the same thing all the time. But someday you'll find a young woman to marry, and it will be for more than just her fine cooking, I'm sure."

He took another bite and winked at the widow. She elbowed him in the ribs, and laughed. "Eat up, my dear. You could use a little more meat on your bones. Someone should take better care of you, young man." Mrs. Higgins took a sidelong glance at Harriet, who pretended not to notice, but was gratified by the suggestion.

The little group ate up every bit of the dish, and then Mrs. Higgins and Oliver returned with ginger cake, custard, and warm rum sauce. They talked and laughed and ate until they could eat no more.

"Mrs. Higgins, you could cook for the King of England and he wouldn't find any better," Harriet said. "Now, I'm afraid that Aunt Edna's carriage will be returning for me soon, but first I have a little something with which to wish you a Happy Christmas." She picked up her reticule and produced a tiny wrapped box, which she handed to her friend.

"Why, you needn't have done that, but thank you, Miss Walters." Mrs. Higgins tore off the wrapping and opened the box to reveal a dainty pair of seed pearl earrings on gold wire hoops. Her eyes grew misty. "Aren't they lovely? I haven't had a new pair of earrings since I got these old hoops thirty years ago. I'll try them on right now so we can all see how well they look." Mrs. Higgins pulled the earrings from the box and fastened them to her ears. "What do you think, Oliver?" she said, turning her head for him to admire.

"They look very nice, Auntie."

"Well, as long as we're handing out presents, I have a little something for you, too, Mrs. Higgins," Ash said, jumping up from the couch. "I left it in the pocket of my coat. I'll be back directly."

He strode out of the room and returned with a slim box trimmed with a red satin bow. "Happy Christmas, Mrs. Higgins," he said, handing it to her with a short bow.

"Another present for me? This is a memorable day," the widow said with a huge smile. She held the box up to her ear and rattled it.

"What's in it, Auntie?" Oliver asked, his eyes shining.

"I don't know, my boy. Shall I open it?"

"Yes, please," he said.

Mrs. Higgins untied the ribbon, removed the lid, and withdrew a pair of brown leather gloves. "Ooh, aren't these handsome, and ever so soft. Let me try them on." She pulled them over her hands and held them up for all to admire. "They have a nice warm lining, too. Won't I look smart going to church on Christmas Day with my new earrings and gloves! Thank you both very much," she said, kissing Harriet and Ash on the cheek.

"You're very welcome," they chorused with glad smiles.

"Now, Oliver, I have a little something for you, too," Harriet said. She handed him a package, and Oliver opened the box to find a brightly-painted wooden top.

"Thank you, Miss," he said, plunking down in the middle of the floor to play with it. The adults were just helping themselves to another bowl of punch when there was a knock at the door.

"Oh dear, I'm afraid that the carriage is here already," Harriet said with a frown. "I'll just tell the driver that I'll be a few more minutes." Returning a moment later, Harriet looked worried. "The wind is rising and it's still raining. Can I offer you and Oliver a ride to the school, Mr. Ash? We can all squeeze in together."

The schoolmaster had stood when she entered the room, and shook his head. "That's very kind, Miss Walters, but I do not wish to take you out of your way."

"Not at all. Just let me carry these things to the kitchen, and I shall be ready to go at once," she said, bending over the table and picking up empty dishes.

Ash beckoned to the boy. "Come along, Oliver. If you take the tray and I carry the punch bowl, we can help Miss Walters clear and save your aunt a few steps." Mrs. Higgins protested, but they insisted that she remain on the couch while they took the leftovers to the kitchen. When they came back down the hallway, however, Mrs. Higgins was waiting for them by the front door with their outer things.

"Happy Christmas, Oliver, and I'll see you on Sunday when your father comes," she said, helping the boy into his coat and muffler.

"Happy Christmas, Auntie," he replied, kissing her cheek before skipping out the door.

"Happy Christmas, Mrs. Higgins, and thank you again for a wonderful party," Ash said. He pointed to the mistletoe tacked to the ceiling and bent to kiss the old woman upon the cheek.

"Why, thank you, young man. First a marriage proposal, and now a kiss. I reckon that the young ladies have to watch out for you!" she said. Ash smiled and nodded before following Oliver outside.

Harriet hugged her friend and said, "Have a wonderful holiday, Mrs. Higgins. I'll see you when I get back."

Mrs. Higgins held her close. "You have a good holiday with your mother, my love. I know how much you've missed her. And don't forget to give Mr. Ash a Christmas kiss, too," she added, pulling away and winking at Harriet. "I think that he would be better off with someone younger and prettier than me."

Harriet smiled and shook her head before hurrying out into the rain. Ash waited beside the vehicle to help her in. Once she was settled beside Oliver, the schoolmaster climbed in, and Harriet arranged a seal-skin rug over their laps.

They were quite cozy as the carriage made the short drive to the school. The driver drew up to the gate, where Hubbard greeted them with a lantern and an umbrella. Oliver climbed over Harriet to Ash, who swung him out to the gatekeeper. Taking Oliver's hand, Hubbard waved at Harriet before hurrying the boy across the courtyard.

"Happy Christmas, Oliver," Harriet called after him. He turned to wave before disappearing into one of the buildings.

Harriet was bent toward the door when Ash turned toward her. Suddenly, they were very close, their knees touching. Ash reached for her hand and held it between his own.

"Have a happy Christmas, Miss Walters. You know, you made Mrs. Higgins very happy today," he said with a sparkle in his warm, hazel eyes.

"So did you, sir. You're a kind man," Harriet said rather breathlessly.

The schoolmaster gazed into her eyes, and then bent to kiss her gloved hand. Without another word, he sprang from the carriage and shut the door, giving a cheery wave before dashing across the courtyard. Harriet sank back in her seat and hugged herself as the carriage carried her home.

Chapter Thirteen

Aunt Edna was anxious to finish the preparations for the house guests arriving the following Wednesday, and Harriet was tireless in assisting her aunt, running instructions down to Cook, helping Grace to air out the spare bedrooms and linens, placing orders at the butcher and grocer's shops, decorating the gardener's wreaths with ribbon, nuts, and berries, and running over to Mrs. Evans' home to borrow everything else that they required. The old nursery was being readied for Aunt Edna's four grandchildren and their nanny, and accommodations were being prepared for Caroline's maid and her husband's valet. Every year Aunt Edna could not imagine how everything would be ready in time, and yet every year she managed.

Harriet knocked on her aunt's door on the evening preceding their guests' arrival. When she was given permission to enter, she discovered Aunt Edna propped up in bed with a cup of chamomile tea, studying the list of tasks yet to be completed.

"Good evening, Aunt. I hope I do not disturb you."

"Harriet, did we borrow those extra candlesticks from Mabel?" her aunt said without looking up.

"Yes, they're on the dining room sideboard."

Aunt Edna dipped her quill into an inkwell and ticked another item from her list. "Good," she said, finally looking up at her niece. "Well, come in and sit down. What do you want with me?"

Harriet sat on the edge of the bed and withdrew a flat package wrapped with paper and ribbon from behind her back. "I wanted to give this to you before the house is filled with people tomorrow. Happy Christmas, Aunt."

Aunt Edna exclaimed happily as she took the present and tore open the wrapping paper. Inside she found a leather-bound journal with pressed flowers on the first and last pages.

"Why, Harriet, what a pretty little thing. I haven't kept a journal since I was a young woman, but it will do for the household accounts. Here, go into my wardrobe, and you'll find something for you. It's the box covered in blue paper."

Harriet found the gift and carried it back to the bed. Aunt Edna said, "Happy Christmas, Niece. Go ahead and open it."

Harriet pulled off the paper, opened a hat box, and found a beaver felt hat within, the brim trimmed with fur. "Why, it's beautiful! Thank you so much," she said.

"You need a good warm hat to wear to your sister's home, child. I'm glad that you like it. Have you finished your packing, by the way?"

"Everything is ready except for a few last minute additions."

"And you have the sweetmeats for the children, and the gifts for the adults?"

"Yes. It was very thoughtful of you to send them."

"Well, I do not usually send gifts at Christmas, but since you're visiting your sister and saving me the postage, I thought that I would be generous this year."

"Yes, Aunt," Harriet said with a rueful smile.

"Well, you had better go to bed. You'll need your rest for our guests tomorrow and for your journey on the following day."

"Goodnight," Harriet said, getting up from the bed and impulsively kissing the old lady on the cheek.

Aunt Edna waved her away. "Off to bed with you. Goodnight, Harriet."

The next morning passed in a flurry of last-minute preparations, but by mid-afternoon, Harriet and Aunt Edna were dressed and waiting in the drawing room as Caroline, Gerald, and their children arrived.

"Caroline, my dear – welcome," her mother said, rising to kiss her. "Gerald, you look well. Do you remember your cousin, Harriet Walters?" Harriet rose and shook hands with them while the four children lined up to give their grandmother a peck on the cheek.

Caroline Springer was a small, calm woman whose every word and movement was a model of economy. Her husband was a tall, languid man who sank back into his chair as if he had no intention of ever getting up again. The children sat primly upon the couch from the oldest to the youngest, the youngest a male child who looked solemnly about the room like an infant owl. Thinking of her sister's boisterous horde, Harriet marvelled at their restrained behaviour and could not refrain from glancing at them every few minutes to ascertain if their good manners had evaporated like smoke up a chimney.

Caroline and Aunt Edna caught each other up on family news while Mr. Springer puffed upon his pipe and Harriet listened. Then Harriet was asked to provide an account of her mother and sister's family, and of her life since arriving in Rexton. The room's unrelenting stillness made Harriet conscious of the sound of her own voice, and she feared that the Springers would find her recitation dull.

A half hour later, the children were dismissed to the nursery, and Caroline and her mother worked on their needlepoint. Mr. Springer laid his head upon the back of his chair and slept, while Harriet struggled to stay awake herself. It was a great relief when the drawing room door sprang open and Grace ushered Sinclair into the room. Harriet's brother-in-law strode over to embrace her, pulling her from her chair and up off her feet.

"Sister, it is good to see you again," he said, examining her at arms' length. "You look very well. You've changed your hair, and it is most becoming."

"Thank you, Sinclair. It's wonderful to see you again, too."

He released her and turned to greet Aunt Edna. Taking her hand, he said "Happy Christmas, Aunt. Mother, Helen, and the children all send their love."

"Thank you," she said, maintaining her distance lest he embrace her, too. "You do remember my daughter and her husband?" Sinclair bowed to his cousin and shook hands with her husband, who had been jolted awake by the gentleman's energetic entrance. Going to stand with his back to the fire, Sinclair rubbed his hands together.

"It's a chilly day. Your fire is most welcoming, Aunt. So, Harriet, how have you been occupying yourself since last I saw you?" Harriet repeated her story, not concerned that she would be boring her audience this time.

Dinner was produced early and consumed quickly, with Sinclair exclaiming over the savoury ham and delicious apple and hazelnut torte until a smile was coaxed from Aunt Edna. The company passed a quiet evening together, Harriet and Sinclair bidding their cousins goodbye at the end due to their early departure the next morning.

When they arrived at Sinclair's house in the late afternoon of the following day, the gentleman preceded Harriet into the sitting room, announcing, "Here she is, Mother, safe and sound." Mrs. Walters sprang from her chair and flew into Harriet's arms, overjoyed at seeing her daughter again.

"Harriet, how was your journey? You did not catch a chill, I hope? I have missed you so much, my dear. How is Edna? Come and sit beside me," the fond mother said.

The children raced to cling to their father's trousers and to their aunt's skirts, practically toppling Harriet before she could sit down. Helen said from her chair, "Now children, do not cling to your Aunt so," but Sinclair scooped up the small offenders and, seating himself in a large armchair, plopped them onto his lap.

Harriet kissed her sister before joining her mother on the sofa and clasping her hand. "Mother, you look well. You are rosier and a little plumper since last I saw you. Before I forget, Mrs. Evans sends her regards."

"Mabel Evans. Yes, I remember her from my youth. She and Edna were always together as girls. I'm glad that they have found each other again."

"Mrs. Evans has become a dear friend to me, too, as have some of the elderly ladies from the parish. One lady is a particular dear – Mrs. Higgins. I've written to you about the two parties I attended at her home."

"Yes, I was astonished to hear that you were making parish visits, Harriet. You were never comfortable doing so at Willoway."

"I have new duties to perform in Rexton."

"You see, Mother," Helen said, "I told you that you did not have to worry about Harriet. It sounds as if she has been both busy and useful these past few months."

"And what has been occupying you since my last visit, Helen?" Harriet asked.

Sinclair cut in before his wife could reply. "The usual things. The baby had croup, Helen's dog wandered off and produced another litter of pups, Nanny left and had to be replaced . . . ."

"Yes, it has been very eventful here," Mrs. Walters said.

"Mother is teaching the twins to play the pianoforte. No doubt we will have a concert while you are here," Sinclair said.

"I could not have taught them," Helen said. "You were always more musical than I, Harriet. I never had the time to practice."

"Never mind, Helen, you were good at so many other things that musical ability was never missed."

"That's true," her sister replied.

Harriet's week-long visit flew by. The day after her arrival was Christmas Eve, and the children were wilder than usual in anticipation of Father Christmas' arrival. When it came time for them to go to bed, all four adults trouped upstairs to say goodnight with severe admonitions that the children must go to sleep, or Father Christmas would not come. Kisses were exchanged and a song or two were sung before the adults could escape back downstairs. Returning to the sitting room, the adults lit the yule log, drank from the wassail bowl, and were very merry before winding their way upstairs to bed.

The children rose early on Christmas morning and had claimed their portions of sweetmeats, oranges, and toys before the sun appeared on the horizon. Harriet distributed Aunt Edna's sweets to the children, and was amused to discover that her aunt had gifted Helen, Sinclair, and her mother with religious tracts recommended by Reverend Simons. The family walked to church together, and when the children were finally shepherded into their pew, Harriet was glad to sit in peace on the end where she could enjoy the service and sing the good old yuletide hymns. Back at home again, the family kept busy with games, carol-singing, and a large goose dinner followed by a blazing plum pudding. A few close neighbours stopped by in the evening to wish the family "Happy Christmas," and it was late before they finally went to bed. The rest of the week was occupied with skating parties, card parties, impromptu dances, and a general over-indulgence in food and drink.

Harriet took the opportunity to speak privately with her mother, and was relieved to find that her spirits had improved. Mrs. Walters derived comfort from Helen and her family. Sinclair was more solicitous of Mrs. Walters' needs, it was true, but Helen was an affectionate daughter who included her mother in all of her plans. The children also loved their grandmother, and the time and attention she lavished on music lessons for the twins not only benefitted the girls, but helped Mrs. Walters to feel useful. By the time that Harriet said farewell at the end of the holidays, she was satisfied that her mother was placed as happily as possible, given their financial circumstances.

Harriet was quite ready to return to the peace and quiet of her aunt's home by the end of her visit, however. The Springer family had already left Rexton by her return, so Harriet and her aunt were both able to recuperate from their exertions over the holidays. They were not entirely idle, however; they welcomed in the New Year with a dinner party at Mrs. Evans' house, where Harriet was finally coaxed into playing and singing as part of the evening's entertainment. Her performance was enthusiastically applauded, and she was able to face the possibility of future performances with some composure.

Life resumed its familiar pattern during the winter months. Harriet continued with her charitable visits, attended Sunday services, socialized with Mrs. Evans, and tried to satisfy her aunt's whims. She occasionally encountered Mr. Ash at the lending library or on outings with his pupils, and was able to snatch a little conversation with him after church on Sundays. Infrequent contact was not conducive to improving their acquaintance, but the possibility that she might turn a corner and suddenly find the schoolmaster standing before her gave Harriet's forays into the village an added spice.

Aunt Edna and Harriet had lived together for several months by then, and Harriet had blossomed with added responsibility. She had grown up in her sister's shadow, and her pursuits and influence at Willoway had been limited by her own feelings of inadequacy. In Rexton, however, Harriet was her aunt's ambassador and a stalwart member of the Women's Association. As her social circle expanded in the village, Harriet became aware of the high opinion in which she was held. In turn, she developed a higher regard for herself, and her increasing confidence was reinforced by improvements in her appearance. Harriet was initially troubled by her aunt's extravagance in purchasing her new clothes, but the young woman's quiet satisfaction with her own reflection soon overcame the pricking of her conscience. Mrs. Evans' daughter observed the improvement immediately upon her arrival for the promised visit in April.

"Why, Harriet," she exclaimed, "you look quite handsome in that gown. It's new, isn't it? I approve. You look fashionable enough even for London society."

"Thank you, Diane," Harriet said as Aunt Edna raised an eyebrow and Mrs. Evans beamed.

"I was thinking the same thing, Diane," her mother said. "My, you've just put an idea into my head. Harriet once told me how much she would like a visit to London. Well, why not take her there this spring? Diane, you wouldn't mind cutting short your visit here, would you? What would you say to entertaining Harriet and me in London?"

"Mother, what a marvellous idea! I would be thrilled to have you and Harriet stay with me. What about you, Mrs. Slater? There's room enough for you, too."

Mrs. Evans turned to her friend. "What an idea, Edna! It's been ages since your London visit. Why not come? It would do us old matrons a world of good to have adventures in London again."

"But our own homes are more comfortable."

"Oh pooh. Don't act so old, Edna."

"But I am old, and so are you, Mabel. Far be it from me to tell you otherwise, if you want to have adventures at your age. You always were more unsettled than I, gadding about the continent and all."

"But Edna, think how much you would enjoy a few months' change. And our expenses in London will be quite insignificant since we'll be lodging with Diane."

"That's very true, Mrs. Slater. There will be practically no expense at all, and you can spend the money you save on little fripperies for yourself," Diane said.

"Don't be impertinent, girl. I'm not interested in fripperies."

Harriet had been overjoyed at the prospect of a trip to London, but doubt began to flicker across her face. "If Aunt Edna does not wish to go, I don't think that I should leave her on her own. And who would visit my parish widows? Perhaps we should forget the whole scheme," she said reluctantly.

Aunt Edna shrugged, and Mrs. Evans glared at her. "Now wait, Harriet, there must be someone who can temporarily assume your responsibilities. Don't give up on London so easily," Mrs. Evans said.

"Well, there is Mother," Harriet said uncertainly.

The lady's face brightened. "What a brilliant idea, Harriet! After all, Edwina grew up here, so Rexton is like a second home to her. I'm sure that she would enjoy a quiet visit with Edna after living with Helen's large family these past eight months. It would be grand for you to see your sister again after – what – four years, Edna?"

"It has been five years."

"Five years! Incredible. It's high time that you had a nice long visit with your sister, and you will not have to leave your own home to do it."

"Mother is accustomed to making parish calls," Harriet chimed in.

Aunt Edna looked from Diane and Mabel's excited faces to Harriet's hopeful one. "I imagine a visit with Edwina would not be unpleasant. I suppose that I could write to her by the afternoon post," she said.

"Certainly you can," Mrs. Evans said. "That is generous of you, Edna. I'm sure that Edwina will accept, so we will make plans to depart as soon as we hear back from her."

"What? Do you mean to leave before she arrives?" Aunt Edna demanded.

"I would not mind spending a day or two with Mother before we leave, if it doesn't interfere with your plans, Mrs. Evans," Harriet said.

The lady smiled. "Of course, my dear. I've not set eyes on Edwina for several years myself. Diane, why not write home of our intentions while Edna writes to Edwina, and we shall lose no time at all. Oh Harriet, I'm quite thrilled for you. Your first trip to London!" Mrs. Evans was delighted to see Harriet's eagerness in her shining eyes. "Come, Diane, let's go home. I've got so many plans to make." The two ladies promptly left with promises to see Harriet the next day. Harriet threw herself onto the sofa and embraced her aunt.

"Oh, I'm so happy! Thank you, thank you for agreeing to let me go to London."

Aunt Edna patted Harriet's back before detaching herself from her niece's arms. She shook her head at Harriet's beaming face. "Imagine being so excited at visiting an over-crowded, dirty old city like London. I hope that it doesn't disappoint you, Niece."

"How could it? There will be so much to see and do. Do you know that I have never been anywhere larger than a town before?"

Aunt Edna studied her for a moment. "Well, you're a level-headed girl, and I'm sure that you won't do anything too foolish with Mabel there. I suppose that you're entitled to one great adventure before you settle down."

"What about you, Aunt? Have you had any great adventures?"

"Adventures? What would I be doing with adventures?" Aunt Edna sputtered. But, after a moment, she winked at Harriet. Harriet laughed, kissed her aunt's hand, and sprang up from the sofa.

"I'm going to examine my wardrobe and decide what to pack," she said before running from the room.

Aunt Edna wrote to her sister that very morning, urging her to come for a visit and to waste no time in making the journey. Mrs. Walters responded that she would arrive in three days' time, and enclosed a note for Mrs. Evans, thanking her for so generously including Harriet in her plans. Mrs. Walters was to arrive on Friday, and Harriet, Diane, and Mrs. Evans were to leave for London on the following Monday.

Harriet spent a harried two days preparing for the journey, helping Aunt Edna to prepare a room for her mother, and saying goodbye to her friends. She worried about communicating her plans to Mr. Ash; it would be unthinkable to leave without seeing him, but how could she arrange a meeting? She did not wish to be so forward as to send him a note.

"No doubt I will see him after service on Sunday," she thought. "I will find a few minutes alone with him then. It will have to do."

Harriet visited with Mrs. Evans and Diane on Thursday, and they were full of instructions and advice. "Don't bring too much, Harriet," Mrs. Evans said. "We can purchase anything you need in London. Diane's chariot cannot handle too much luggage with the three of us in it, and she brought so much with her." She clapped her hands together. "What a good time we shall have. I'm looking forward to seeing some dear old friends again, particularly Colonel York. I've been worried about him since his wife passed. The colonel's wife was an extraordinary woman, and he seems lost without her. How is he, Diane?"

"He's tolerable, Mother. His life revolves around his club and his horses. His valet takes good care of him, and I suspect that many of London's spinsters and widows have amorous aspirations for him. He is not interested, however – his loss is still too recent – but I agree with you, he seems a touch sad. Edward has a brandy with him some evenings at the club."

"Poor man. Well, I will look him up on our arrival, and have him take us to dinner and the opera. He used to find that entertaining."

"Will your son be home from school, Diane? I look forward to meeting both him and your husband," Harriet said.

"You'll certainly see Edward when he is not required at the House, but Steven will not be home yet. Trinity term is not finished until June. But you will certainly see him then."

Mrs. Evans said, "I will enjoy seeing my grandson again. I think it was a year ago Christmas when last I saw him, Diane."

"That was his first year at school. Remember how excited he was to tell us about his teachers and friends? Of course, Steven is a little more blasé this year."

"No doubt. He would not want his friends to think him too eager or unworldly."

Diane laughed. "Heavens, no, that would not do."

Harriet glanced at the clock on the side table and rose from her chair. "Is that the time? I must be going. There is so much yet to be done with Mother arriving tomorrow. I promised Aunt that I would check her room after Grace finished preparing it today. Aunt Edna does not let on how eager she is to see Mother again, but I know that she is." Harriet bustled out of the room and down the hallway with Mrs. Evans following her.

"Now, don't worry about a thing, Harriet. Diane has made all of our travel arrangements and, knowing Edna, I am sure that your household is flawless. Your mother and Edna always got along well. Edna bossed your mother, and Edwina was so accommodating."

Harriet laughed and turned to Mrs. Evans. Her friend said, "We're going to have such a good time together in London, my dear. I can hardly wait to show you the city and to introduce you to some of my friends. I love Rexton, but the old city holds a special place in my heart, too."

"I'm more grateful to you than I can say, Mrs. Evans, for arranging the trip and for smoothing the way with Aunt Edna. I'm so thrilled about seeing London that I lie awake at night, wondering at my good fortune."

Mrs. Evans kissed her cheek. "God bless you, Miss Walters. You deserve some fun in your life. Now, off you go and try to sleep tonight. I will see you at church on Sunday. Give my love to your mother."

"I will. Goodbye," Harriet called, stepping out the front door and into the waiting carriage.

Chapter Fourteen

It was early Sunday morning and Grace was just bringing up the tea when there was a rapid knock upon the front door. She answered it and abandoned the tea tray to scurry up the stairs to Aunt Edna's room. Aunt Edna asked her to call Mrs. Walters, who knocked upon her daughter's door minutes later.

"Harriet, are you up? Harriet?"

Harriet opened the door in her dressing gown. "Yes, Mother, I'm up. What is it?"

"Dearest, come with me to your aunt's room. There is bad news." Harriet clasped her mother's hand and they rushed down the hallway. Mrs. Walters rapped on her sister's door and entered without waiting for a response. Aunt Edna sat on a chair beside the bed in her dressing gown and cap. She turned numb eyes to Harriet.

"What is it, Aunt?" Harriet asked, falling to her knees and taking her aunt's hand.

"Diane just sent one of the servants to inform us. It's Mabel. Her maid could not wake her this morning, so they fetched the doctor. Mabel is dead." Tears streaked down Aunt Edna's face as Harriet embraced her and began to sob.

An hour later, Rogers ushered Aunt Edna and Harriet into Mrs. Evans' room. The curtains were drawn, and Diane sat in a chair beside her mother's bed while Reverend Simons murmured prayers.

"Diane, I am very sorry," Aunt Edna said, stopping at the foot of the bed to nod at her before turning her gaze upon the earthly remains of her life-long friend. Harriet stepped around her aunt and made her way to Diane, who stood to embrace her. Tears began to flow down Diane's face, and Harriet patted her back and helped her to sit. Reverend Simons continued his prayers while Harriet talked quietly with Diane. Finally, Harriet turned toward the bed. Mrs.

Evans rested there, her hands folded upon the bedclothes and her face as peaceful as if she were just asleep.

"Dr. Mackenzie said that her heart failed during the night. She would not have suffered at all," Diane said.

Reverend Simons closed his prayer book and looked up at the women. "She was one of the pillars of our community, and a good woman. We will pray for her at this morning's service. Will you be coming this morning, ladies?"

Diane uttered an emphatic "no," while Aunt Edna said "yes" just as forcefully. Harriet looked at her aunt; her posture was perfectly straight and her face was icily composed. Aunt Edna bent to pat her friend's hand. Sighing, she said, "I'm ready to leave now, Harriet."

"Of course, Aunt," she replied, quickly kissing Diane's cheek and whispering a goodbye. Harriet paused for a moment to lay one hand upon Mrs. Evans', and then followed her aunt from the room. They climbed back into the carriage and returned home, where Harriet's mother was waiting for them in the morning room.

"I asked Grace to serve tea and toast as soon as you came back," Mrs. Walters said, taking her sister's arm as Aunt Edna slowly entered the room. "Come and sit down, Edna."

They two women sat together on the sofa, where Mrs. Walters motioned for Harriet to join them. Grace arrived with a breakfast tray and placed it on the table before them. Mrs. Walters poured out the tea and added sugar to their cups.

"How was Diane?" she asked, handing around a plate of toast and preserves.

"She's very upset, of course," Harriet responded. "She told me that Mrs. Evans appeared in perfect health yesterday evening. Diane had no inkling that her mother was unwell." After a pause, she murmured, "I just cannot believe that Mrs. Evans is gone." Her eyes began to tear, and Mrs. Walters took her hand. Harriet rested her head upon her mother's shoulder while her mother consoled her. When Mrs. Walters looked up, she noticed her sister staring off into space.

"Drink your tea, Edna," she said, gently. The women sat quietly together until it was time to leave for service.

Reverend Simons announced Mrs. Evans' passing from the pulpit, and requested prayers for her and for her family. The congregation turned as one to look at the empty stall where the good lady had once sat. When the service was over, Aunt Edna marched out of the church without stopping to speak with anyone, pausing only to acknowledge Reverend Simons at the door. Following her mother and aunt down the stairs, Harriet noticed Mr. Ash detach himself from the school group and advance toward her.

Harriet turned to her mother. "If you do not mind, Mother, I would prefer to talk with a friend before walking home on my own. I feel the need of some fresh air."

Mrs. Walters looked toward the approaching young man. "Is that the schoolmaster you have written to me about?" Harriet nodded. "All right dear, I will take Edna home and try to get her to rest. Take your time."

Harriet hugged her mother gratefully, and Mrs. Walters left to follow her sister. Ash caught up with Harriet and removed his hat.

"I'm terribly sorry for your loss, Miss Walters," he said with sympathy in his eyes. "Mrs. Evans was a dear friend to you and to Mrs. Slater, and I am sure that you feel her passing keenly."

"Thank you, sir," Harriet said, her eyes beginning to moisten again at these kind words. She averted her face.

"I wonder if you will allow me to escort you home?"

"That would be very kind."

Ash offered her his arm and led Harriet away. His kindness prompted another wave of emotion, and Harriet was unable to speak for a few moments. The schoolmaster did not say a word until Harriet regained her composure.

Finally, she was able to say, "Do you know, Mr. Ash, I cannot think of anyone who was more alive than Mrs. Evans, or more joyous. It seems impossible that she is dead. I cannot credit it yet."

He squeezed her hand upon his arm. "It was so unexpected. It's not surprising that you cannot."

Suddenly, Harriet stopped. "Oh, you do not know! I was going to tell you after church today. Mrs. Evans was taking me to London! We were going to leave tomorrow with Mrs. Fitzwilliam. It was all arranged very quickly over the past week. I told Mrs. Evans months ago that I longed to visit London, and she seized the opportunity to take me. We were to stay with her daughter and her family. That was the kind of woman Mrs. Evans was – generous and impetuous. Oh, how I shall miss her! And poor Aunt Edna. What shall she do without her friend?"

Harriet's vision blurred with tears, and she feared she would be overcome with grief right there in the street. She trembled as she fought to control herself, her face averted. Two women from the parish passed them and looked back at Harriet.

"Come, Miss Walters, let us walk in the park a little," Ash said, guiding her the short distance to the park entrance and down a tree-lined path. Some of the trees wore plump pink blossoms, and early spring flowers flourished in the beds. Ash led Harriet to a private corner and seated her on a bench underneath a tree. Harriet searched her reticule for a handkerchief to dry her face. Taking a few deep, calming breaths, she met the young man's eyes and gave him a weak smile.

"Thank you for your kindness, sir. I am better now."

Ash sat down beside her and took her hand. "It's a very fresh loss, Miss Walters. You were brave to appear in public so soon afterward, but perhaps it was a little too hard on you?"

"Aunt Edna wished to come to service this morning to honour Mrs. Evans, and I wanted to support her. She is very strong – stronger than I, it would seem."

"No doubt she is more familiar with loss than you are. Perhaps grief becomes easier to endure with practice? I have not lost anyone dear to me yet, so I cannot judge. But tell me, there was another woman with you today whom I did not recognize. She left with your aunt."

"That was my mother. She was going to stay with Aunt Edna during my visit to London. I'm so glad that she is here. Perhaps she will be able to console Aunt Edna. Certainly better than I could."

"I'm glad that she is here with you, Miss Walters. I was concerned that you would have to bear your aunt's grief as well as your own."

Harriet nodded. "I would like to introduce you to my mother sometime. I have written to her about you."

He smiled and released her hand. "I would very much like to meet her." After a pause while the two gazed out across the lawn, he said, "I know that your loss overshadows everything else right now, but you must be disappointed at losing the trip to London, too. Did I tell you that I visited London just before I came to Rexton?"

"Did you, Mr. Ash?" Harriet asked, glad of the diversion. "No, you didn't mention it. What did you see on your visit?" The couple lingered on the bench while Ash described the London he had experienced.

Harriet would always remember that day with mixed emotions: the pain of losing Mrs. Evans, her gratitude for Mr. Ash's kindness, and the wonder of seeing London through the eyes of a historian. When he left Harriet at her aunt's door, her heart felt more at ease than she had thought possible. Mr. Ash's company had given her an hour's respite, and she felt ready to resume her burden and to help comfort her aunt as she entered the house.

Chapter Fifteen

The funeral service was held later that week at St. Michael's. Mr. Fitzwilliam was not able to escape his parliamentary responsibilities in time to attend his mother-in-law's funeral, so Diane was left to cope with all of the arrangements herself. She leant heavily upon Harriet's arm as the procession, comprised of Diane, Harriet, Harriet's mother, and Aunt Edna, followed the casket into the church with Rogers and the rest of the household servants following at a respectful distance. Mrs. Evans was laid to rest with her parents in the Rexton family plot. Mr. Evans' remains were interred in London, where the couple had been residing at the time of his demise.

Diane invited Aunt Edna and Harriet to meet with Mrs. Evans' solicitor the following Monday for the reading of her mother's will. Harriet assumed that they were included because Mrs. Evans had left some small bequest to her old friend. The two ladies were admitted into the morning room on the appointed day, where Diane waited with the solicitor.

"Thank you for coming, Mrs. Slater, Harriet. Do have a seat," Diane said in a low voice, not bothering to rise from the couch. She turned to the gentleman standing beside her and nodded.

The ladies sat, and the lawyer began by introducing himself. "How do you do, Mrs. Slater and Miss Walters? My name is Harvey Burton, and I acted as Mrs. Evans' solicitor while she was in residence here in Rexton. You were asked here this morning because you are both beneficiaries of Mrs. Evans' will. The will is relatively new, having been signed and witnessed on January 18th of this year. I will avoid reading it aloud in its entirety in favour of relating the primary points to you."

"Mrs. Evans names Mr. Edward Fitzwilliam, the deceased's son-in-law, as her executor. There are some small monetary bequests left to the younger servants and to her favourite charities, and more ample sums to her cook and butler, who have served her faithfully for over ten years. A donation is made to St. Michael's Church to purchase a new organ. To Mrs. Edna Slater, she left her silver dining candelabrum, her silver service, her Devon Rose china dish set, and a Venetian cut-glass punch bowl with matching glasses. Mrs. Evans comments in her will that Mrs. Slater always borrowed these items at Christmas, and now 'she will have to keep them for herself.'" Aunt Edna snorted and her stony expression softened in amusement.

"Now, to deal with the two properties that are part of Mrs. Evans' holdings. One of them is a country estate in Hampshire consisting of one hundred and sixty acres, the principal residence, and the outbuildings, which Mrs. Evans inherited from her father. There is a tenant farmer in place, and Mrs. Edward Fitzwilliam habitually occupies the residence during the summer months. Mrs. Evans leaves this property to her daughter to do with as she so desires." Diane nodded with a sad smile.

"The second property is the house in Rexton that came to Mrs. Evans through her mother and, in recent years, was Mrs. Evans' principal residence. Mrs. Evans has willed the ownership of the house and its residual contents – that is, those contents which are not specified in other bequests – to Miss Harriet Walters."

Harriet gasped, Aunt Edna started, and Diane's hand flew to her mouth. Mr. Burton paused to allow them time to recover.

"Mrs. Evans comments that Miss Walters may choose to reside there, or sell the property and use the proceeds, as she so desires. Mrs. Evans also asked me to deliver this letter to Miss Walters." Mr. Burton withdrew a sealed envelope from his leather case and passed it to Harriet, who accepted it wordlessly. He reseated himself and continued.

"Now, Mrs. Evans comments in her will that the maintenance of the house and the employment of servants, et cetera, is not insignificant, and that she wishes to provide Miss Walters with an annuity so that she may comfortably reside in the house if she so chooses. Therefore, she leaves Miss Walters one hundred shares in the Arlington Bank, Bond Street, London which her deceased husband, Mr. Richard Evans, owned until his death. At the current rate of interest, this should provide Miss Walters with an annual income of approximately three thousand pounds." Harriet's eyes opened wide in astonishment as she tried to digest this news.

"Finally, Mrs. Evans wishes to leave her remaining one hundred Arlington bank shares to her grandson, Stephen Fitzwilliam, in trust until his twenty-fifth birthday, and the contents of her bank accounts, safety deposit box, and remaining stocks and bonds to her daughter, Mrs. Edward Fitzwilliam." Mr. Burton finished reading and looked up. "This sums up the disposal of Mrs. Evans' estate. I have a copy of the will for your husband, Mrs. Fitzwilliam, which I will post to his London residence today. Are there any questions?"

Diane sprang to her feet and cried, "Harriet, how could you!" before turning and running from the room. The others remained seated as they listened to Diane rush down the hallway and clatter up the stairs to the second floor.

Mr. Burton removed a card from his wallet and presented it to Harriet, who still clutched Mrs. Evans' letter. "If you have any questions, ladies, or wish to consult me concerning the execution of Mrs. Evans' will, please do not hesitate to visit me in my chambers. Good day. It was a pleasure to meet you both."

Harriet automatically answered, "Thank you, Mr. Burton," as he bowed and left the room. Still dumbfounded, she turned to her aunt, who considered her thoughtfully.

"Well, Niece, that was a poke in the eye for Diane. It looks like Mabel got her way after all."

"What do you mean, Aunt?" Harriet asked.

"I'm sure that Mabel's letter will explain everything to your satisfaction." Aunt Edna rose from her chair. "Come, Harriet, let us go home and give Diane a chance to lick her wounds in private. I cannot wait to see Edwina's face when I tell her that her daughter is an heiress." Aunt Edna smiled grimly as she took Harriet's arm and pulled her from the room.

Chapter Sixteen

A letter from Mrs. Richard Evans to Miss Harriet Walters

January 15, 18__

"My dear Miss Walters,

This letter has been delivered to you by my solicitor, Mr. Burton, on the occasion of the reading of my will. You have been informed by now of my bequest to you. I am sure that you are surprised, and am wondering what on earth possessed me to do such a thing.

I have already expressed my gratitude to you for the difference you have made in your aunt's life. It gladdens my heart to see Edna happy again. You have become her lifeline to the outside world; in caring for you, she takes an interest in life again. I have also grown close to you over these past months and have felt privileged to be your friend and confidant. I am very fond of you and, I must admit, worried about your future. I have told you before, Miss Walters, of a similarity in our experiences: you, too, are a spinster dependent upon a relative for your living and without expectation of marriage. I was more fortunate than you because my people had property and means. I would have inherited a home and enough money to make me independent, at the very least. But you, to be blunt, would have been dependent on your relatives all of your life.

Why should that be, whilst I have the means to help you? Society might wonder at my leaving a portion of my estate outside of my family, but should I let convention interfere with what I know in my heart to be right? Diane does not need the money. She had a generous marriage settlement, and she and Mr. Fitzwilliam enjoy a very comfortable life. I have left her the Hampshire estate, which she is accustomed to using as a summer home, but is also profitable in its own right. Diane will have no reason to complain, and I have left her a letter explaining my actions. Perhaps it was cowardly of me not to warn her of my intentions, but I did not wish to quarrel with her and leave unhappy memories behind.

Please forgive me for this indulgence, Miss Walters. To think of you enjoying your own home, perhaps living part of the year in London or travelling to see some of the world's wonders, gives me great happiness and peace. You were always keen to hear stories of my own travels. Perhaps you will wish to marry now that financial constraints are smoothed away. I might recommend Mr. Ash; you seem fond of each other, and he is a worthy young man. I can imagine the two of you exploring Roman ruins, or perhaps visiting some exotic location together. Egypt? The Orient? Whatever you please. Whatever you choose.

It has been a pleasure to know you, my dear Miss Walters. Have a happy life.

Yours most affectionately,
Mabel Evans

Aunt Edna sat sewing on the drawing room sofa while her sister peered out the window. Without looking at her, Mrs. Walters said, "I'm worried about Harriet. She's been walking in the garden for hours now. Do you think that I should go out to her?"

"No, Edwina, I do not. I think that you should leave the girl alone and let her think. She has a lot to consider."

Mrs. Walters seated herself beside her sister and picked up her sewing. Jiggling the toe of her shoe, she frowned.

"I just do not understand what Mabel could have been thinking. What outrageous behaviour, to leave such a valuable property and income away from her own family."

"I'm sure that Mabel could do whatever she liked with her own money. Diane will not miss it – she's wealthy enough. What I want to know is what Harriet will do with it."

"Really, it would be very odd if she takes up residence in Mabel's home. If she does, you must not think her ungrateful, Edna. I know that she is very thankful for the home you provided for her here."

"I don't doubt the girl's gratitude, Edwina. Just between you and me, Harriet has been more attentive than my own children have been, and I think very highly of her. She is not at fault in this situation. This was all Mabel's doing, and Mabel did it out of kindness. Harriet is steady. I doubt that she will do anything hasty or foolish with her inheritance."

"I agree with you. Harriet has always been practical and reliable. But she has lived a quiet and sheltered life. She has never been responsible for her own decisions before. This inheritance will make her quite independent. Poor child. She must be very confused right now."

Aunt Edna looked up at her sister. "Don't fuss so, Edwina. Things will turn out fine."

Mrs. Walters turned to peer out the window again, and started. "I just saw Harriet go by. She's coming inside."

"Now, Edwina, calm down. Pick up your sewing, and try not to look worried."

When Harriet entered the room, her cheeks flushed from the cool spring air, the sisters were bent over their needlepoint. "Hello Mother. Hello Aunt," she said. "The sun is setting and I thought that it must be time for dinner soon. I am ravenous."

Aunt Edna glanced at the mantle clock. "Grace should be announcing dinner any time, now, but never mind that, for a minute. Take a seat, Niece. Your mother and I want to talk with you. Obviously, you've been considering your inheritance all afternoon. Have you decided what you're going to do with it?"

Harriet joined her mother and aunt upon the sofa. "I've not decided yet. I've been thinking that it would feel odd to live in Mrs. Evans' house. You don't want me to leave you, do you, Aunt?"

"Of course not. I'm used to you now, Harriet, and you've been very useful in the running of my household. I don't want you to go."

Harriet leaned over to squeeze the lady's hand. "Thank you," she murmured. Aunt Edna patted her arm. Harriet turned toward her mother. "Mother, would you like to live in Mrs. Evans' home?"

"Good gracious, child, what would I do all by myself in Mabel Evans' home? That house is too big for me."

"I thought not, but I wanted to ask you anyway. I suppose that I could close up the house and leave it as it is for now, as long as I paid the servants' wages?"

"I suppose you could, but that would be very wasteful," Aunt Edna replied.

The drawing room door opened and Grace entered with a curtsy. "Excuse me, ma'am, but Mrs. Fitzwilliam is here to see Miss Walters."

"Mrs. Fitzwilliam? What can she want? Never mind, show her in please, Grace," Aunt Edna said.

"Oh dear, I hope that she's not still upset with me," Harriet said, taking her mother's hand.

"Now, Harriet, show a little spine. You've done nothing wrong," Aunt Edna said.

Diane swept into the room and Harriet rose to greet her. "Oh, Harriet, it's so good to see you," Diane said, embracing her. "Staying in Mother's house all by myself is very melancholy. Everywhere I turn, there are memories that tear at my heart. I simply had to get away for a while and spend time with friends."

Diane released Harriet and turned to the other women. "How are you bearing up, Mrs. Slater? You look well. And Mrs. Walters, I have not seen you since the funeral. It was kind of you to come that day." Diane seated herself on a chair. "With the funeral over, there is nothing more for me to do here. I shall be returning to London soon. But I know that life will be difficult, even with my usual routine to distract me."

"Would you like a cup of tea, Diane?" Aunt Edna interjected. "Harriet, ring for Grace."

"Oh no, don't bother on my account," Diane said. "I know that you dine early, and I had a bit of cheese before I came. I will not take too much of your time. There was just a little matter I wished to discuss with Harriet." She turned to the young woman. "I was thinking that, even with Mother's passing, it's a shame that your visit to London should be postponed."

"Diane, the trip to London has been the last thing on my mind," Harriet cried.

"Of course, but life must go on, must it not? I was remembering today how excited and pleased Mother was at the prospect of showing you the city. Do you recall the list she composed of places to see? I still have the list, Harriet. Why not come back to London with me, and I will show them to you? Mother would have wished it." Diane smiled, but Harriet looked distressed.

"I'm not sure that a visit would be appropriate under the circumstances, Diane. It would seem disrespectful to your mother's memory."

"Nonsense. How could fulfilling Mother's dearest wish be disrespectful? Besides, you would be doing me an enormous favour. I know that life will be very dreary once I return to London. Mr. Fitzwilliam will be absorbed with parliamentary matters, and my son will be away at school. Of course, I would not dream of doing anything frivolous during my mourning, but visiting museums and galleries is educational, is it not? There's nothing disrespectful about educating oneself, is there, Harriet?"

"No, not when you put it that way. But are you certain that I would not be in your way at such a sorrowful time?"

Diane leaned forward to take Harriet's hand. "Harriet, I would love for you to come. We will console each other, and it will do us both a world of good to be distracted from our grief. It's unhealthy to wallow in the darker emotions, don't you agree?"

Harriet still felt uncertain about the propriety of the visit and did not respond. Diane said, "I know what we shall do. Think about it and come to dinner tomorrow, Harriet. That should give you adequate time to decide."

Relieved that Diane did not require an immediate answer, Harriet smiled. "Thank you. Please don't think me ungrateful for not answering right away, Diane. I will let you know my decision tomorrow."

"Excellent," Diane said, rising, "Goodbye, Mrs. Walters, Mrs. Slater. It's good to see you both again."

The sisters murmured their goodbyes as Harriet escorted Diane from the room, returning a minute later with a frown. "Mother, my mind is in a whirl. What shall I do?"

Aunt Edna responded, "You haven't asked for my opinion, Niece, but I will tell you what I think, all the same. I should accept Diane's offer and go to London."

"Really, Edna? Do you think that is appropriate?" Mrs. Walters asked, her mouth gaping open.

"I hate to say it, but Diane has a point. If you stay here, you'll mope over Mabel's death, plus you'll worry about the inheritance. If you go to London, you will be distracted from your worries and return home with a fresh perspective. I think that the change will do you good, Harriet."

"But Aunt Edna, how can I leave you here alone?"

"There is nothing that you can do to shorten my grieving, although I know you mean well. I will grow accustomed to Mabel's passing in my own time. Meanwhile, I will not be alone – Edwina will be here with me. Go ahead, Harriet, go to London. Just be wary of Diane. I wonder what lies behind her invitation? Do not let misplaced guilt interfere with good judgement. Look after your best interests, Niece."

Harriet turned to Mrs. Walters. "What do you think, Mother?"

"Well, I suppose that Edna is right," her mother said. "Don't worry about your aunt and your duties here in Rexton, dearest. I will take care of things for you."

"You are both so good to me," Harriet said, hugging them both. "Thank you for your advice. I will think upon it."

But when Harriet woke the next morning from a troubled night's sleep, there was still one person she wished to consult before making her decision. Fortunately, it was Thursday, the day Mr. Ash took his pupils to the bakery to spend their allowances. Harriet went to the shop at mid-afternoon, and was relieved to see the schoolmaster and his pupils through the bakery window. She knocked on the glass, and Ash looked up in surprise. She motioned for him to join her outside, and he hastened out to her.

"Miss Walters, what a surprise! How are you?" he said with a warm smile.

"I'm well, thank you, sir. I'm not on an errand for Aunt Edna today. I've come to ask you for some advice on a personal matter. I would not interrupt you in your duties if it were not urgent. Might I possibly join you on your walk back to the school?"

The young man glanced inside the shop window before returning his gaze to her. "Yes, of course. Let me gather the boys together, and we shall be with you momentarily."

Harriet waited while Ash shepherded his pupils back into the street. The boys had their purchases out of their sacks in seconds, and began devouring them.

Ash said, "Everyone, mind your manners, please. Remember to give way to anyone who wishes to pass you. I'll be walking behind with Miss Walters, but I'll still have an eye on you. Off you go, then."

As they walked, Harriet told Ash of her unexpected inheritance, and of Mrs. Fitzwilliam's invitation to visit London. He was astonished at first, and then grave, but listened without interrupting her. Harriet waited for his opinion when she had finished. It was slow in coming.

"Miss Walters, I am very happy for you," he finally said.

"Thank you. The inheritance came as such a shock. I had no inkling of Mrs. Evans' intentions. I still cannot take it all in. I must have more time to consider before I decide what to do with the inheritance. But tell me, sir, do you think that I should go to London?"

The young man kept his eyes on the horizon as they walked. "I know how much you would like to see London, Miss Walters, and opportunities to go, forgive me, will not be plentiful given your circumstances."

"You're right, sir," Harriet said with a sigh. "I envy you your masculinity. Men can pick up and go anywhere they like, if they have the means. A single woman wishing to travel must be chaperoned by a friend or a relative, and Mrs. Fitzwilliam is the only person I know living in London."

"I don't know Mrs. Fitzwilliam very well. Is she a responsible person?" Ash asked, turning to her.

"Yes, and she has always been kind to me."

The schoolmaster nodded. "How long will you be away?"

"Our original plan was to stay until the end of June. After that, London becomes too warm, and everyone who can heads for the country."

"Then you will not return until after my departure for Bath this summer."

"Yes. We would not see each other for quite some time, I fear."

Ash nodded again and kept his eyes on the boys. "Well, since you ask, I think that you should go, Miss Walters. I agree with your aunt that the change would be beneficial to your state of mind, and I know that you will greatly enjoy the visit."

Harriet nodded. "That's true."

"Of course, I did not associate with 'society' when I was in London. I expect that you will have that opportunity as a guest of Mrs. Fitzwilliam."

Harriet grimaced. "I had not thought of that. That is a strong argument against my going."

Ash glanced at her with a startled expression. "Why?"

"Come now, Mr. Ash, can you imagine me surrounded by society? I'm sure that if I attended a fashionable gathering, I should end up hiding in a corner somewhere. I would much rather remain here amongst friends then associate with London society."

Ash frowned and stopped. "Nonsense, Miss Walters. You're an intelligent, well-spoken, engaging young woman, and much better company than the typical, empty-headed, self-absorbed women calling themselves 'society.' Please do not allow yourself to feel socially or personally inferior to anyone you meet in London." He gazed at her earnestly before resuming their walk. Harriet was warmed by his flattery.

"Thank you, sir. I will do my best to follow your advice. I fear, however, that I will not have many interests in common with Diane's friends. Perhaps I shall find some elderly scholars to associate with instead," she said with a smile.

The boys had reached the school gate and run on ahead. Ash said, "You will certainly be exposed to a wider variety of people than you have had the opportunity to know here in Rexton. No doubt, travelling in the Fitzwilliams' circle, you will meet titled men – men of power and wealth."

"Oh my. I don't know what I will have to say to such men," Harriet said with a worried face.

"Your life has changed. You are an heiress now. You deserve to take advantage of the opportunities that Mrs. Fitzwilliam can offer you."

Harriet was displeased with his words; they had an ominous tone. "My life does not have to change, Mr. Ash. I would enjoy a visit to London, but I'm certain that I will be glad to return to Rexton afterward."

The young man blinked and looked away. "I think that you have made your decision, Miss Walters. Enjoy your London visit and take advantage of its opportunities. This visit may be crucial to your future happiness."

"Thank you for your advice," Harriet said, still feeling uneasy.

He took her hand and spoke more gently. "Take good care of yourself, Miss Walters. You are an independent woman now." He released her, bowed, and began to walk away.

"Do have a good holiday in Bath, Mr. Ash," Harriet called after him. The schoolmaster nodded and waved before disappearing through the gate, leaving Harriet to hurry home to tell her mother and aunt of her decision.

Chapter Seventeen

Rogers showed Harriet into the drawing room to see Diane later that day. Diane laid her book aside and rose to greet her.

"Harriet, I'm so happy to see you. Do come in. It has been such a pleasant day. Did you walk, or did Mrs. Slater send you in her carriage?" She motioned for Harriet to sit and joined her friend on the sofa.

"No, I walked. I wanted the exercise."

Rogers returned carrying a silver tray with a decanter and glasses. He placed it on the table beside the two women and left, closing the door behind him.

"Would you like a glass of sherry?"

"Yes, thank you."

Harriet accepted the glass and waited while Diane poured one for herself.

"So, Harriet, is a toast in order? Can we drink to your trip to London?" Diane asked.

Harriet smiled brightly. "Yes, we can."

Diane returned her smile. "I'm so glad. I wrote to Fitzwilliam yesterday that I should be very dull if Miss Walters does not stop with us this spring. He will be pleased to hear that you are coming."

"Thank you, you are very kind."

Diane raised her glass. "To the first of what I hope will be many visits to London, Harriet."

Harriet clinked her glass with Diane's. "To London."

The two women made plans over dinner, Diane exclaiming over the wonderful places she would show her friend. It all seemed like a dream come true to Harriet. By the time they returned to the drawing room, they were discussing how soon they could be ready for their journey.

"Our preparations should not take longer than two days," Diane said. "You had already decided what to bring before Mother died, so the packing should not take long. Your mother is here, so you have no responsibilities to deter you. We are as free as birds." Diane sat back in her chair and crossed her ankles, the picture of indolence.

Harriet shrugged. "You're right, Diane. There's nothing to detain us. Two days' preparation will suffice." She glanced at the table clock. "It's getting late and there is so much to do tomorrow. I should be going."

Before she could stand, however, Diane clutched her arm. "Before you go, Harriet, there is still a small matter which I should like to discuss with you." Harriet sat down again and waited for Diane to say more. "Actually, it's a favour which I would request of you."

"Of course – you are doing so much for me already. What can I do for you?" Harriet asked in an eager tone.

Diane leaned toward her. "It concerns a necklace of Mother's to which I have a great personal attachment. Father gave it to Mother on my birth. It was one of the few pieces of jewellery that Mother actually wore. That is why it was not with her other jewellery at the bank. I'm sure that she would have given it to me on this visit had she realized how ill she was, but, of course, she had no idea."

"Do you mean her pearl and diamond necklace, Diane?" Harriet asked.

"Yes, that very one. I was sure you'd noticed Mother wearing it."

"Yes. As a matter of fact, she's wearing it in the portrait of the two of you that hangs in her bed chamber."

Diane's hand rose to her mouth and her eyes looked shiny. "You're right. She *is* wearing it in the portrait. I had forgotten."

"Where did she keep the necklace?"

"Here. There is no reason why you shouldn't know this, now that you've inherited Mother's house. Do you see the flower painting hanging on the far wall?" Diane asked, waving at the picture.

"Yes."

She leaned toward Harriet and whispered, "Well, it actually conceals a wall safe."

"Really? I had no idea."

"Of course not. Rogers has the combination, and he told me that Mother usually kept the necklace in the safe."

"I see," Harriet said.

"Do you, Harriet?" Diane asked with anxious eyes. "Mother left you the house and its contents. Legally, the necklace is yours, but I'm sure that you can see how important it is to me. It would mean so much to have Mother's necklace, for sentimental reasons. You understand, don't you, Harriet?"

"Certainly, Diane. You must have the necklace."

"Oh, I knew that you would understand," Diane said, grasping Harriet's hand. "You have such a sympathetic nature. Of course, I could have gone through legal channels to get the necklace – no judge would have denied me – but that's not necessary between friends, is it, my dear?"

"No, of course not," Harriet said with a smile, happy that she could do this favour for Diane.

The older woman patted Harriet's hand and released it. "Now, since we will be leaving for London so very soon and I shall probably never set foot in this house again, shall we seize upon the moment to retrieve the necklace?" She rose and pulled the bell rope for Rogers.

Harriet jumped to her feet. "Please don't say that, Diane. You're welcome to visit your mother's home whenever you choose."

Diane smiled. "That is kind of you, Harriet. It is hard to be turned out of this house when it holds so many happy memories for me, but what can I do? It was dear Mother's decision to give it to you, and we must respect her wishes." Harriet felt uncomfortable, as if the fault were somehow her own, but said nothing.

Rogers entered the drawing room and bowed. "Rogers, we are looking for Mother's pearl and diamond necklace. I assume that it's in the safe?" Diane asked.

"Yes, madam. Mrs. Evans always returned the necklace to the safe when she was finished wearing it for the day."

"Excellent. Please be so good as to open the safe," Diane said, waving her hand.

Rogers turned to Harriet for her approval. "Miss Walters?" he asked. Diane frowned and turned to Harriet.

"Certainly. Yes please, Rogers," Harriet stammered.

The butler bowed and sailed across the room with Diane and Harriet trailing behind him. He paused before the picture and swung it aside, revealing a small safe set into the wall. Standing squarely before it, Rogers rotated the dial back and forth until the door clicked open. Reaching inside, he removed a green velvet pouch, closed and locked the safe, and presented the bag to Harriet.

"The necklace, Miss Walters," he said with a short bow.

"Thank you, Rogers," she replied. The butler nodded and left the room. Harriet handed the pouch to Diane, who opened the drawstring and allowed the contents to spill into her hand. Out tumbled Mrs. Evans' pearl and diamond necklace, two strands of flawless pearls with a diamond set after each tenth pearl. Diane's eyes brightened.

"Thank you, Harriet. It's just as I remembered it. I can picture Mother wearing it now." She put the necklace back into the pouch and drew the drawstring together. "Now, it is late and we have so much to do over the next two days. Shall I have Rogers call the carriage for you?"

"Thank you. I am rather tired," Harriet said.

"Of course you are, Harriet. All this excitement must be wearing for you. I don't know how I'll sleep tonight myself, thinking of the adventures we shall have together in London."

On the short ride home in Mrs. Evans' carriage – "My carriage now, I suppose," Harriet said aloud – she spared a moment to think about the necklace. It had all happened so quickly that she hoped she had done the right thing. Perhaps she should have consulted with Mr. Burton and had the necklace transferred to Diane legally?

Another thought occurred to her. What if Diane had found the necklace among Mrs. Evans' things? Would she have taken the jewellery without mentioning it? Dismissing the thought as unworthy, Harriet turned her attention to all the preparations she still had to make for the journey, and let the matter of the pearl and diamond necklace drop from her mind.

Chapter Eighteen

The trip from Rexton to London took three days with the hired horses, and Harriet was both weary and excited when the carriage rolled to a stop in front of Diane's Brook Street home. After the driver had helped her down, Harriet craned her neck to admire the three-storey, brown brick house with its Palladian-style windows. A black wreath hung upon the front door, a reminder of the family's recent loss. The door opened and a footman emerged to assist the driver with the pile of luggage, most of it Diane's, while a butler waited for the two women to mount the front stairs.

"Welcome back, madam," the corpulent, silver-haired servant said with a bow. "Please accept my deepest condolences on the loss of your mother."

"Thank you, Symonds. This is our guest, Miss Harriet Walters."

Symonds made a second bow. "A pleasure to meet you, Miss Walters."

"Is Mr. Fitzwilliam at home?" Diane asked.

"The master left instructions that he will be home at five o'clock, madam."

"Very well. I will conduct Miss Walters to her room myself. Please instruct Cook to send up tea and sandwiches. We are both famished."

"Very good, madam." The butler stood aside to allow Diane and Harriet to pass into the black-and-white tiled foyer. From there, Diane led Harriet down a tiled hallway and up a broad, curving staircase to the second floor.

"You'll be just down the hall from my room," Diane said, ushering Harriet into her bed chamber. Harriet's eyes trailed from one feature to another in the lovely room. The pale blue walls were accented with gold and white trim, while delicate plaster moldings embellished a lofty ceiling. The slender wooden furniture was in the latest style, with a black and white marble fireplace and a floral screen adding to the room's elegance.

"How beautiful, Diane," Harriet said. "I shall be very comfortable here. Thank you."

Diane smiled. "I'm glad, dear. One of the maids will be up shortly to unpack and to help you dress." She embraced Harriet and then drew back to gaze into her eyes. "I'm so happy to have you with me during my time of sorrow."

"I'm glad to help, Diane."

Diane released her. "I'll let you rest for now, but I'll be back in half an hour to bring you down for refreshments. We shall have a quiet evening in with Fitzwilliam tonight, just the three of us. I'm so tired that I'm sure I shall retire directly after dinner."

"As shall I."

"Until then . . . ," Diane said, exiting the room.

Diane and Harriet were sipping their second cup of tea when Edward Fitzwilliam strode into the drawing room. He was a bantam rooster of a man, the same height as his wife, and his coiffed hair with its stiff curls was just as elaborate. Harriet noted that he wore a black cravat to mark his mother-in-law's passing. Edward kissed his wife on the cheek.

"My dear, I am so sorry. I was greatly distressed that I could not get away to join you for your mother's funeral. The journey back to London must have been most trying. How did you fare?"

"The roads were muddy, Edward, but that is the danger one faces when travelling in the spring. As you can see, I have brought home my dear friend, Miss Harriet Walters."

Edward bowed. "Miss Walters, how kind of you to accompany my wife home. I am sure that your presence here will be a great consolation to Mrs. Fitzwilliam."

"Thank you," Harriet said

"Will you have a cup of tea and a beef sandwich, dear?" Diane asked. "Do sit down and I'll pour for you."

"Thank you. I have not had anything since breakfast," he said. Edward perched on a chair across from his wife and ate his refreshments.

"My husband works too hard while the House is in session and neglects himself dreadfully, Harriet. I'm delighted that he has come home early this evening and is not dining out. The food at his club is not always consistent."

"My constituency does not care if I dine on pheasant or on bread and cheese, Diane."

"No, but they will care if you become ill and cannot attend to their needs. Adequate food and rest is essential to your health."

Edward nodded and sipped his tea. "My wife and I have this conversation frequently, Miss Walters. Fortunately, I have her to oversee my personal needs while I labour at more important matters."

"Fitzwilliam champions the modernization of our great city," Diane said with a smile.

"By 'modernization,' Miss Walters, my wife means the improvement of basic living standards to a level where commerce can flourish. 'Sanitation, transportation, and employment' are the three planks of my political platform. We cannot continue in this country as we have in the past. The Dark Ages have been banished and great changes are coming. Machinery will soon do the work of ten men, resulting in dramatic increases in production. Business will thrive, and London is the seat of England's economy. People will come flooding to us, from the lowly dock worker to the bank owner. Where will we house these people, Miss Walters? What will they eat? How will they be transported?"

"I'm sure I don't know, Mr. Fitzwilliam," Harriet said, shrinking back in her chair.

Edward nodded, rising to his feet and pacing the floor. "Neither do most of my colleagues in the Commons or in the House of Lords, unfortunately. Firstly, we must abolish the plague breeding-grounds where the poor and unemployed dwell to ensure a healthy and plentiful workforce. Secondly, we must improve the roads and waterways to expand transportation, resulting in a reduction in the cost of food and fuel."

Diane beamed at her husband. "Fitzwilliam is a great planner, Harriet. I'm sure that one day you will be honoured to say that you knew Edward Fitzwilliam."

Edward waved one hand modestly and sank back into his chair. "Not at all, my dear. Understand, Miss Walters, that I do not seek greatness. I am merely a servant of this glorious city we are proud to call our home. I understand that this is your first visit to London?"

"Yes, sir."

"I envy you seeing it for the first time. What will you visit first?"

"I am taking her to St. Paul's tomorrow, dear."

"An excellent choice. A triumphant example of British architecture."

"Yes. I'm also planning a dinner party to introduce her to some of our closest friends on Saturday evening. Nothing too extravagant, of course. It's too soon after Mother's passing."

"Of course not, my dear. You must not overtax yourself. I am sure that our friends will not expect too much of us."

"No, they are kind. But we must stir ourselves and not be too dull for Harriet's sake."

Harriet sat forward in her chair. "Please, Diane, do not concern yourself with dinner parties and introductions on my account. Such things matter little to me. I should be glad to meet some of your friends, to be sure, but only when you are ready."

Diane smiled at her husband. "Didn't I tell you that she is a dear, Edward?" She patted Harriet's hand. "No, Harriet, we will proceed with the dinner. I cannot wallow in grief – Mother would not have approved. Just a few of our closest friends, ten or twelve at most. I will invite Colonel York. Mother was speaking of him so close to the end, and we have not seen much of him this year. She particularly wanted you to meet him, so I will be carrying out her wishes."

"Yes, I remember that your mother spoke very highly of the colonel."

"He is a fine old gentleman, Miss Walters, although rather backward in his thinking, I fear," Edward said. "So many of our elders choose to live in the past."

"Good, it is settled," Diane said. "I will issue the invitations tomorrow morning before we go out. It will give us all something to look forward to." Little did Diane realize how far from the truth that sentiment was for her guest.

Chapter Nineteen

Harriet came down to join Diane on Saturday evening before the first guests arrived. She wore her best gown, a fine white muslin with a pleated skirt trimmed in blue and pink floral embroidery. Diane's maid had dressed Harriet's hair in an intricate style of braids and curls which made her conscious of every turn of her head. Diane wore a flat black silk that emphasized the whiteness of her skin. Coupled with long black gloves and black plumes in her fair hair, her appearance was arresting.

"How nice you look, Harriet. Is that a new gown?" Diane asked.

"Yes, one of the dresses Aunt Edna had made for me," she said, checking the clasp on her necklace.

"Your pearls are very sweet," Diane added.

Harriet glanced down at the strand of seed pearls. "Thank you. They were a gift from Father."

"Simple jewellery can be the most elegant, but more colourful stones would better set off your rich hair."

"I'm afraid that they are all I have, other than a mourning ring and a garnet brooch of my grandmother's."

"Well, you look very nice, dear, but I shall take you to my dressmaker to have some new gowns made. One must wear the latest fashions when one is in the city. I can also recommend one or two jewellers whose merchandise is superior.

Harriet looked doubtful. "I've never really bothered with jewellery before."

"Nonsense, Harriet, it is the details that finish a lady's appearance. You will want to look your best now that you are in society. You never know who might be watching. It could be someone interesting." Diane gave her a knowing look.

"Who is interesting, my dear?" Edward asked, strolling into the salon.

"Who's to say, Edward? It could be a military or a naval officer, or a gentleman with a country estate. Perhaps even a bank owner, like Father. Harriet is a woman of consequence now. Many people will want to be introduced to her."

"Hmm, I see. Miss Walters is on the lookout for a husband this spring, is she?"

Harriet blushed. "I fear that Diane is teasing me, sir."

Symonds entered the salon with a bow. "Mr. and Mrs. Warner, and Colonel York, sir." He stood aside, and the lady and two gentlemen appeared. Diane swept forward to greet her guests while Fitzwilliam waited to shake hands with the gentlemen.

"Mrs. Warner, it is so good to see you again," Diane said. "Mr. Warner, Edward has been telling me of your latest land bill. It's high time something was done about that neighbourhood. Colonel York, it's been too long. You look very well, sir."

Fitzwilliam drew Mr. Warner aside to discuss a point of parliamentary business, leaving Diane to entertain Mrs. Warner and the colonel. The lady gazed pointedly at Harriet, who lingered a few steps behind her hostess. Diane extended a hand to her friend.

"Mrs. Warner, Colonel York, let me introduce Miss Harriet Walters of Rexton to you. She was a dear friend of my poor mother, and has granted me the consolation of a visit. This is her first trip to London, and she is so looking forward to seeing some of our famous landmarks. Harriet, Mrs. Warner's husband is in the House with Fitzwilliam, and you have heard Mother speak of Colonel York."

"How do you do, Mrs. Warner and Colonel York," Harriet said with a curtsy. Mrs. Warner smiled and the colonel bowed.

"How wonderful, Miss Walters – your first trip to London," the lady said. "My, it's been years since my first visit. What mischief we girls got up to." She giggled girlishly, which was disconcerting in a woman so firmly ensconced in middle age.

The colonel remained a step behind the knot of ladies. Harriet felt his glance and looked up to meet his eyes. He was a tall, spare gentleman with white hair combed back from a craggy face, and warm, brown eyes. Harriet noticed his black arm band and guessed that he wore it for Mrs. Evans. As Diane and Mrs. Warren reminisced about earlier London seasons, Harriet detached herself and stepped toward the colonel.

"We had a friend in common, Miss Walters," he said in way of a greeting.

"Yes, Mrs. Evans. She spoke very highly of you and Mrs. York."

"My wife was a remarkable woman, Miss Walters. She taught music at a young ladies' academy in Paris before we were married. I am convinced that she could have had a career as a soloist if her parents had not opposed it."

"Indeed? Was your wife a Parisian? Mrs. Evans didn't mention it."

"No, she was born right here in London. Mabel introduced us, in fact."

Symonds entered the room to announce the arrival of four more ladies and gentlemen.

"I fear that our hostess will be claiming you soon, Miss Walters. I would like to speak to you about Mabel sometime, if I may. She was a dear lady."

"Yes she was, Colonel. I would enjoy talking about her."

He made a short bow and stepped aside as Diane approached with the other guests. Harriet stood quietly by and smiled at appropriate points in the conversation until it was time to enter the dining room. She was seated next to a young dandy named Augustus Bell, a handsome, broad-shouldered man with raven-black curls and devilish, dark eyes. He chatted about horse racing during the soup course, a sport about which Harriet knew nothing. Happily, Colonel York sat on her other side, and when Bell began arguing the merits of two popular jockeys with a gentleman across the table, the colonel drew her into conversation.

"I am curious to know how you met Mabel," he said. Harriet told him how she had come to live in Rexton with her aunt, and of her friendship with Mrs. Evans. The colonel reciprocated by telling her how he had met the lady through her younger brother, Jack, while he and Jack were at school together. A few years later, the colonel had visited Mrs. Evans at her house in London, where she had introduced him to his future wife.

"Mabel was always so lively and so curious about people. It was her great ambition to travel, so her husband took her on a tour of the continent the year after they were married. He was a partner at his bank by then, and a busy and important man, but he took six months away from work to travel with Mabel. He was happy to indulge her whenever he could."

Harriet smiled. "It sounds as if their union was a happy one."

"It was, although they had a few difficult years when they were trying to start a family. She and Richard gave up on more children after Diane was born – the failures were too heart-breaking. But Mabel was always an optimist, always ready to try something new. I greatly admired that lady, and I'm going to miss her."

Harriet nodded. "I wouldn't be visiting London if it weren't for Mrs. Evans. The trip was her idea."

"Is that so? Was Mabel planning on coming with you?"

"Yes indeed. She was particularly excited about introducing me to theatre and opera. I've never been to either, you see."

"No? What will you do about that now? Diane can't take you – she's just begun mourning." Harriet shrugged. "You can't come to London without attending a few performances. That would be disgraceful. Miss Walters, I have a suggestion. If you would permit it, I would be happy to escort you to any production that you would care to see. My wife and I used to attend the opera regularly when she was still alive, although I haven't felt much like going since her death two years ago. I haven't wanted to go alone, but I would be delighted to escort you. Would you do me the honour?"

Harriet smiled with delight. "Colonel York, you are very kind. I would be happy to attend either the theatre or the opera with you."

"But Miss Walters, we must see both. Let me think – what is on offer this season?" They bent their heads together to discuss which performances they should attend, Harriet deferring to the colonel's superior knowledge since she was only familiar with the works of Mr. Shakespeare. Colonel York decided that she must see both a Shakespearean play and a modern farce, and had to spend some time convincing Harriet that she was not imposing upon his generosity. They continued their conversation until Diane rose and the ladies returned to the salon.

The gentlemen joined the ladies half an hour later, and the guests split into groups to make up card tables. Harriet did not care to play cards, however, and listened to their conversations from one of the settees. The young dandy from dinner, Mr. Bell, sat down beside her and crossed his legs. Harriet moved over a bit to put some space between them.

"How do you do again, Miss Walters? I was berating the colonel over brandy and cigars for monopolizing you throughout dinner. Whatever were you two discussing all that time?" Harriet coloured and looked down at her lap; she was not accustomed to such forward conversation from a gentleman. He remained silent, however, and she looked up. Bell smiled.

"That's better. I don't like it when ladies pretend to be timid. It's too hard to make conversation. But excuse me," he said, noting the blush in Harriet's cheeks, "bless my soul, you really are shy, aren't you?" When Harriet still did not answer, he added, "You will have to forgive my impudence, Miss Walters. I do not mean to make you uneasy. Let's see. I guess that I should own up to listening in to your dinner conversation. You were talking about opera and theatre with Colonel York, weren't you?"

"Yes," Harriet answered, thinking that the young man was very insolent to speak to her so familiarly and confess to eavesdropping, too. The young dandy laughed, displaying two perfect dimples.

"That was a decidedly unfriendly look you just gave me, my dear. You must guard against showing your emotions so openly. Please allow me to begin again. Miss Walters, I understand from our hosts that this is your first trip to London. How do you like the city so far?"

"I have not seen very much beyond St. Paul's Cathedral and a few of the shops on Bond Street, Mr. Bell. I look forward to seeing Westminster Abbey and St. Margaret's Church tomorrow."

The gentleman held up his hands in mock horror. "Two churches in one day, and the only other sight you've seen the Cathedral! Really, Diane, are you trying to turn Miss Walters into a nun?" he called to his hostess across the room.

Harriet shrank into her seat, embarrassed about being teased before the entire company. "Hush, please," she whispered. Bell grinned at her.

"What's that, Augustus?" Diane asked, glancing at him over her shoulder.

"I was just wondering why Miss Walters is only seeing churches on her visit. How dreary that must be."

Diane turned to drape an arm over the back of her chair. "Miss Walters' tastes are loftier than yours, Augustus. She appreciates architecture and history. Besides, I am newly in mourning. I cannot take her dancing."

"No, but I can. What a capital idea! If Colonel York can take Miss Walters to the theatre, I shall take her to a ball at Almack's. What do you say to that, Miss Walters? Would you care to waltz with me?"

The gentleman held out his arms as if to dance with her that very minute, and Harriet shrank away from him in alarm.

"Leave Miss Walters alone, you fool. Harriet, come sit beside me," Diane ordered.

"Now Diane, don't scold," Bell said in a petulant voice while the other ladies tittered. Harriet fled to Diane's table, where Colonel York was seated. The gentleman stood.

"Please, Miss Walters, take my place," he said.

Harriet sank into his chair with relief and smiled up at him. "Thank you, Colonel. You are very kind," she said.

"Not at all. May I get you a cup of coffee?"

"Yes, thank you." The colonel left on his errand while Harriet was dealt into the game.

Later that evening when the others had gone home, Harriet, Edward and Diane climbed the stairs to bed. Harriet had a dull headache and was weary from the effort of smiling and trying to make polite conversation. The Fitzwilliams' guests were acquainted with Harriet's situation, and had been curious to know what Mrs. Evans' little heiress was like, so Harriet had been the centre of attention all evening. Edward wandered off to his dressing room while Diane escorted Harriet to her door.

"I think that went well, Harriet. Did you have a pleasant evening?"

"Yes, thank you. Everyone was very kind, especially Colonel York."

"I'm so glad. I think you've made a friend there, my dear. The colonel is not generally so gregarious in company, but he certainly leapt to offer you his place at the whist table when Augustus was teasing you."

Harriet frowned at the memory. "Yes, Colonel York was very gracious, but I did not care very much for Mr. Bell's manners," she said.

"Augustus often plays the clown in company, and it can be rather trying to those who do not share his sense of humour. The trick is to tease him right back."

"I'm afraid I'm not very good at teasing, Diane."

Diane laid her hand upon her friend's shoulder. "You are unused to society and to what is considered 'witty repartee,' Harriet. You are out of your element here, but all you want is practice. I know that it was difficult for you to meet so many new acquaintances this evening, but you will become more comfortable with society in time."

Harriet nodded. "You're probably right, Diane. I shall do better, as long as I do not have to face Mr. Bell again anytime soon. Good night."

"Sleep well, Harriet."

Chapter Twenty

Harriet was not to have her wish, however. The very next day, after having toured Westminster Abbey and St. Margaret's Church, she and Diane discovered the gentleman on a bench outside St. Margaret's, two bunches of spring daisies lying on the seat beside him. When he spotted the ladies, Bell sprang to his feet and bowed.

"Ah, I thought that I would see you today if I waited long enough," he said, presenting his flowers. Diane smiled and accepted hers with a mock curtsy while Harriet only nodded.

"How clever of you to find us, Augustus. What brings you here?" Diane asked.

"Just the desire for your company, Diane. How were today's churches, Miss Walters? Did they live up to your expectations?"

"Westminster is very impressive, and I thought St. Margaret's charming."

"I'm so glad we did not disappoint," he replied, offering each lady an arm. Harriet hesitated before laying her hand in the crook of his elbow. Bell smiled down at her and gave her hand a pat before leading both ladies to their carriage.

"Now, you've been shut up inside stone walls long enough. It's a beautiful spring day. What do you say to a carriage ride in Hyde Park?"

"What a delightful idea, Augustus," Diane replied, "but how will we accomplish that? How did you get here this afternoon?"

"I came in my carriage," Bell replied, pointing to a curricle with a roan-coloured gelding cropping the grass behind Diane's carriage.

"You have not thought this through, Augustus. The three of us cannot fit into your curricle, and if you ride with us, who will drive your vehicle?"

Bell frowned for a moment. "I have it," he said, his face brightening. "I shall play coachman for you two young ladies, and your man can follow in my curricle."

"Nonsense. You, our driver?" Diane laughed while Harriet frowned and shook her head.

"Why not? It should prove very entertaining. Here, my good man," he said to Diane's servant, "get down from there, if you please." He untied his own horse and handed the reins to the driver. The man grinned, touched his hat, and climbed into Bell's curricle.

"Ladies," Bell said, handing Harriet and Diane up into their carriage. Harriet climbed in with reluctance. She was afraid that Mr. Bell would appear a perfect jackanapes in public. The gentleman bounded into the driver's seat and, with a whistle and a snap of the reins, drove away at a smart pace with Diane's driver following in behind.

Once they arrived at Hyde Park, Bell doffed his hat and called a greeting to whomever he recognized driving or strolling by. Several people made derisive comments or hooted with laughter as they recognized the driver. Harriet thought the joke unseemly given Diane's recent mourning, but Diane was obviously enjoying the escapade, waving and smiling at acquaintances. After a half hour's leisurely drive, however, Bell grew bored with the joke and drove them home. He stopped in front of Diane's house and helped the ladies to descend. Diane smiled, but Harriet would not meet his eyes. Diane's driver had driven the curricle at a more sedate pace and arrived just in time to attend to the horses while Bell escorted the ladies to the door.

"You are an excellent driver, Augustus. If my driver ever leaves me, perhaps you would consider the position?" Diane said.

The gentleman swept off his hat and bowed. "I cannot think of a better use of my time, Mrs. Fitzwilliam," he replied, kissing her gloved hand. Diane broke off a daisy from her bouquet and tucked it into his lapel before going into the house. Harriet was about to follow when Bell blocked her path. Harriet looked around uneasily, just in time to see the butler discreetly closing the front door.

"How did you like the park today, Miss Walters?" the dandy asked, leaning against the railing.

Harriet paused and folded her hands over her skirt. "I hardly took any notice of my surroundings, to be truthful, sir."

"You did not seem to enjoy my little joke."

"I wonder what Mrs. Fitzwilliam's friends will think of us parading around the park with her mother so recently deceased?"

Bell sat down at her feet and rested back on his elbows. "Diane's friends will think nothing of it. They are used to me playing the fool. Only the sanctimonious will think my prank unseemly."

"But why would you expose Mrs. Fitzwilliam to any kind of censure, sir?"

"Bah, Diane does not give a snap for anyone so stuffy."

"But her husband is a Member of Parliament, and some of his constituents may feel differently about what constitutes unseemly behaviour."

Bell tilted his head back and squinted up at her. "Hmm, you do have a point, Miss Walters. I would not want to cost Fitzwilliam any votes. What do you suggest I do to remedy the situation?"

Worried that he might think of something outrageous, Harriet blurted, "Do nothing, Mr. Bell. Don't do anything which may draw further attention to the Fitzwilliams."

"You're quite right. Soon another fool will do something equally or even more ridiculous, and no one will remember today's small transgression. On the other hand, if I were to dive off London Bridge, people will consider me a madman and congratulate Diane on her narrow escape from an association with a lunatic."

Harriet sighed. "If you're not going to be serious, sir, I shall go in." She pushed past him and went into the house.

Bell laughed and shouted, "Goodbye, little Miss Prim," before she could close the door.

Chapter Twenty-One

Diane had already made an appointment for Harriet to see her dressmaker, but decided to take an inventory of Harriet's wardrobe before the visit, from undergarments and gowns to hats, boots, and coats. She shook her head when she saw her friend's meagre collection, and insisted that they take immediate action to supplement its deficiencies. The ladies spent two days visiting the shops, with Harriet's head in a whirl as Diane instructed her on style, fabrics, cut, and embellishments. Diane completed this fashion pilgrimage by taking Harriet to an exclusive jeweller in Ludgate Hill, where the two ladies were conducted into a private room. The proprietor, a Mr. Peters, chose a selection of items for Harriet to consider, from simple jewellery appropriate for morning calls, to necklace, bracelet, and earring sets for more formal occasions. Harriet's eye was caught by a spectacular diamond and sapphire necklace, and she returned to this piece when everything else had been examined.

"Oh, Diane, it is exquisite. I have never seen anything so beautiful before," Harriet enthused, staring at the necklace in its velvet case.

Diane smiled at Peters. "My friend has lived in the country for most of her life. She has not had the opportunity of seeing such beautiful stones and settings before." The proprietor acknowledged the compliment with a bow.

"Dare I try it on?" Harriet asked. Within a moment, Mr. Peters had whisked the necklace from its case and clasped it around her neck, moving a table-top mirror in front of her so that she could admire the piece. Harriet's hand trembled as she touched the necklace, mesmerized by the glittering gems.

"Diane, it's much too grand for me," she said, wrenching herself away from her reflection.

"Nonsense, it looks wonderful on you."

"Where would I wear it?" Harriet asked, peeking back into the mirror.

"Hasn't Colonel York offered to take you to the theatre and the opera?"

"Yes . . . ."

"Think how it would set off your white silk gown with the ostrich feathers. You'll look magnificent."

Harriet hesitated. "May I ask the cost, Mr. Peters?"

The proprietor bent and whispered the figure into her ear. Harriet's eyes flew open.

"No, I couldn't. It would be too indulgent to spend so much money," she said, hurrying to unfasten the clasp. Diane covered Harriet's hands with her own, however.

"Now, dear, think of it as an investment. I found two very handsome necklaces and a bracelet of mother's at the bank that I don't remember her ever wearing, not to mention the pearl and diamond necklace. You see, even mother believed in jewellery as an investment."

"But, Diane, see that pretty little cameo? I would feel much more comfortable wearing it."

"Fine, but take them both. Enough. I shall not listen to any further argument. You have the means, and I would be remiss not to convince you to buy the sapphires."

Harriet considered for a moment before acquiescing. She had a vision of herself in her new gown, the jewels sparkling on her skin, and she liked it. For once, she would appear as grand a lady as Diane and her friends. Peters laid the necklace back in its case, picked up the tray with the other trinkets, and left the room to wrap her two purchases.

Diane smiled. "I am pleased by your good sense, Harriet. Now, I must find a new gold chain for my topaz cross while we are here."

A week later, Harriet had an appointment to go to the opera with Colonel York. She dressed and came down to the salon early that evening, sitting stiffly on one end of the couch while Diane sat doing her needlepoint on the other. When Colonel York entered the room,

Harriet rose to her feet eagerly. The colonel stopped in the middle of his greeting to gape at her, and she coloured.

Harriet wore her new white silk gown with the under and over dresses trimmed in ostrich feathers at the shoulder and hem. Her arms were encased in long white gloves that stretched to the slit sleeves. Her hair was tucked into a turban also trimmed with ostrich feathers, and the diamond and sapphire necklace glittered against her throat.

"Doesn't she look lovely, Colonel?" Diane inquired. The gentleman recovered his composure and strode forward to greet them.

"You look very well, Miss Walters," he said before taking Diane's proffered hand. Harriet remained silent, doubtful of the sincerity of his compliment.

"You look very distinguished yourself, Colonel," Diane said. "What a handsome ruby stickpin you are wearing. I have never seen it before. Is it new? I must say, I do envy the two of you your excursion tonight. Fitzwilliam is at the House, so I shall have a quiet evening alone at home. Well, do not let me keep you. The traffic around Covent Garden can be very trying on opening night. I shall not wait up, so stop for refreshments afterward, if you choose. Have a wonderful evening."

"Thank you, Diane, I'm sure that we will," Harriet murmured.

The colonel escorted the young woman to his carriage, and she sat quietly by his side as he manoeuvred the vehicle into the street. Once they were underway, Harriet gathered her courage and said, "I shouldn't wonder that you stared on seeing me this evening, Colonel."

The gentleman started. "I beg your pardon, Miss Walters. Did I stare? My apologies, I did not mean to."

Harriet's hand touched the stiff curls protruding from her turban. "Do I look foolish in this ensemble? I once saw a pet monkey attached to a grand lady by a chain around its wrist. The monkey wore a gold turban and a red coat. I feel rather like that monkey now."

The colonel coughed and squirmed in his seat. "Come now, Miss Walters, you mustn't ask me that. I know nothing about ladies' fashions. I'm sure that you're just not accustomed to wearing these new, fancy styles. By the way, that's a splendid necklace you're wearing."

Harriet's hand fluttered to her throat. "I'm afraid that the clasp will come undone, and that it will slip off without my noticing. I wish that I had left it behind. I don't know how women dare wear such expensive jewellery outside their homes."

"If it makes you feel any better, I promise to keep an eye on it all evening," the colonel said with an earnest face.

"Thank you, sir," Harriet said with a small smile before falling silent again. She watched the passing buildings while the colonel looked at her out of the corner of his eye.

"Miss Walters," he said after a few minutes, "I must admit that ladies' fashions are incomprehensible to me. I don't see how you can be comfortable with all the frills and feathers that your sex wears. But don't worry about how you look this evening. Diane will know just what should be worn to an opening night at the opera. You'll fit right in with the other ladies, you'll see." He smiled reassuringly, and Harriet relaxed a little.

"Thank you," she replied. "I shall try to feel a little less like a monkey."

But when the couple had taken their seats at the Royal Opera House and Harriet had begun to glance about the auditorium, she forgot to feel self-conscious. She stared at the crowd of people crammed into the enormous space, her eyes taking in the rows of boxes and balconies rising toward the magnificent inlaid ceiling. The men and women chirped and preened, the ladies wielding their fans so vigorously that they resembled a flock of birds about to take flight. When the curtain rose, however, Harriet forgot about them to focus on the stage.

The opera was sung in Italian and Harriet was unable to translate much of the libretto into English, but the singers' florid acting enabled her to follow the story. She had never heard such singing before, and didn't know what to make of all the flourishes and heroic high notes. When she was not watching the spectacle on the stage, however, Harriet found equal entertainment in watching her neighbours: the little flirtatious smiles from behind a lady's fan, the nods of acknowledgement from one superior-looking person to another, and the snores of a patron sound asleep. She wondered if the stately-looking woman in the box above the stage saw any of the performance since she appeared to spend the entire evening looking through her lorgnette at the occupants of the other boxes.

During the interval, Harriet took the colonel's arm and they ventured through the press of people strolling toward the theatre entrance. A few people greeted Colonel York, and he introduced Harriet as a visiting friend of Mrs. Fitzwilliam. Harriet noticed her clothing and jewels being surreptitiously appraised by the other females. After the third such encounter, Colonel York whispered, "You see, Miss Walters, I told you that you would pass muster." He winked, and she laughed, thinking that the colonel was right in equating her clothing to a uniform; the uniform of wealth and privilege.

After the opera, the gentleman treated Harriet to a late supper at a nearby inn. As they were eating their meal, he asked the young woman if she had enjoyed her first opera.

"To be honest, I am not sure," she replied. "I have been to private musical soirées and a few concerts, but nothing to equal the grandeur of tonight's performance. What did you think of the singing, Colonel?"

"My wife educated me in music a little, but I do not pretend to be a judge of vocal quality. That being said, I thought that the tenor was fine." The colonel hummed a piece from one of the arias. "What did you think of the soprano?"

"She was very – loud." Her friend guffawed, and Harriet smiled down at her plate, pleased that her companion had enjoyed her small joke. "I am curious," she continued, "to see if the audience at *Romeo and Juliet* is more inclined to watch the performance."

"But Miss Walters, you forget the purpose of going to such entertainments. The theatre and the opera are convenient places for society to meet and to pursue their affairs. Only the wealthy would pay these ticket prices and completely ignore the performance. Perhaps those who attend the cheaper theatres are the true devotées."

"I think I begin to comprehend, sir. It does not signify if one understands opera and theatre. Being seen at a performance is what is important. Appreciating the art form is not required."

Colonel York nodded and smiled. "Well done, Miss Walters. You are a quick learner."

Harriet shook her head and ate her meal.

Chapter Twenty-Two

Diane's carriage was at Harriet's disposal and she was always willing to accompany Harriet into the city, but for every visit to places of cultural importance, Harriet paid the price in social calls and entertainments at home. Diane was the perfect helpmate for her husband's political ambitions; she utilized social functions to charm and influence people who could be useful to Edward, and she was vigilant in exploiting every opportunity. Of course, Diane expected her guest to participate in these entertainments as well.

It was not that Harriet was reclusive by nature. On the contrary, she enjoyed the companionship of good friends and close relatives, but she was not comfortable with strangers. For Diane's sake, however, she hid her discomfort behind a mask of affability and attempted to mix with her friend's crowd. And she was successful because she posed no threat to anyone: she was well-dressed but not pretty, unobtrusive, and not in pursuit of a husband. She was also a patient listener, and spent many an evening trapped beside a fond mother bent on recounting her offspring's admirable qualities, or by one of Edward's political allies boasting of his accomplishments.

Occasionally, Diane introduced Harriet to someone whose friendship she valued. One of these people was Abigail Pope, the daughter of Dr. Richard Pope, a physician and Edward's second cousin. At twenty-two, Abigail kept house for her widowed father and older brother, who was studying to become a doctor. Abigail's appearance was unremarkable. She was of middling height and a little stout, with freckles and sandy brown hair. The family was comfortable financially – Dr. Pope's patients were drawn from the prosperous merchant class – but not wealthy enough to attract any suitors for Abigail.

Harriet first met Abigail when the young woman called to express her condolences on the death of Diane's mother. Later, when all three members of the Pope family came to dine, Harriet discovered that Abigail did not bother to join in conversation in which she had no interest. After dinner, Harriet found herself sitting alone with the bored young lady while the other four played cards.

Abigail must have found Harriet worthy of conversation, for she said, "I understand that you study history, Miss Walters. Are you interested in any particular period?"

"In English history in general, Miss Pope, although lately a friend has piqued my interest in the Roman occupation of England."

"I know very little about the subject myself. My interest lies in science. In medicine, in particular. Hardly surprising considering what my father and brother do. The human body is endlessly fascinating to me. I have been reading Father's medical books to learn more about it."

Harriet was startled. It was improper for a female to read medical books. "Does your father know that you read his books, Miss Pope?"

"Of course. I ask him or my brother for explanations whenever I do not understand something. My father did not like me reading them at first, I admit, but he no longer objects. A friend of my mother's once tried to break me of the pursuit, but she was unsuccessful. My mother died when I was twelve, you see, and this friend undertook my education in the traditional female pursuits. She was distressed to learn of my medical reading, but could not prevent me from doing what I liked when father was not at home. She supervised my entry into society when I was eighteen, but abandoned her plan to prod me down the path to marriage and motherhood in the end. What could she do, after all? I had no offers." Abigail made this bald statement without any sign of embarrassment, which Harriet found incredible.

"Do you have no intention of marrying then, Miss Pope?" Harriet asked after clearing her throat.

"Yes I do, when I have found the right situation. I am healthy and strong, and my knowledge of medicine, plus my own personal inclination, compel me to a life of service. My ambition is to marry a missionary so that I can put my medical knowledge to use in some uncivilized country – perhaps China or Africa – while my husband spreads the gospel."

Harriet's eyes opened wide in astonishment. "Miss Pope, won't you be afraid to live in a foreign country where you will know no one but your husband and will not even speak the language? I could not undertake such a plan."

Abigail shrugged with the indifference of youth. "I am not a conventional woman, Miss Walters. But then, neither are you, from what I understand. You are a spinster with an independent income which allows you to live as you please. You are interested in history – an uncommon interest in a woman – and you're staying in London with the only person you know, a friend of very brief acquaintance. Your actions indicate an adventurous nature, a characteristic that I share with you, but on a grander scale." Harriet had nothing to say to this.

"You still look askance at me, Miss Walters. Come now, men undertake professions in foreign locales all the time. They generally do so to conduct business or to soldier. Is my motive not more worthy? And yet, I will not deceive you that my ambition is altruistic. What is the alternative? To be smothered in a marriage where my husband will do my thinking for me? To have child after child to increase the likelihood of a male heir? To fashion a little life for myself, when I can use my love of medicine to accomplish greater things? Certainly my plan is the better way." Abigail's eyes shone, and her voice grew louder as she rhapsodized on her subject. Her father heard her and looked up from the card table.

"I hope that Abigail is not boring you, Miss Walters?" the gentleman said. "She can chatter exhaustively on a favourite topic. One would not think so to see her sitting in a room full of people without a word of conversation passing her lips, but she can." He smiled indulgently at his child.

"No, Dr. Pope, I'm quite enjoying our conversation."

"How nice," Diane said, smiling at Harriet. No doubt she had witnessed that exact behaviour from her husband's cousin in the past and was thankful that Abigail had found a sympathetic listener.

Abigail said, "Go back to your cards, Father. All is well."

When the card game had resumed play, Harriet leaned toward her new friend and said in a low voice, "Do your father and brother know of your intentions?"

"No, and I would gain nothing in trying to enlist their help. Father would not approve, and my brother, while kind, does not have any imagination. They will miss me when I am gone, but Father can afford to hire a housekeeper. Father recently applauded my joining a missionary fund-raising committee at the church – he thinks that I am assuming my proper duties at last. Little does he know that my true purpose is to meet male missionaries. I am patient, Miss Walters. One day I will find a man who will appreciate my medical knowledge, and will treat me as a partner in our marriage. Meanwhile, I educate myself in the areas that I think will be most useful in my new life."

Harriet sank back into her seat. "Well, it is an ambitious plan. I wish you all the luck in fulfilling your dream, Miss Pope. And I thank you for confiding in me."

Abigail smiled. "Not at all. You appear trustworthy, and sometimes I just long to talk to someone about my scheme. By the way, I understand that you visit the British Museum on occasion. I would be pleased to accompany you on your next outing. The museum is an excellent place to study other cultures."

Harriet was happy to agree, and Abigail began accompanying Harriet on outings that they found mutually educational. Dr. Pope and Diane encouraged their friendship, thinking that Harriet might have a gentling effect on Abigail, but the opposite was true. Harriet did not share Abigail's pragmatic approach to marriage, but the idea that marriage could be used to promote one's talents and inclinations was revolutionary to Harriet. She was not so naive as to doubt that both men and women married for financial and social gain, so it seemed reasonable that Abigail should marry a missionary to put her medical knowledge to use. That Abigail was actively working toward her own happiness was admirable.

While Harriet and Abigail's friendship blossomed, Diane's son, Steven, came home from Oxford for the summer holidays. He popped into the morning room without any warning one day.

"Well, Mother, here I am," was his nonchalant greeting.

Diane sprang up from her chair with an exclamation and rushed to embrace her son.

"You silly child, why didn't you write to tell me that you were coming home today?" she scolded, standing on tiptoe to kiss his cheek.

"Because I like to see your face when I surprise you," he replied, beaming down at her. "It's gratifying to know that I am missed."

Diane smiled happily at him. "Imp," she said.

"You look as beautiful as ever, Mother, although it's sad to see you in mourning."

"I know, darling," Diane said, patting his cheek, "but it must be endured. Now, let me introduce you to our guest, Miss Harriet Walters. I've written to you about Harriet's friendship with Grandmother." Stephen turned to Harriet with a bow, and she observed that he had inherited his mother's blond good looks.

"Miss Walters, I am delighted to know you," he said with a welcoming smile. "Grandmother wrote of you to me, too."

"Your grandmother spoke of you with both pride and fondness, Mr. Fitzwilliam. She said that you were a man of high intellect, and that you planned to follow your father into Parliament one day."

Steven grinned. "My grandmother was flattering me, I fear. I enjoy literature and the classics, and I have a good memory for poetry, but I have to work hard for my first classes."

"Don't be modest, Steven. You've always been a clever child," Diane said. "In that you take after your father. I was never of a studious bent. Speaking of your father, I shall send him a message to be on time for dinner tonight."

When the family and Harriet sat down to dine that evening, they were in a festive mood.

"Well, my boy, how did you get on this term?" Edward asked.

"Not too badly, Father," Steven replied around a mouthful of beef.

"Did you meet the Warners' son?" Diane asked. "Mrs. Warner and her daughter dropped by for a visit just last week, and Meredith was asking after you. She came out into society this season, you know."

"Did she really, Mother? Last time I saw Meredith, she was a little girl with ribbons trailing down her back."

"Yes, she did. By the way, Mrs. Warner is holding a private dance this Friday. She hoped that you would come if you were home. Her invitation extended to Harriet."

Harriet fumbled her fork, and it clattered onto her plate. "I think that she was just being polite, Diane. She does not really expect me to come," Harriet said.

"Nonsense, Mrs. Warner thinks highly of you, dear. You mustn't stay at home just because I'm in mourning. Wait, I have a wonderful idea." Harriet waited, dreading to hear any idea of Diane's that involved social engagements. "Steven, why not take Harriet to the ball? I'm sure that she will feel more comfortable with a member of the family there."

Steven and Harriet gazed at each other across the table, Harriet frowning at this turn of events. The young man raised his eyebrows.

"I would be happy to escort you, Miss Walters, if you would care to come with me."

Edward added, "What a good idea, Diane. No doubt some of the parliamentary crowd will be there as well. It will be an opportunity for Steven to make some worthwhile connections. You can never start building a political career too early."

"But Diane," Harriet said, "I'm sure that Mr. Fitzwilliam would have a more successful evening unencumbered by my company. I will know so few people there. I will be of no use to him."

"I know dear, but that is why one goes to balls – to meet people."

Harriet gazed forlornly at the table.

"Don't look so wretched, Harriet," Diane said with a laugh. "You silly thing, most people enjoy dances. What if you were to bring Abigail with you? Then you would have someone to sit with while Steven is dancing. It wouldn't do Abigail any harm to socialize more, too. I'll send Mrs. Warner a note asking her to invite Abigail first thing tomorrow morning. You wouldn't mind escorting both ladies to the ball, would you, Steven?"

"Of course not. I would be happy to." Steven smiled at Harriet, who couldn't help grimacing back at him. "Escorting two such admirable ladies will make me the envy of all of my friends."

Harriet searched his face for any hint of irony, but his expression was innocent. "What an enjoyable evening we shall have together, Miss Walters," he added.

Chapter Twenty-Three

Harriet hurried over to Abigail's home as soon as she was free the following afternoon, but she was too late; Abigail had already received the invitation.

"I understand that I have you to thank for this invitation, Miss Walters?" Abigail said when Harriet was shown into the library. Abigail had been reading a book at the desk. She pulled out the opened invitation from under a stack of papers and pushed it across the desk toward Harriet.

"I'm afraid so, Miss Pope. Diane thinks we shall keep each other company while Steven dances with all of his admirers. I do hope that you don't mind going?"

Abigail stiffened. "While Steven is dancing?"

"Yes, he is to escort us. I imagine that he will be popular with the young ladies looking for husbands this season – he is handsome, charming, and wealthy."

Abigail deflated in her chair.

"Is something wrong, Miss Pope?" Harriet asked.

"Wrong? No," Abigail said, sitting up again. "I'm just never sure what to wear on these occasions. With all the young girls trying so hard to make an impression, it seems pointless to dress up."

Harriet brightened, relieved that her friend was not upset with her. "I know just what you mean. I usually end up sitting in a corner of the ballroom with some of the mothers, although I suppose we can count on a dance apiece with Steven Fitzwilliam. Maybe we'll surprise Diane and be the belles of the ball after all."

"Maybe . . . ," Abigail said with a frown.

Harriet was puzzled. What was troubling her friend? "Excuse me for prying, Miss Pope, but is it the prospect of going with Mr. Fitzwilliam that disturbs you? Are you not on friendly terms?"

"Steven? Oh yes, we get along fine. I've known him since we were both infants. My mother was fond of Diane, and our families were constantly together while we were children. We still see each other regularly."

"I see. Well, at least you and Mr. Fitzwilliam are old friends. Your presence will smooth away any awkwardness I would have felt alone with him. You have accepted Mrs. Warner's invitation, haven't you?"

"Yes, the footman was told to await my response, so I was forced to accept right away."

"Good." Harriet settled more comfortably in her chair and looked about the room. She had visited Abigail at home before, but had never been shown into the library. She saw a comfortable, well-used room furnished with a table, a desk, and three chairs. Quantities of books overflowed two large bookcases and were stacked upon every available surface. Harriet smiled, imagining all three Popes working together in the library.

"I wonder, Miss Walters, if you would do me a favour?" Abigail asked. "Will you come upstairs and help me to find something suitable to wear? It's been four years since I dressed for such an occasion, and I was never very good at it. You, on the other hand, are always fashionably dressed."

Harriet smiled in amusement. "Thank you, Miss Pope. While I do not think of myself as 'fashionable,' I have learned a trick or two from my dressmakers. I would be happy to assist you."

Abigail rose. "Good. Let us see to it right away."

When Harriet was shown into Abigail's room, she looked around in surprise. She had expected the decorating scheme to be simple and even a little austere, but the room had a soft, feminine feeling to it. The walls were papered in a cheerful yellow floral, the furniture was dainty, and a pretty, painted screen covered the hearth. A pair of framed watercolours hanging over the mantle displayed a deft hand and a harmonious use of colour.

Abigail noted her surprise. "The room was my mother's," she said.

"What a lovely place," Harriet replied, wondering if there was more to her friend than she had supposed. Did Abigail harbour a sentimental streak, preserving her mother's room as a way of honouring her memory, or did she hide a soft, feminine side not apparent in her masculine manner and opinions?

"Yes, Mother had excellent taste – unlike her daughter. But come and sit here while I pull some things from my wardrobe."

Harriet sat down on the bench Abigail indicated, and examined the gowns her friend proceeded to lay out on the bed. Not surprisingly, the dresses were simple and dark in colour, the kind of wardrobe that a woman more concerned with functionality than style would prefer. Actually, they were just the sort of gowns that Harriet had worn while living at Willoway. There were two muslin dresses that Abigail had worn to Diane's home, but nothing was particularly becoming or elegant enough for a ball.

"Well, that's all there is," Abigail said, gesturing to the heap upon the bed. "I don't see anything likely. Do you?"

"I'm afraid not. But what did you wear for your introduction into society? Do you have anything left over from that season?"

"It was four years ago. If there's anything left, it will be in that trunk." Abigail knelt down before a sturdy trunk and removed two white muslin gowns. She shook them out and held them up for Harriet's inspection. Harriet was dismayed; the gowns were plain and unremarkable.

"My mother's friend would have liked me to wear something fancier, but I saw no reason in wasting good money on something that would have made me look ridiculous. The gloves are still serviceable, though," she said, pulling out a pair of elbow-length, white gloves.

Harriet smiled. "Well, at least you have gloves."

"Wait," Abigail said, digging down through some undergarments, "I think there must be shoes, too." She drew out a pair of white kid pumps with pink rosettes.

"Very nice," Harriet said with a nod. Abigail smiled. "But gloves and shoes are not enough, and I don't think that either of the white gowns will do." Abigail sighed and sank down upon the floor. "Let me think," Harriet added. "There are still four days left before the ball. I'm afraid that I don't see anything here for you to wear, unless something can be altered. Show me that top gown again."

Abigail drew the dress from the pile and passed it to Harriet, who studied it doubtfully.

"I'm not sure, Miss Pope. Perhaps if we took this to Diane's dressmaker, she could suggest something? If we leave right now, we could reach the shop before it closes."

"Do you really think that Diane's dressmaker will want to bother with me when she has so many other clients?" Abigail asked.

"Of course. I've been to the shop on more than one occasion, and all sorts of women patronize it. Young and old, thin and plump, fashionable and . . . not quite so fashionable. A well-made dress can go a long way toward disguising a woman's flaws, believe me." She stood and helped Abigail from the floor.

"Fortunately, money is not a problem. Father is always encouraging me to expand my wardrobe. Very well then, Miss Walters, I will put myself in your dressmaker's hands. Let us see if she is up to the challenge."

On the evening of the ball, Abigail arrived at the Fitzwilliams' house early to take advantage of the hair-dressing talents of Diane's maid. Harriet was already dressed, and hovered in the background while the maid assisted Abigail. She swept the young woman's hair up onto her head, adding curls and a fullness that softened the square contours of her face. As a final touch, the maid pinned a sweet little bonnet on top of Abigail's hair that Harriet had chosen from the milliner's. When Abigail was finally dressed, Harriet called Diane in to see the results.

Catching sight of her cousin, Diane smiled with delight. "Why, Abigail, you look charming!" she said. "What a pretty dress you're wearing." The dressmaker had used Abigail's white muslin as an under-dress, topping it with a tailored overskirt and jacket that had a slenderizing effect upon her figure. Lace at the wrists and throat, and the delicate pink of the overlaying fabric, helped to feminize the outfit and complemented the soft rose in Abigail's cheeks.

Abigail stared back at her admirers. "I don't look foolish?" she asked.

Harriet said, "Absolutely not. You look wonderful. Come and see for yourself," drawing her friend to the full-length mirror.

Abigail gazed at herself, turning this way and that, before finally smiling at her reflection.

"I do look pretty," she said over her shoulder. Diane nodded while Harriet beamed at her friend.

"It just takes a little more effort, my dear," Diane said. "You could always look this attractive, if you wanted to."

Ignoring Diane, Abigail said, "Hadn't we better be going? Where is Steven?"

"He's been waiting in the salon for the last half an hour," Diane replied. "Gather your things and hurry down to him. The carriage is waiting at the front door."

Sweeping down the stairs to the salon, the young ladies paused in the doorway to collect Steven. He put down the book he had been reading and sprang up from his chair, a delighted grin upon his face.

"Cousin, is that you? You look beautiful," he said, winning another smile from Abigail. "Give me a twirl so that I can have the full effect." Abigail obliged, and when she had stopped, he said, "You're like a beautiful butterfly emerging from her cocoon." He took her hand and kissed it, causing Abigail to blush. "Do you remember the last time I kissed you, Cousin? You pushed me off my chair onto the floor for my trespass."

Abigail laughed – a rare, joyful sound. "I certainly do remember. You were four years old, and you had asked me to marry you because I was the only girl you knew. Then you kissed me right on the mouth! I was furious at your impudence."

He held her hand and laughed with her before noticing Harriet waiting at the door. Steven regarded her appreciatively, bowed, and said, "Miss Walters, you look lovely, too, if I may say so." Harriet was wearing a pretty new confection from Diane's dressmaker.

"Thank you, Mr. Fitzwilliam. You look very well, too. I find myself actually looking forward to a ball, for once."

"Excellent. So am I," Steven said. "Shall we go?" Tucking his cousin's hand into his arm and offering the other to Harriet, the three young people departed into the soft summer evening.

Chapter Twenty-Four

The ball was very well attended that evening, forcing Harriet, Abigail, and Steven to wait in the press of people pushing their way into the ballroom. The guests were either friends of the Warners' children, or political allies of Mr. Warner's in attendance with their stylish wives. The air was already close, and the more mature guests had claimed the cooler side of the room beside the open windows. The gentlemen debated the government's latest increase in the spice tariff, their bickering adding to the overall din, while their wives gossiped about their families. The young ladies making their debuts that season were grouped in knots that formed and reformed as newcomers arrived, all the while keeping watch on the unattached bachelors who leaned against the walls.

Steven found chairs for Harriet and Abigail near the dance floor, and was immediately hailed by Meredith Warner and her three giggling companions. Meredith introduced Steven to her friends, and he reciprocated by presenting them to his two female companions.

"Of course you've met Miss Walters, Miss Warner. I presume that you also know my cousin, Miss Pope?"

Miss Warner smiled brightly at each of them in turn, but Harriet knew from the girl's immediate dismissal that she was not considered a contender for Steven's attentions. Harriet was not offended; she supposed that she seemed very mature in comparison to Miss Warner's tender eighteen years.

"Miss Pope, it has been some time since last we met," Miss Warner said. You are looking very well. I visited your father at his office only last week."

Abigail gazed back at her. "Did you? I hope that you are not ill, Miss Warner?"

"Me? No, I am always in excellent health."

"But you said that you were visiting my father at his office."

"Oh, not for myself. I was helping Mother with my younger brother, Percy. He has his annual spring cold."

"Do you mean that he has a cold every spring?"

"Why, yes, for the past three years, as I recall."

"Was he feverish?"

"No, I don't think so."

"What about his cough?"

"Yes, he had one."

"No. I mean, was his cough wet or dry?"

Miss Warner took a step backward at this barrage of questions, while her young friends stared at Abigail. "I really have no idea, Miss Pope."

"Very interesting," Abigail said. "It is possible that your brother's colds are caused by an ambient irritant, although his repeated illnesses may be indicative of a weak chest. Well, I'm sure that Father has it all in hand." She looked about the room. "I see that the other couples are gathering for the first dance. Shall we join them, Steven?"

Steven smiled and offered her his arm. "Of course, Abigail. Please excuse us, Miss Walters. Ladies." He nodded at Miss Warner and her friends and led his cousin out onto the floor.

Miss Warner, looking bewildered, only had time to say, "What odd questions," before she was claimed by her dance partner. Harriet, amused by the exchange, was left alone in her chair.

She watched Abigail and Steven as they danced, curious to see how they would conduct themselves on the floor. Her friend's lack of enthusiasm for Steven's company prior to the ball was all the more puzzling because the two cousins seemed to get along so well.

Steven was an accomplished dancer, and he kept up with his partner quite easily while calling greetings to his friends. Dancing was obviously not one of Abigail's strengths, however. If pressed, Harriet would have described her friend's dancing as enthusiastic rather than graceful, but Abigail shrugged off her mistakes and seemed to be enjoying herself. Harriet shook her head; there was no understanding Abigail's earlier reaction.

When they had finished, Steven fetched some glasses of punch before escorting Abigail back to Harriet. Harriet drank hers quickly because she was engaged to Steven for the next dance. As she drank, a sturdy young man with a barrel-shaped chest and startlingly bright red hair approached them. He greeted Steven with a rollicking, "What are you doing in polite company, Fitzwilliam?"

"Avoiding you, Gwinn," Steven answered with a grin, slapping the man on the back. Turning to Abigail and Harriet, he added, "Ladies, this scoundrel is a friend of mine, Harold Gwinn. He is a student at the London School of Medicine. Harold, this is Miss Walters, and my cousin, Miss Pope."

"Your cousin? How could someone as unfortunate-looking as you have such an attractive relative, Fitzwilliam? Charmed, ladies," he added, bowing to each in turn.

"You think my cousin's appearance unfortunate, sir?" Abigail asked indignantly.

"Truly, I do. Just look at him, ladies. Such a puny specimen of a man. He has to put rocks in his pockets whenever there's a stout wind blowing."

Harold turned to Abigail. "Miss Pope, I was just chatting with the daughter of our hosts, and she had some fascinating things to say about you. When I saw that you were part of Fitzwilliam's party, I hurried over in hope of an introduction."

Abigail frowned. "What did Miss Warner say about me, sir?"

"She said that not only are you the daughter of her family physician, but that you personally take an inordinate interest in medical matters."

"Indeed? Well, it's true. There is no point in hiding it. I read medical books. Do you think that improper?" Abigail's voice rose at the end of her question and her face flushed. Harriet took a step closer to support her friend.

"Improper? Heavens, no. I am studying to be a physician myself. That a bonny young woman such as yourself should have the intelligence and character to be interested in medicine is commendable. Shall we discuss our mutual interest on the dance floor?"

Abigail hesitated, speechless for once, and glanced at her cousin. "Oh, he's not particularly dangerous, my dear. I can vouch for your safety," Steven said. Mr. Gwinn crooked his arm at Abigail, who took it after a moment's hesitation and was swept away.

"Come, Miss Walters, it's our turn to dance," Steven said, leading her onto the floor. They began the dance in silence, Steven smiling to himself.

Harriet said, "You look pleased, Mr. Fitzwilliam."

"I am indeed. Delighted with myself, in fact."

"Why are you so pleased? Is it concerning Miss Pope and Mr. Gwinn?"

"You have hit the bull's-eye, Miss Walters. I have always thought how well-suited the two of them were for each other. As a matter of fact, I've gone so far as to speak of Abigail to Harold. Priming the pump, as it were. He evidently liked what he saw tonight, and used his conversation with Miss Warner as an excuse for speaking to my cousin. And she was so ready to start an argument with him that I'm sure she will be more talkative than usual."

Harriet was impressed. "Bravo. You've done well with your matchmaking so far, Mr. Fitzwilliam."

"Oh, do call me 'Steven.' After all, we're living in the same house together."

"Very well, Steven. And you may call me Harriet."

He made a little bow.

"You know Miss Pope very well, don't you," she said.

"Of course. She's like a sister to me. She has always been so independent, but I think that she uses her independence to mask her loneliness. Gwinn has the personality to draw her out of her shell, and he is a good man. I would be thrilled if a romance developed between them."

Harriet thought of her friend's plans to marry a missionary. "Do you think Miss Pope open to the possibility of a romance?" she asked.

"I have seen the opinions of young ladies change direction like a weather vane in the wind." Steven winked. "It all depends on who is doing the persuading."

Harriet smiled and managed to wink back. "I hope you're proved right. Every woman deserves some romance before she settles into the yoke of marriage."

Steven pretended to be shocked. "Harriet, how risqué of you." This time Harriet's wink was more effective as she danced with the handsome young man.

Chapter Twenty-Five

Despite Diane's plan, Harriet spent much of the ball alone. Mr. Gwinn danced two sets in a row with Abigail before they disappeared into the garden, and Steven was kept busy squiring young ladies around the dance floor, although he promised to return to Harriet in time for supper. Bored, Harriet left her chair to walk in the garden.

It was a lovely June evening. Rain had fallen earlier in the day, and the air was moist and sweet. There was no moon, but the garden path was amply illuminated by flickering torches. Harriet strayed from the path to bury her face in a raised patch of sweet pea, only to hear a feminine giggle somewhere close by. She peered across the path and spotted a gentleman and a lady occupying a secluded bench sheltered between two trees. The man embraced the woman, attempting to steal a kiss. The lady protested, but none too vigorously. Harriet tiptoed back to the path, but not before her foot slipped and dislodged a stone. The woman heard the sound and averted her face, but the man turned toward Harriet. She stiffened. The man was Augustus Bell. They stared at each other for a moment, and then Augustus deliberately winked at her. It was a very different wink from the kind that she and Steven had exchanged earlier that evening. Harriet gasped, and scurried back to the house.

Once inside, she ventured into the refreshment room, but recognized no one she could join. She accepted a cup of fruit punch from one of the liveried servants and drifted back into the ballroom. Steven was dancing with one of Miss Warner's giggling friends, and Harriet was amused by the fixed smile upon his face. Steven was too much of a gentleman to let the world see how much he suffered from the shrill voice pitched at his ear.

"What do you find so amusing, Miss Walters?" inquired a voice right beside her own ear. Harriet started, turned, and discovered Mr. Bell standing directly behind her.

"I-I didn't know that you were here tonight, sir," she stammered.

Raising one eyebrow, the gentleman replied, "We both know that that is untrue." Harriet blushed and did not know what to say. "Feeling shy again, Miss Prim?" Bell asked.

"Please do not call me that."

"I shall never call you that again if you will honour me with the next dance." He stood too close for Harriet's comfort, an impertinent smile upon his face. Harriet took exception to his expression; obviously, he thought her too afraid to dance with him.

"Thank you. That would be very pleasant," she responded icily.

"Well, it could be," Bell said, considering her for a moment before turning on his heel and sauntering away. Confused, Harriet watched him approach the musicians. Bending over one of the seated players, Bell said something in the man's ear and handed him a coin. The violinist nodded, and Bell headed back toward her.

Harriet turned away so that he would not see her watching him. She was dismayed that Mr. Bell had asked her to dance. Better to remain a wallflower than to be jeered at by this roguish man.

A pause ensued as the music ended and the dancers strolled off the floor in search of their next partners. Bell caught up with Harriet and took her arm. "Please excuse my absence, Miss Walters. I was requesting something special for the next dance."

"Do you have a favourite, Mr. Bell?"

"Yes. The next dance will be a waltz. Have you ever waltzed, Miss Walters?" he asked, leading her toward the floor.

Harriet stopped in her tracks. "No. Never."

She had seen this daring new dance performed, and had marvelled at the gracefulness of the dancers as they whirled about in each other's arms. She did not think that she could duplicate their gracefulness, however, nor did she want Mr. Bell to hold her so closely.

The gentleman said, "It is not difficult. Waltzing has a gliding movement not unlike ice skating. You have skated before, haven't you?"

"Yes, but not for years."

"I'm sure that it will all come back to you. Just follow my lead." He pulled the reluctant lady onto the floor and turned to face her, waiting for the music to begin. When it did, he offered her his hand. Harriet took it reluctantly, and Bell pulled her in closer. He seized her other hand and placed it upon his shoulder, reaching his own around her waist to grasp the small of her back. Harriet shuddered, and Bell snorted.

"This is a dance, Miss Walters, not an assault," he said. Harriet jerked her head up to glare at him. "That's better. You're more attractive when you show a little spine. Now, the waltz steps form a square. I take a step forward, and you take one back. We step to the side, and then reverse. It's not very hard. Let us give it a try."

"See, it's not so difficult," he said when they had successfully traced a square. Harriet glanced up at him, and they shared a brief smile before she gazed back down at her feet. "Now we're going to do the same thing in reverse. Let's begin." Together they slowly traced another square.

"Excellent. We have completed one circuit. Now, for a second." They practised the steps over again until Bell began moving in time to the music and sped up. Harriet was able to follow him as she matched her steps to the rhythm of the music.

"Very good, Miss Walters. You're a natural. But now you must raise your head and look about the room. If we all watched our feet, we would crash into each other."

Harriet obeyed and began noticing the other dancers. Some of them were beginners, like her, but others were cutting in and out of the other dancers and whirling about gracefully. "Oh, how elegantly they move!" she exclaimed.

"Exactly. Now we shall try to duplicate them," Bell said, launching them into the middle of the floor. Harriet squealed in alarm and concentrated all of her attention on her feet, but after some practice, she began to relax and enjoy herself. Bell was a gifted dancer, guiding her with a light pressure upon the back. He did not call out greetings to his friends, as Steven had done, or even talk. He focused all of his attention upon her, his dark eyes sparkling with pleasure.

Eventually the dance came to an end, and Bell released her. Together, they turned to applaud the musicians. "There. Wasn't that exhilarating?" he asked, lowering his mouth to her ear.

"It was both frightening and wonderful. You are an excellent teacher, sir."

"Ah, at last there is something you approve of in me." Surprised, Harriet stared at the gentleman, and he nodded. "Yes, I have spied disapproval in your eyes on more than one occasion. Just recently in the garden, for example. You don't have a very high opinion of me, do you, Miss Walters?"

"I hardly know you."

"But you don't like what you see, do you?"

"Really, Mr. Bell, what can I say?" Harriet said, looking away.

"The truth, you little hypocrite." He moved closer, and Harriet could smell spirits on his breath. "Perhaps I will call you that from now on, since I have promised not to call you 'Miss Prim.'" Nothing to say? Never mind. If you can be taught to waltz so beautifully, perhaps you can be taught not to be so correct all the time. Maybe I will make that my target this summer. To show you how to squeeze a little pleasure from life."

Harriet was embarrassed by his intimate words and said nothing. Bell's presence overwhelmed her. How had she ever thought this masterful man a clown?

"Have you been looking after Harriet for me?" Steven asked, suddenly appearing at her side. Harriet was relieved by his return and took a step toward him.

"Her friends have abandoned her, so I have snapped her up," Bell said, confronting the younger man.

"Not abandoned her. Unfortunately, other duties have interfered with our evening, but I have returned to take Miss Walters to supper. Look, here come Abigail and Harold." Harriet looked across the room and saw her friend, looking happy and excited, returning upon Mr. Gwinn's arm. Steven turned back to Bell.

"Will you join us for some supper, sir?"

"I'm afraid not. My presence is expected in the card room. But thank you for the invitation." He nodded and turned to Harriet. "And for the waltz, Miss Walters." He took her hand and kissed the tips of her fingers. "I hope to see you again very soon," he said, staring down into her eyes. Glancing back at Steven, he added, "Give my regards to your mother, Fitzwilliam," before walking away.

Harold said, "My stomach is complaining of neglect. Let's get some food." He turned on his heel and left with Abigail again before giving the other two a chance to join them.

Steven laid his hand upon Harriet's shoulder. "Is all well with you? Did Bell say anything to upset you?"

"No, I'm fine," she replied, meeting his eyes before glancing away.

He took a step closer and lowered his voice. "I've known him for years. Mother finds him amusing, but I know that others find him arrogant and erratic. He can talk a lot of nonsense. I hope that he hasn't made you uncomfortable?"

"A little, I admit."

The young man took her hand and placed it on his arm, covering it with his own. "Don't worry, Harriet. If Bell's attentions are unwelcome, I shall speak to Mother about him."

"Oh, I wouldn't go that far, Steven. I'm just not very good at talking nonsense to people," Harriet said, lifting her eyes to his face.

"That is one of your many admirable qualities, Harriet." He smiled at her before leading her from the ballroom in search of supper.

Chapter Twenty-Six

Harriet did not see Abigail in the week following the Warners' ball, but they met again at the dressmaker's shop on Saturday. Harriet was accompanying Diane on a fitting, while Abigail wished to purchase another dress. Harriet noticed that her friend still wore her hair in the more becoming style she had adopted on the night of the ball.

"Why, Abigail, two new dresses in as many weeks! That does show promise," Diane said. "Let's see what they have ready-made." She and the shop owner began discussing two possibilities, giving Harriet and Abigail time to talk alone.

"I expected to see you at the lending library last Thursday, Miss Pope, but you didn't come," Harriet said.

"I do apologize. I was at the taxidermist with Harold."

"The taxidermist," Harriet replied a little shrilly. "Whatever were you doing there? Is Mr. Gwinn having a pet stuffed?"

"No. The taxidermist is a friend of Harold's, and he promised him the heart of the bird he is preserving. Harold was eager to show it to me."

"How astonishing. Why should you want to look at a bird's heart?"

"Not just look at it, Miss Walters. Dissect it, too. It was fascinating to see its construction. Studying the hearts of animals helps us to understand the workings of the human heart. Of course, Harold attended the dissection of a human body at the university as part of his studies. He said that it was one of the formative moments of his life."

"I'm sure that it must have been very interesting."

"Truly. I told Harold how disappointed I was that I shall never see a human dissection, and he promised to dissect a pig for me at the first opportunity." Abigail smiled brightly. "He's a very generous person – and brilliant."

Harriet smiled back at her besotted friend. "Yes, he seems a remarkable man."

"Who's a remarkable man?" Diane asked, joining them.

Harriet glanced at Abigail, wondering what to say, but the young woman's blank expression gave her no hint. "I was talking about Harold Gwinn, Diane. Steven introduced us to him at the ball last Saturday. Mr. Gwinn is studying to become a physician.

"Really?" Diane said. "I don't believe that Steven has introduced him to us."

Abigail said, "They met last Christmas at the theatre."

"Hmm," Diane said, studying Abigail as the young woman gazed impassively back at her. "Well, to change the subject, I was talking to Edward earlier this morning about renting a boat for a picnic on the river tomorrow afternoon. Now that Parliament has adjourned, we should take advantage of this fine weather. Would you care to join us, Abigail? Perhaps we could invite Mr. Gwinn to come along, too?"

"That would be agreeable," the young woman said, her face breaking into a smile.

"I'm so glad. You'll come, won't you, Harriet?"

"Thank you, it would be a great pleasure."

"Excellent. I'll have Steven make the arrangements. We'll send the carriage to fetch you at one o'clock, Abigail. You could wear your new dress. Let's choose a parasol to go with it, shall we? We don't want any more freckles on that sweet nose of yours." The young woman sighed, but let Diane lead her away.

In the end, Abigail purchased a white parasol and both of the dresses. Diane had her fitting, and the three ladies were back on the street when a familiar figure came strutting toward them.

"Look, it's Augustus," Diane said as the gentleman caught up with them and bowed.

"I must be going. I have another appointment. I'll see you tomorrow," Abigail said, leaving before Bell had time to straighten.

"Adieu, sweet lady," he shouted after her, kissing his fingers and waving. Heads turned and passersby stared. Turning back to Diane and Harriet, he added, "Well, people are not usually so blunt in avoiding me."

"You mustn't let Abigail's bad manners offend you, Augustus," Diane said. "She treats us all the same way."

He nodded and looked at Harriet. "You look well today, Miss Walters."

"Thank you, sir, as do you," she said, striving to sound more composed than she felt. Harriet was unsure how she felt about the gentleman; one moment he was mocking her, and the next, teaching her to waltz.

"Ah, a second compliment. I think I shall swoon," he said, applying the back of his hand to his temple and rolling his eyes. Harriet couldn't resist smiling at him.

Diane looked from one friend to the other before saying, "Augustus, we're having a picnic upon the river tomorrow afternoon. Abigail and Mr. Gwinn are invited, and Steven and Edward are coming, too. Would you care to join us?"

"A pleasure outing, eh? Will Miss Walters be coming?" he asked, turning to the lady.

"Harriet? Of course," Diane replied.

With his eyes still upon Harriet, the gentleman said, "Then I will come. Thank you for the invitation, kind lady." He kissed Diane's hand and attempted to do the same with Harriet's, but she snatched it back before he could.

Bell shook his head at her and bowed. "Adieu, ladies. I shall meet you at the dock."

"Be there by two o'clock," Diane called after him as he strolled away. She turned to Harriet. "My, my, what was that all about?"

"Shall I call the carriage?" Harriet asked, waving at the driver before Diane had a chance to respond. He handed them in, and they settled themselves for the ride home.

"I assume you saw Augustus at the Warners' ball last Saturday," Diane remarked.

"Yes, for a little while. We had one dance together. It was of no consequence."

Diane smiled. "He's very handsome," she said.

"Yes, but that characteristic smirk of his is not very attractive," Harriet said with a frown.

"Harriet, such harsh words!" her friend said with mock surprise. Harriet shrugged and looked away. "Of course he doesn't have any money," Diane added. "He loses at cards too often. But then, you have money. I wonder if it will be enough?" Harriet stared at her and remained silent. "There have been plenty of women in his life, you know. No doubt there will be many more. But when a man has such a large appetite, mistresses can be a blessing."

"Diane!" Harriet exclaimed, open-mouthed.

Diane shrugged. "I have heard rumours. He could at least be a pleasant flirtation for you, Harriet. I suppose that you have not had many flirtations in your life?"

"Of course not."

"No? Well, you never know. He might be willing to settle down if he thinks that you have enough money. You cannot afford to be too particular at your age, dear. Let me give you a little advice, Harriet. Don't discount him out of hand. You might come to a very comfortable arrangement between you."

"I doubt it," Harriet replied, her eyes fastened on the passing scenery.

Diane laughed. "This is a new outspoken side of you I've not seen before. I like it, Harriet. Very well. Just think on it. See how you like Augustus after the picnic tomorrow."

Sunday dawned with an early morning fog that burned off in time to reveal a cloudless, blue sky. Abigail arrived at the appointed hour, and rode in the carriage with Harriet and the Fitzwilliams. Symonds and one of the maids followed behind in a hired carriage with the copious picnic supplies.

When they reached the docks, the servants quickly descended to prepare the pleasure barge that had been secured for the afternoon with two deckhands assisting them. It was furnished with tables and chairs, and had an awning to protect its guests from the sun. The captain and Harold Gwinn, who was already on board, welcomed them. There was no sign of Bell, however.

Edward checked his pocket watch. "What time did you tell him to be here, Diane?" he asked, frowning and snapping the case shut.

Diane leaned against the rail, shading her face from the sun with a black lace parasol. "Don't worry, dear. You know Augustus. Time doesn't matter to him. Give him a few more minutes, and if he still hasn't come, we'll set off without him." Edward nodded and left to talk with the captain.

Steven had made himself comfortable in a deck chair. "That's odd," he said, lifting his head.

"What is, dear?" Diane asked.

"Do you hear music? Hey there, Harold, have a look. Is someone playing music out on the dock?" he called. Harold, who was standing in the stern with Abigail, turned to check.

"Someone certainly is, Fitzwilliam," he called. "Here comes the tardy Mr. Bell with the entertainment."

Harriet, who had been watching another barge pull away from the dock, bent over the rail to see, and laughed at the spectacle before her. Bell, dressed in a straw hat, open-necked shirt, and white pantaloons, was prancing down the dock in time to a jig being played by a fiddler. Diane laughed and waved her parasol in greeting.

"What's your little fop doodle up to now, Diane?" Edward asked, rejoining her at the rail.

Diane turned and covered his mouth with her gloved hand. "Hush, dear, he might hear you."

"Ahoy, shipmates," Bell shouted. He doffed his hat and waved it over his head.

"Who have you got there, Augustus?" Diane called.

"This is my new friend, Mr. O'Malley," he shouted back. "He's consented to provide musical entertainment for the afternoon." Mr. O'Malley made a short bow and held up his bow and fiddle.

Harold and Abigail came forward to join the rest as Bell and his fiddler climbed aboard. Edward turned to the captain, who had come to see what all the commotion was about, and said, "We're all here now, Captain. You can cast off."

"Very good, Mr. Fitzwilliam. We'll be underway in a minute."

The two deckhands scrambled to untie the ropes, and soon the barge was pulling out onto the river. The sun sparkled upon the water, and a pleasant breeze rippled the ladies' dresses. If the river's odour was unpleasant, the breeze helped to dispel it. The guests made themselves comfortable upon chairs and cushions while the butler served wine and fruit.

"Here, Mr. O'Malley, do you know any popular tunes?" Harold asked. "I wish to thank my hosts for their hospitality with a song."

"Really, Harold, I didn't know that you sang," Abigail said.

"We haven't known each other long, Abigail. There's a lot you've yet to learn about me," Harold said with a grin.

"Yes indeed, Abigail," Steven said. "Harold is always singing, even though people beg him to stop. He's known as 'Harold the Horrible Troubadour' around the city."

"Ach, you're wrong there, Fitzwilliam. People love my singing," Harold said.

"Why not let your audience judge?" Steven countered. "What do you say, everyone? Shall we have a song from Harold?"

"Please do, Mr. Gwinn," Diane said.

"Here, Abigail. You better cover your ears," Steven warned.

"Enough of that," Harold said, climbing to his feet. "Whenever you're ready, Mr. O'Malley."

The fiddler nodded and launched into a popular Scottish air. Harold took off his hat, folded his hands behind his back, and began singing in a clear, strong tenor. The song was about a broken-hearted swain and the sweetheart who had jilted him, and the young medical student sang it most effectively, wringing a sigh from Harriet at the end. The picnickers broke into applause, Abigail the most enthusiastic of all, while Steven stamped his feet upon the deck. Harold bowed and sank down upon a cushion at Abigail's feet.

"You have an artist's soul, Mr. Gwinn," Bell said. "Now, who's next?"

"What about you, Steven?" Harold asked, accepting some grapes from Abigail. "I've heard you sing a ditty or two in drinking establishments, although nothing you'd want to perform in front of the ladies." Steven grinned and looked at his mother, who was instructing Symonds to serve the rest of the food.

"You used to have a pleasant voice when you were a boy, Steven," his father said.

"Do you remember the duet we sang two Christmases ago, Father?"

"I do, and we weren't too bad, as I recall."

"Oh, do sing it again," Diane said. "Harriet hasn't had a chance to hear you sing together yet."

"I will if you will, Father," Steven said.

The two men conferred with Mr. O'Malley. Standing side-by-side, they sang an Oxford school song popular with Edward's generation. The song was slightly ribald, and drew laughter from their audience.

The party wore on with an easy flow of food, drink, and laughter, everyone enjoying themselves. Diane was called upon to sing, as was Bell, but Abigail flatly refused. As a penalty, she was asked to dance a jig instead, and was still protesting when Harold jumped up and pulled her to her feet. He took her hands and they danced together, the fiddler playing so spiritedly that the pins fell out of Abigail's hair. It took Harold several moments to recover them after the dance had ended.

"Whoosh," he panted, "I've been studying too hard and not getting enough exercise."

"Be careful, Gwinn. The ladies will not admire you if you lose your figure. A handsome doctor is a prosperous doctor," Bell said.

"I think that the most Harold can aspire to is distinguished," Steven retorted to a bellow of laughter from the gentlemen. Abigail protested that Harold was quite the most handsome man of her acquaintance, which drew guffaws and the comment that love must truly be blind.

Harriet sat on a cushion with her back braced against the rail, enjoying the sun on her face and the breeze stirring her skirts. She laughed at the others' antics and appreciated the singing, particularly Mr. Bell's. He sang an old folk tune her father used to sing, his eyes closed and his head resting on the back of his chair. Her complaisance was disturbed, however, when Diane suggested that Harriet should take a turn performing.

"Oh no, I couldn't," Harriet said, the heat rising in her face. It was difficult enough to sing with a pianoforte to hide behind, but singing in such an exposed, casual manner would be torturous.

"Come now, Harriet, everyone else has sung for his supper," Diane said. "All but Abigail. Or would you prefer to dance a jig?"

Harriet couldn't do that either, however. How ridiculous she would look bobbing up and down with everyone staring at her. Mr. O'Malley drew his bow across the strings to make a rude, raucous noise that made Diane and Edward laugh.

From where he was sitting, Bell said, "Miss Walters shall not dance a jig. Jigs are for farmers and peasants." Harold and Abigail exchanged an amused look at his remark. "No, Miss Walters is a lady and shall dance something more elegant – and with a partner. Will you dance with me, Miss Walters?" Bell rose to his feet and extended his hand. He smiled, and Harriet saw that his suggestion was meant as a kindness to save her the embarrassment of dancing alone.

She summoned up all of her courage to say, "Yes, Mr. Bell. Shall we waltz again?" Taking his hand, she placed her other hand upon his shoulder while the others stared. The servants hastily pushed back the chairs to make an impromptu dance floor, and Mr. O'Malley began playing a melody with a waltz tempo. Harriet felt self-conscious with all eyes upon them, but Bell whispered, "Just look at me, Miss Walters," before taking her in his arms and sweeping her onto the floor.

It did not take long to regain the rhythm they had found together at the ball, and Harriet forgot the rest to enjoy the pleasure of the dance. At first she kept her eyes upon Bell's, but as her confidence grew, she closed them. It felt as if they were flying through space together, swooping and turning like birds. She could feel his firm hand guiding her, and felt ready to follow anything in his arms.

Finally, Mr. O'Malley drew out the song's last sweet notes, and they slowed to a stop. Harriet opened her eyes, and Bell said, "Well done, Miss Walters!" They smiled at each other as even the deckhands broke into enthusiastic applause.

Harriet became aware of Abigail at her side. "Miss Walters, you looked wonderful," her friend said. "Mr. O'Malley, could you play that tune again? Harold and I would like to try."

Edward and Diane also joined in, and soon all three couples were waltzing with varying degrees of proficiency. Steven even tried to coax the house maid onto the floor, but she shook her head and hung back, and he was forced to cut in on his father. When the fiddler had exhausted his repertoire of waltzes, he broke into a lively jig, and Bell led Harriet back to the chairs for a rest. Symonds came forward to offer wine to the two thirsty dancers, and Bell clinked his glass against Harriet's.

"To the pleasure of dance."

"To dance," she agreed.

Harriet took a swallow of wine while Bell studied her. "You look happy and at peace today," he remarked.

Harriet nodded as she stretched her legs out in front of her. Lifting her face into the breeze, she smiled. "I feel very content."

"Good, I'm glad. Dancing makes me happy, too."

Harriet looked at him. "And yet, I have never felt this kind of pleasure in dance before."

"I could try to claim credit by saying that it was due to your partner, but I believe that waltzing has a freedom and spontaneity that country dancing lacks."

"I agree with you, sir. Everything else feels so prescribed upon the dance floor."

"Not just there, Miss Walters, but in life in general. Sometimes I feel so caged by the city." He studied her. "Do you ride, my dear?"

"I often rode in the country."

"What would you say to a ride in Hyde Park? It would give us another small taste of freedom."

"On horseback?"

He laughed. "Yes. You on your horse and me on mine."

"I would enjoy that."

"Good. Will tomorrow suit?"

"Yes," she agreed impetuously. "At what time?"

"Not too ungodly early, if you please. Shall we say two o'clock?"

"It may be too warm by then. What would you say to nine o'clock?"

Bell groaned. "I'm not usually out of bed by then."

"Why ever not? It's so much fresher in the morning."

"But I'm not usually abed until two or three in the morning."

"Then make an early night of it tonight. How can you not feel sleepy after all this fresh air and exercise?

Bell gazed at her with laughter in his eyes. "Eleven o'clock, then."

"Ten, and don't be late like you were today."

"Fine, little Miss Dictator. That shall be your new name for now." Harriet sat back, delighted to have won the skirmish.

Bell turned to watch the others dancing. "We are much more accomplished than they, don't you think?"

"Much," Harriet said with satisfaction.

Chapter Twenty-Seven

Bell was merely a half hour late when he called for Harriet the following morning. He declined the butler's invitation to wait inside, and was astride his horse when she greeted him. Diane had insisted earlier in Harriet's stay that she purchase riding clothes for just such an occasion, so she was properly outfitted in habit, boots, gloves, and hat. Harriet forgot to scold the gentleman for his tardiness when she beheld his horse, a tall, dappled-gray gelding with magnificent musculature.

"Oh, Mr. Bell, what a beautiful animal," she exclaimed, hurrying down the front stairs while Bell patted the horse's shoulder.

"Yes, I am fond of the creature. We've been together for two years, now. I call him 'Onion.'"

"'Onion?' What a peculiar name," Harriet said, running her hand down the animal's flank. The horse turned to look at her over his shoulder.

"Yes, he has a peculiar appetite, too. His real name is 'Hephaestus' Hammer.' Rather a difficult name to say, wouldn't you agree? Wouldn't people snigger if they heard me say, 'Get up, Hephaestus' Hammer.' You like 'Onion' better, don't you boy?" The horse snorted and bobbed his head.

"How clever! It's as if he knew what you were saying."

"I'm sure that he does. One of us has to be intelligent enough to get me home at the end of the night. What about your mount?"

Harriet turned to a rangy chestnut mare waiting with one of the stable boys. "Steven tells me that her name is 'Cinnamon.' This is my first time up on her." Harriet handed her crop to the stable boy, who helped her to mount. The animal nickered softly as Harriet scratched her withers. "Anything I should know about her before we leave?" she asked the stable boy.

"The mare's steady, Miss, but a real goer if you ask her. She's got heart."

"Excellent. I'm sure that we shall get along well. Shall we go, Mr. Bell?"

The gentleman nodded and set off at a leisurely pace down the street with Harriet following. They refrained from conversation until turning into the park, where they could ride comfortably side-by-side.

"Shall we head to Rotten Row for a gallop?" Bell asked.

"Yes, please."

"I know that you are a country woman, Miss Walters. I've heard a little of your history from Diane, but I should like to know more. Tell me about your childhood."

Harriet spent the next half hour talking about her childhood and how she had come to live with her aunt in Rexton. She also described her friendship with Mrs. Evans, and the peculiar way in which she had become an heiress. Bell listened with his attention entirely focused upon his companion.

"I did not give you credit for your courage before, Miss Walters," he said when she had finished. "You left your home and everyone you loved to live with an aunt in a place you hardly knew. And here you are in London with people you did not know even a year ago. You have had adventures."

"Yes, and they have changed me. I am not the same person I was a year ago."

"How so?"

Harriet gestured impatiently. "I was a mouse – a crab – scuttling away to hide whenever people took notice of me. I had so many fears, and I'm struggling with them still, but at least I put myself forward a little more now. But enough about me. Tell me about yourself, Mr. Bell."

"Talking about myself is not one of my favourite pastimes."

"But I would like to know you better. Where did you grow up, for example?"

"On a country estate in Gloucestershire."

"Not so very far from my Somerset. You were a country lad, then?"

"Yes."

"Brothers and sisters?"

"Two older brothers and three younger sisters.

"Are your parents still alive?"

"Very much so."

"How did you come to live in London?"

"My family owns a large estate in Gloucestershire, and I was superfluous to its operation with two older brothers content to help. I was left to my own amusements when I was a boy, and got into several scrapes. My father decided that I should take up soldiering – teach me some discipline, so he thought – so he purchased me a commission in the cavalry. I served with them for five years and fought against the French, but found army life dull when we were not actively engaged. After an indiscretion with a general's wife, I sold my commission and returned to London. I've been here ever since – four years, now."

"Do you see your family anymore, Mr. Bell?"

"Sometimes. I was home fourteen months ago for a visit. Mother sends for me whenever she's feeling sentimental. I may be the black sheep of the family, but not to the point of disinheritance. Also, my grandmother left me an annuity, so I live as I please."

"I see," Harriet said as the horses plodded past some deer grazing on a nearby hill. "I remember that you spoke yesterday about feeling confined by the city. Do you ever intend to leave London? Perhaps you could move to a small town, marry, and start a family."

"Marriage – a woman's solution to all of life's ills."

"Do you find a bachelor's life so satisfying, then?"

"Bravo. You've hit the nail on the head, Miss Walters. I admit that the bachelor life has begun to pall. All of the little escapades and flirtations are not as diverting as they once were. My only source of excitement these days is gambling. The thought of leaving London and starting fresh somewhere else has crossed my mind. Who knows, maybe I'll leave England for India, or even the colonies."

"That sounds very adventurous, sir."

"In that respect we are similar, Miss Walters – just on a different scale."

"That's funny. Miss Pope once said something very similar to me."

"Miss Pope is an independent-minded female. No doubt she'll have her adventures, too."

They arrived at Rotten Row and watched a horseman and carriage driver racing against each other, the carriage horses thundering after the rider.

Bell sighed. "It's too crowded for a really good run. You always have to be on the lookout for some neophyte who can't control his horse and gets in your way." He glanced up at the overcast sky. "The wind is rising and the clouds are beginning to threaten. I would not be surprised to see rain before we can get you home again."

Harriet had been absorbed with their conversation and unaware of the darkening sky and the wind that caught at her veil and whirled the dust around them. "Perhaps we should set off for home straightaway, sir?"

Bell considered her for a moment. "You are a country woman, Miss Walters. Surely you are not afraid of a little rain?"

Harriet's eyebrows rose. "I have been drenched before without melting."

"Wonderful. You appear to be a good horsewoman."

"What are you thinking, Mr. Bell?"

"Only, shall we race the weather home?" He pointed his crop toward a hill. "I believe that Brook Street lies in that direction."

"You mean, race across the park?"

"Exactly. Let's get off the drives and head overland. Only yesterday we were talking about freedom, Miss Walters. Would you like to experience some?"

Harriet studied the lay of her surroundings before smiling at her companion. "I'm an excellent horsewoman, and the stable boy said that my mount has some 'go.' I've never raced the weather before, but I should like to try. Lead the way, sir."

Bell grinned, saluted Harriet with his crop, and whirled Onion around. "Hi, Onion. Get up!" he shouted, digging his heels into the animal's sides. The horse reared and started forward. Harriet laughed and dashed after him on Cinnamon.

Bell's gelding was big and strong and began pulling away from the mare, but she didn't like being left behind. Soon Harriet was galloping neck and neck with Bell, the horses thundering across the grass and flinging up clumps of sod behind them. A bolt of lightning forked across the horizon, followed seconds later by the rumble of distant thunder. Bell paused on a hill to get his bearings before pointing to the east and tearing off again, Harriet at his heels.

They raced across the park, dodging carriages and pedestrians wherever their route intersected a pathway. Bell was a fearless rider. He splashed through creeks, jumped hedges, swerved around trees and statuary, and even barrelled through a herd of cows. Harriet did not know the park and had to react quickly, but she was equal to the task. Bent over her horse's neck with her hat pushed back from her face and her skirts flying, Harriet urged Cinnamon forward. Just as the entrance to the park came into view, the storm broke and rain came pelting down. Bell and Harriet had to slacken their pace around the carriages, horsemen, and pedestrians scurrying to get out of the rain at the park entrance.

The pair turned onto a city street and maintained a steady trot, breaking into a canter wherever the streets straightened and became clear. The wind drove the rain at them, but Harriet felt exhilarated rather than uncomfortable. Riding in the storm was exciting and reckless and unlike anything she had ever done before. At last they reached Brook Street, stopping their streaming horses in the drive before the Fitzwilliams' door.

Bell turned in the saddle and called, "That was a capital ride, Miss Walters." Staring at each other, they burst out laughing. Both were sodden and mud-splashed, rain dripping from their pink faces. Bell jumped down from his horse and led both animals to the railing, where he secured them. Turning to Harriet, he held up his arms. She kicked her feet free from the stirrups, grasped the gentleman's shoulders, and allowed herself to be dragged from the saddle. Once she was on the ground, Bell put an arm around her shoulders and they ran to the front door. The gentleman pounded on it with his fist, Symonds opening it moments later. They laughed at the startled expression on his face as Bell pushed past the butler, his arm around Harriet's waist.

"Have someone look after our horses, will you Symonds?" Bell asked. "They've been ridden hard and are soaking wet, just like us. Is Diane anywhere about?"

"Yes, sir, she's in the morning room."

"Don't worry about us, Symonds – we know the way," he called over his shoulder. The butler stared opened-mouthed as Harriet and Bell staggered down the hallway, leaving a muddy trail in their wake. Bell pushed open the morning room door and they paused, dripping, on the threshold. Diane jumped up from her writing desk at the unexpected intrusion.

"Good heavens, what's happened to you two?" she exclaimed.

Harriet and Bell giggled, Harriet collapsing against her companion's shoulder as they took a step into the room. "You'll have to forgive the mess we're making on your carpet, Diane," he said. "We were out riding and got caught in the storm."

"I can see that, you goose. You're both drenched." She went to the bell rope and summoned help.

"You won't get Symonds. He's having the horses looked after," Bell said. One of the maids came hurrying into the room.

"Don't worry about me, Diane," Harriet said, tugging her hat from its pins, her hair a straggly mess around her shoulders. "I'll run upstairs and change my clothes." She patted Bell's arm and said, "I'll see you in a little while," before turning to go into the hallway. He grabbed her hand and pulled her back, giving it a kiss. She met his eyes and smiled before turning away.

"Well, Augustus, what have you been up to?" she heard Diane ask as Harriet stepped into the hall. She laughed and dashed up the stairs to her room.

Chapter Twenty-Eight

By the time Harriet returned downstairs, sponged, dressed, and hair re-pinned, Bell was feasting on sweet buns and ham with Diane. Harriet was starving after the morning's ride, and filled a plate of food for herself. They laughed about their ride in the park as they ate, before turning to other topics.

"Colonel York is taking me to see *Romeo and Juliet* on Thursday evening at the Theatre Royale," Harriet said. "I've never gone before."

"To *Romeo and Juliet,* or to the Theatre Royale?" Bell asked.

"To either, actually."

The gentleman raised his eyebrows, and Harriet laughed. "You forget that this is my first visit to London, sir. There were no opportunities for theatre-going in Willoway. My acquaintance with Mr. Shakespeare's plays all comes from books."

"What can I say, Miss Walters, except that I envy Colonel York."

"Have you seen this production yet, Augustus?" Diane asked.

"No, not yet, although I should like to. I am fond of those two young lovers."

"Sword fights, passion, daring a family's wrath to steal the pretty daughter – yes, I can see the attraction for you," Diane said with twinkling eyes.

Bell smiled and made a half-bow. "My reputation precedes me."

"Oh, definitely."

Bell wiped his mouth with his napkin and stood. "I fear that I must drag myself away, ladies. I have an appointment with my barber. Thank Fitzwilliam for the loan of his clothes, and tell him that I will have them returned, cleaned, tomorrow. Adieu, my dears." He bowed over each woman, kissing their hands before departing.

Harriet smiled after him while Diane sank back into her chair, stirring her tea. "Well, what do you think of Augustus now, Harriet?" she asked.

Harriet turned to look at her, the smile disappearing. "He is very amusing," she said.

Diane paused before placing her spoon upon the saucer. "That's a change from your earlier pronouncements, Harriet. I was under the impression that you found him clownish."

Harriet finished her bun and put down her plate. "Perhaps I have changed, Diane. Everyone changes, you know."

"Maybe life in London is broadening your horizons?"

"We shall see. Now, if you'll excuse me, I have some correspondence to attend to in my room." Harriet rose and left, Diane gazing thoughtfully after her.

When Colonel York was shown into the salon on Thursday evening, Harriet rose to greet him as Diane closed her novel.

"Colonel, it seems so long since last I saw you, but it's only been a week," Harriet said, offering her hand. The colonel took it, studying her.

"Why, Miss Walters, don't you look fine," he said. Harriet wore a beautiful midnight-blue gown with capped sleeves slit open to display her fair arms. Two white plumes adorned her rich, walnut-coloured hair, and the diamond and sapphire necklace glittered at her throat.

"Thank you, Colonel. You look very handsome in your evening dress, too," Harriet replied. "Would you care to sit for a moment?" She indicated the chair beside Diane.

"Just for a moment. How are you tonight, Diane? How are Fitzwilliam and your son?"

"We're all well, Colonel. Thank you for asking. What have you been doing since last we saw you?"

"I've been visiting a friend in the country."

"Good. I hope that it was cooler there than it has been in the city. It was uncomfortably warm this week, don't you agree, Harriet? Perhaps we shall leave for the country a little earlier than usual this summer."

The gentleman said, "The weather was fine, Diane, especially in the evenings. But then, I'm sure that you ladies are more sensitive to the heat than I am." Even in his black evening dress, the colonel appeared cool and comfortable.

"I don't doubt that we are, Colonel. Well, don't let me keep you. I'm sure that Harriet is excited about seeing her first theatrical performance and doesn't want to be late."

"Yes, I'm very much looking forward to it. The story is so exciting, and seeing it performed will make it even more so."

Colonel York stood and offered Harriet his arm. "Well, let's not delay then, young lady. Good night, Diane."

"Good night, Diane. Don't wait up for me," Harriet echoed as she took the colonel's arm and followed him from the room.

As they drove to the theatre, Harriet asked her friend about his visit to the country. "Do the people you were visiting live very far away, Colonel?"

"About fifty miles north of London, Miss Walters. He's an old army friend – a major. He's lame as the result of a war injury, and his wife has her hands full looking after him. I visit once a year to reminisce about our old campaigns, while his wife takes the opportunity to visit her sister."

"How nice that you can give her a little holiday."

"It's a holiday for me, too. Gives me a chance to get away from the city."

"Were you born in London, sir?"

"Egad, no. I was born and raised in a small town in Kent. My wife, however, was born in London and always preferred city life. When I retired from soldiering, it was natural to settle here. When I lost her, there didn't seem any point in uprooting myself. I don't know where else I would go."

"What about your family in Kent?"

"I've got a brother and his family there. He had a parish for years, but he's retired now. The children are all grown and have their own homes, but his wife is still alive. Unfortunately, my brother and I are not close."

"I'm sorry to hear that, sir. As enjoyable as these three months in London have been, I miss my mother very much and, oddly enough, my aunt. I used to find her intimidating before I grew to know her better, but she really is a dear. Life in London is so much more interesting than life in Rexton – I'm not sure that I could see all the major attractions if I stayed a year – but as my visit draws to a close, I find that I am looking forward to going home."

"Rexton. That's where Mabel lived, isn't it?"

"That's right. She and my aunt, Mrs. Edna Slater, were good friends."

"Yes, I remember Mabel talking about an 'Edna.' A childhood friend of hers who still lived in Rexton. Well, imagine that. The lady is your aunt. It's a small world, Miss Walters."

"Yes, it is."

Harriet turned to look at the theatre as they drew up before the building. The play was popular, and the performance was well-attended. Colonel York helped her through the throng pouring into the theatre, and progress was slow as they threaded their way to a box on the second tier. Harriet nodded to a German diplomat and his wife whom she had met at Diane's house before taking her seat and looking around. The theatre was huge, and the din of its occupants made conversation difficult. Harriet had feared that they would be late for the performance, but many people were still taking their seats. One elderly dowager entering the box below them had so many plumes attached to her hat that Harriet wondered how her neighbours would be able to see the stage. The younger members of her party helped to adjust her chair, arrange her train, fetch her fan, and any number of other small tasks before the dowager was satisfied. Harriet was amused that one woman could occupy so much space while the rest of her companions were so cramped.

The play began ten minutes late, and absorbed Harriet's attention right from the start. She forgot the heat and the distractions of the crowd in her enthrallment, and started as if awakening from a dream when the lights brightened at the interval. She turned shining eyes to the colonel, who smiled at her pleasure.

"Isn't it a wonderful play, sir? I think that the young actress playing Juliet is perfect, don't you?"

"Yes, she's a pretty woman and very compelling in her part. I look forward to her death scene."

Harriet shuddered. "I don't. But wasn't the balcony scene between Romeo and Juliet enchanting? The garden seemed so real with the moonlight and the fountain. It felt as if real life were unfolding right before our eyes."

"I'm glad that you're enjoying the play so much, Miss Walters. Shall we see if we can manage a stroll during the interval?"

Harriet and Colonel York wended their way past knots of people, nodding at acquaintances and stopping every few feet for snatches of conversation. They had just finished a circuit of the front of the theatre and were headed back to their seats when Harriet saw Mr. Bell in conversation with a lady. As Harriet and her escort approached them, Bell happened to look up and Harriet caught his eye.

"My dear Miss Walters, imagine seeing you here tonight in this crowd," he said. "One can hardly move. Colonel York, I hope you are well. Allow me to introduce my friend to you, Mrs. Gwendolyn Sommer."

Mrs. Sommer was a large, well-endowed woman teetering on the brink of middle age. Her gown had an immodest décolletage and clung to her body. She simpered as she presented a gloved hand to the colonel.

"So pleased to make your acquaintance, Colonel York," she said while the gentleman bowed. She made a half-curtsy to Harriet, who responded in kind. "Miss Walters, I am happy to know you. Are you enjoying the play?"

"Very much so, Mrs. Sommer. And you?"

"This is my second performance, but when Augustus invited me to come tonight, how could I refuse?" She aimed a flirtatious smile in Bell's direction before turning back to the colonel. "I'm sure that I have seen you before, sir. Perhaps we have an acquaintance in common?"

"Mr. Bell and I are both friends of the Fitzwilliams, madam," the colonel replied.

"Edward Fitzwilliam? We're old friends. Perhaps we met at one of his functions?"

"I do not believe so, Mrs. Sommer. I'm sure that I would have remembered you if we had."

"Oh, you are too kind, Colonel." Smiling, she turned to Harriet. "But I'm sure that Miss Walters and I have not met before. How do you know each other, Augustus?"

"Miss Walters is visiting with Diane Fitzwilliam this summer, Gwendolyn."

Mrs. Sommer's eyes gleamed as she stared at Harriet. "Of course. I have heard of you, Miss Walters."

Before Harriet was able to respond, Mr. Bell said, "I'm afraid that we must return to our seats, Gwendolyn. The interval is almost over. So happy to have seen you both, Miss Walters, Colonel York. Enjoy the rest of the performance." He turned his companion around and hurried her away, Mrs. Sommer managing a small wave over her shoulder before the couple were engulfed by the crowd.

"We must get back to our seats, too," the colonel said, offering Harriet his arm and escorting her back in time for the second half.

Harriet was not able to concentrate as fully on the remainder of the play; she was too distracted by Mrs. Sommer's comment. How did the lady know of her? Had Mr. Bell been speaking of her? And what did the lady mean when she said, "Of course I have heard of you"? Had Harriet somehow become a common topic of conversation?

Later that night, after the colonel had taken her for after-theatre refreshments and deposited her at her door, Harriet had difficulty falling asleep. She lay on her back staring at a shaft of moonlight on the bedroom wall, thinking about Mr. Bell. She decided that she did not like him taking another woman to the theatre. Of course, she had no claim upon him; she was not so foolish as to think that. They had waltzed together twice and gone for a ride in Hyde Park, but that did not indicate any marked preference on the gentleman's part for her company. Diane had warned her that there had been many women in his life. He probably dispensed those charming smiles and hand kisses to every woman of his acquaintance. Besides, should she really encourage Bell? Was he the kind of man whose advances she could take seriously? What would Mother think? And Aunt Edna?

Harriet rolled over, smacked her pillow, and settled onto her side. "Don't be a fool, Harriet Walters," she told herself. "You are neither attractive nor young, nor do you have the obvious attractions of a woman like Mrs. Sommer. I'm sure that lady knows her way around a man. Mr. Bell likes excitement and gambling and city life, and you are a country girl who enjoys museums and old churches. Now, put him and his lady friends out of your head and go to sleep." She tried to follow her own advice, but the stars had begun to fade from the morning sky before she finally succumbed to sleep.

Chapter Twenty-Nine

It was mid-June, and Harriet's visit was drawing to a close. Diane had commented on more than one occasion that the summer had been unseasonably warm, and that the family might leave for Hampshire earlier than planned.

Diane was planning a dinner party, and had invited Colonel York, Abigail, Harold Gwinn, and Augustus Bell as her guests. Harriet wondered if the dinner was intended as a fare-well party for her, but her hostess had not shared her intentions, and Harriet did not like to ask. Meanwhile, a streak of hot weather had inspired Diane to hold the party in the garden.

Harriet strolled out of the house before dinner, waiting for the guests to arrive. A table had been prepared in the rose arbour, and a footman hovered over it, laying the settings. The table was draped with white linen, and the glassware and cutlery glinted in the early evening sunlight. A breeze ruffled the tablecloth and wafted the sweet smell of roses to Harriet. The footman heard her step upon the gravel. He looked up, bowed, and withdrew, leaving Harriet to wander over and inspect the floral arrangements.

"It's a beautiful evening, isn't it?" a familiar voice inquired from somewhere nearby. Harriet walked around the arbour and discovered Steven lounging on a wooden bench.

"I didn't know that you were here," she replied. He sat up, and Harriet took a seat beside him.

"The house is rather close this evening," he said. "I had a cool bath before dressing, and decided that it would be more comfortable waiting out here than inside the house."

"Yes, it's much more pleasant outdoors." They paused to watch a pair of sparrows flit in and out of the hedge.

"Will you be leaving us soon, Harriet?" Steven asked.

Harriet reflected for a moment on the most diplomatic response. "Yes. I've been underfoot here long enough, and my mother writes weekly of how much she misses me."

"We will miss you, too. I've enjoyed your company these last weeks. Sometimes school holidays can be excruciatingly dull, with no one under the age of a hundred around the place."

Harriet laughed. "Don't let your mother hear you say that. I'll miss you all, too, but I haven't been the least bit bored during my visit. London is an exciting place."

"What will you do when you get back to Rexton?"

Harriet stretched out her legs and crossed her arms over her chest, aping Steven's posture. "I'm not sure yet. Of course, I'll spend the first fortnight visiting with my mother, coddling my aunt, and catching up on parish visits, but I haven't decided what to do after that. I guess I've been using this visit as an excuse to procrastinate making my plans. I'm very grateful to your grandmother, you know. She has given me the luxury of choice. That's something I've never had before."

Steven nodded. "You are fortunate in your independence, Harriet. I may have the means to be independent – or I will have one day – but one still has obligations to one's family."

"Yes, that's very true. So do I, even with my inheritance. For instance, I wonder if my mother should continue living with my sister, or if I should make a permanent home with her? And if I leave my aunt's home, will she be lonely, especially after just losing your grandmother? I can't just abandon them to follow my own inclinations."

"And if you didn't have those concerns, Harriet? What would you do?"

Harriet sighed. "Travel. I've always wanted to see the continent. But I'll just have to put it off for now. It's already been three months since I last saw my mother and my aunt. It's time I went home."

Steven cocked his head. "You'll have to get through this dinner party first. I hear people coming." Harriet and Steven rose and walked around the arbour just as Diane and Edward arrived with their guests. Diane saw her son with Harriet and said, "There you are. We were wondering what became of the two of you."

Harriet stepped forward to give Abigail a hug. "You look very pretty tonight, Miss Pope," she said, taking a moment to appreciate her friend's transformation. Abigail was glowing on Harold's arm, her cheeks rosy and her eyes sparkling with happiness. "Have you dissected anything recently?" Abigail laughed, Harold winked, and Diane said, "What was that?"

Harriet turned to Colonel York. "How are you this beautiful evening, sir?" she asked.

"You look very well, Miss Walters," he replied. "You are in your element here in the garden."

Harriet smiled while Bell leaned forward to whisper, "Like Eve in the garden of Eden? Does he compare you to that temptress?"

The colonel overheard his remark and frowned while Harriet whispered back, "No, a more likely comparison would be you to the snake." Bell grinned while Harriet took the colonel's arm. "You are sitting beside me at table tonight, sir."

"Delighted," he said as they followed the rest of the party to the arbour. Symonds and the footmen emerged from the shrubbery to pour wine and to serve the chilled soup.

"What a good idea, Diane – dining alfresco," Bell said.

"We do it all the time in the country, Augustus."

"Perhaps you'll make it the fashion here in London, too. Speaking of the country, when are you and Edward headed for Hampshire?"

Diane dipped her spoon into the soup. "We were discussing that earlier today. Normally, we would wait until July, but Edward's calendar is clear for the last two weeks of June. We may go early, but that would mean cutting Harriet's visit short, and we would hate to deprive ourselves of her company." Diane caught Harriet's eye and smiled.

"That would be a great shame," Bell said. "Of course, there is a way out of your dilemma. Invite Harriet to come along to the country with you."

Diane's composure slipped for a moment, but her face relaxed into a smile as she turned to the gentleman. "Of course that would be lovely, Augustus, but I'm afraid that it would not be much of a treat for dear Harriet. County life is no novelty to her, and we shall be a little dull once we have left the city."

"How fortunate that you have me here to advise you, Diane," Bell replied. "There is a simple solution to that difficulty as well. Why not have a country house party in the last week of June? Personally, I would be delighted to get away from the heat and stench of a London summer, and I promise that Miss Walter's entertainment would be my first priority. What do you say, Diane? Why not invite tonight's delightful company to the country for a week?"

Diane continued smiling at Bell, but the smile did not reach her eyes. "What a charming idea, Augustus," she said.

Harriet had heard the exchange and thought it time to intervene. "Diane, you have been so generous to me already, I would not dream of impinging upon your hospitality any longer."

Diane waved her hand. "Nonsense, Harriet. You have been a perfect angel, helping me through my time of need. We would love to have you visit with us in the country, but perhaps it wouldn't be right, with the family in mourning."

"Nonsense, Diane. Just three or four friends and family quietly supporting you through your grief. Nothing to draw anyone's censure," Bell replied. "Why not ask your husband's opinion?"

"Edward?" Diane said. Her husband looked up from a conversation with his son.

"Yes, my dear?"

"Augustus has had a wonderful idea. What would you say to a little house party for our first week in the country?"

"Of course, whatever you like, Diane," he said, returning to his conversation.

"You see? Even Fitzwilliam agrees," Bell said, raising the wine glass to his lips with a mischievous glint in his eyes.

Diane took a deep breath and rested her spoon upon her plate. "Symonds, you may serve the next course," she murmured.

Chapter Thirty

The country house expedition left the following week. Harriet rode in the carriage with her hosts and Abigail, while Steven and Howard followed on horseback. Colonel York was to arrive separately, as was Mr. Bell.

Harriet was curious to see the estate that Mrs. Evans had inherited from her father. She had learned that it was a working dairy farm and not just a holiday retreat. As they drove through the estate park, a rambling, yellow brick building came into view, bordered by sloping, verdant lawns and a copse to the east of the residence. Symonds greeted them at the door, he and the additional staff having preceded the family by two days.

"I hope that you had a pleasant journey, sir," the butler remarked as Edward descended from the vehicle.

"Yes it was, for the most part. Of course, it always takes longer when the ladies are with us. They do like to stop. Yesterday we broke our journey in Winchester so that Miss Walters could attend service in the cathedral."

Harriet did not respond to his complaint, but Diane defended her. "You men are always in such a hurry to get to your destination. We couldn't have driven by without going inside, Edward."

"Yes, ladies like to see the sights," Edward repeated. "And then Abigail had to stop to collect her botanical specimens."

"Thank you again, Cousin Edward. I needed those specimens for my medicinal herb collection," Abigail said.

"The old place looks the same as ever," Steven remarked, arching his back to ease muscles cramped from being in the saddle for two days.

"Yes, Middleton takes good care of it for us," Edward said.

"Middleton is the tenant farmer, Harriet," Diane explained. "His father was my grandfather's tenant before him. I'm certain that they feel they own the place after all these years."

"It's a handsome spot," Harriet said. "I look forward to seeing the rest of the estate."

"I'm sure that you and the young people will want to go for a good long ramble tomorrow," Diane said. "Steven will be happy to take you. But for now, let's go inside and sort out the rooms." The lady took her husband's arm and headed into the house with Harriet and the rest of the company following.

The building was a study in contradictions. It had begun as a farm house, but ensuing generations had expanded and improved upon it as their tastes and budgets allowed. Diane had extended the dining room to accommodate dancing, and remodelled the library to suit Edward's needs. The library had formerly been a dark little nook where previous owners had retreated to work upon the estate accounts, but Edward required a room with grander appointments to entertain his important political friends. An adjoining wall had been demolished, the windows had been enlarged, and several cases of leather-bound books had been purchased to triple the collection. Now gentlemen disappeared into the room for the type of conversation that accompanied expensive cigars and imported brandy.

The guests were installed in a wing separate from the family. Harriet and Abigail had neighbouring rooms, but Harriet was displeased to see Mr. Gwinn and Mr. Bell's rooms just around the corner from her own. It was true that Colonel York was to be in the chamber directly across from the young ladies, and perhaps this mixed style of accommodation was typical of all grand country house parties, but still, she did not like it.

The guests had all arrived by late afternoon, and met at dinner for the first time that evening. Diane's table was impeccable; standards were not lowered because they were in the country. The conversation was very amusing with Steven and Howard telling tales on each other, but people began hiding yawns as the meal wore on. Everyone retired early to bed, but not before Steven had organized a tour of the property for the following morning.

Harriet went down to breakfast early the next day, and was surprised to see Mr. Bell already there. He looked up from his cold mutton and silently saluted her with a cup of tea.

"Why Mr. Bell, I'm surprised to see you up so early. Good morning, Mr. Gwinn," Harriet said as Harold came in behind her.

"I keep country hours when I'm in the country, Miss Walters," Bell said. "Besides, I thought I'd join you and the others this morning." He passed the toast, and Harriet poured herself a cup of tea.

"Have you seen anything of Abigail yet this morning, Miss Walters?" Harold asked as he seated himself.

Harriet forked a slice of mutton onto her plate. "Yes, she poked her head out her door just as I passed, and said to tell you that she would be down as soon as she finished today's journal entry." Harold nodded, and Harriet turned her attention back to Bell. "You're coming on our tour?"

The gentleman shrugged. "Nothing like the sweet smell of a barn." Harriet's eyebrows rose in disbelief as he smothered a piece of toast with strawberry preserves.

Abigail hurried into the room with a straw hat dangling from her fingers, and Steven sauntered in behind her, his hair still damp from his ablutions. "Morning, everyone," he said as Harold rose to greet Abigail with a kiss on the cheek. Harriet gaped at this public display of affection, thinking that the couple had trespassed the bounds of common decency. Perhaps she should advise Abigail to restrain herself in future, even if her young friend regularly flaunted social convention. After a moment, Harriet realized that Bell was addressing her.

"What's that, Mr. Bell?" she asked.

"I was asking if you would mind passing the cheese?"

"Yes, of course."

"Has everyone got what they want?" Steven asked as Symonds entered with a fresh pot of tea. The new arrivals devoured their food and, twenty minutes later, everyone pushed back plates and chairs, ready for the tour.

Lucas Middleton, the Fitzwilliams' tenant, kept the farm in good repair. As Steven led his guests to the dairy, they passed sleek animals fresh from their morning milking grazing in the pasture. Steven introduced them to the farmer, a placid-looking man of middle years, and to his two young daughters, who were busy milking the remaining cows. They observed the family at work for some minutes before departing with a promise to look in on Mrs. Middleton and the younger children at their cottage.

After examining the barn and the horse stable, the company wandered down a path into a wood. Abigail and Harold fell behind the others and vanished, leaving Harriet, Bell and Steven to continue on their own. Harriet half-listened while the two men discussed milk production and crop yields, hearing just enough to know that Mr. Bell was more knowledgeable on the subject than Steven.

"I forget," Harriet thought, "that Mr. Bell grew up on a farm, while Steven grew up in London and just holidays here."

By late morning, the air was warm and still as the sun reached its zenith, even though it was shady under the trees. They came upon a brook, and Harriet wished her companions gone so that she could remove her shoes and stockings and paddle in the inviting water. Bell seemed to read her mind, and sat down upon a rock to pull off a boot.

"Going in wading? What a good idea," Steven said, his eyes sidling in Harriet's direction.

Bell looked up. "Miss Walters, why don't you join us?" he said. "It's a private spot. No one will disturb us here. The water looks so cool, and my feet are damned hot in these boots." He pulled off the other one.

Harriet turned to Steven. "Are you joining him?" she asked.

"It sounds like a good idea," Steven said, hesitating.

Shrugging, Harriet said, "Well, why not."

"Good girl," Bell said, patting a place on the rock beside him. Steven helped her to sit while Bell climbed into the brook. With Bell's back turned and Steven busy with his own things, Harriet took off her shoes, pulled up her skirts, and removed her stockings. Bell offered her a steadying hand as she stepped into the water, with Steven climbing in after her. Harriet paused, letting the refreshing water stream past her ankles while holding her skirts out of the way. Bell kicked a little water at her, and she laughed and kicked some back. The trio waded up the brook some distance until the water rose to their knees and forced them to turn back. Climbing out of the brook at their starting point, they sat upon the grass to wait for their legs and feet to dry. Bell lay on his back, his straw hat pushed over his eyes to shade them from the glinting sun.

"It's a fine day," he remarked to Harriet and Steven. "I feel like a boy again, lying here in the grass. Let me see, there was a song I used to sing when I was just a wee lad." He broke into a familiar country tune, and the other two joined him on the chorus. They sang another song, and then Harriet wandered off to gather a nosegay while the gentlemen remained recumbent upon the ground. Harriet smiled when she heard Mr. Bell's snores, and returned to find both men asleep. She dressed in private and, laughing, left some of her flowers on each man's chest before heading back to the house.

Harriet enjoyed her walk, appreciating the clean air, exercise, and solitude she had not experienced during her stay in London. Striding across the grass, she even pulled the pins restraining her hair and allowed it to bounce upon her shoulders. She felt happy and free, as if the old chains of worry and uncertainty had fallen from her limbs.

When she reached the house, Harriet found Diane and Colonel York drinking lemonade under a tree on the front lawn. She flopped into an empty chair and accepted a glass from Diane.

"Your face is flushed, Harriet, and your hair is all dishevelled," Diane said. "What have you been doing?"

"I've been for a walk and I feel wonderful," she replied, taking thirsty gulps from her glass. Colonel York smiled as she turned to gaze at him. "What has occupied you this morning, sir?" she asked.

"Not much. I strolled down to the stable to look in on my horses before joining Diane out here. It's been a pleasant morning, but I feel the need of some exercise."

"We could play croquet if you like," Diane said, "or lawn bowls."

"Lawn bowls. I was rather good at that at my friend's house. Perhaps I could make further improvements to my game here," he replied.

"What an excellent idea," Harriet said, jumping up. "I've always liked lawn bowls. Will you join us, Diane?"

When Steven and Bell found them an hour later, Harriet and Diane were arguing over whose ball lay closer to the jack while the colonel tried to mediate.

"Now, ladies," he was saying, "we're getting rather heated here, don't you think?"

"No," Harriet said, kneeling on the ground and measuring her ball's position with a piece of ribbon borrowed from Diane's hair. She held the ribbon up for Diane to see.

"Aha, I told you so. My ball is this far away," she said, indicating a point on the ribbon before turning back to measure Diane's ball, "while yours is this far." She pointed to a spot two inches further along the ribbon.

"I think you must be mistaken, dear," Diane said, snatching the ribbon from Harriet, her cheeks flushed and her hat sliding over her left temple. "My ball is closer than yours by a good inch."

"Pardon me, but you must be blind," Harriet said. The colonel threw up his hands and turned away. "Let's pace out the distance between our balls and the jack."

"That won't work, Harriet. My feet are so much daintier than yours," Diane replied. Harriet's hands flew to her hips just as Steven and a chortling Bell started toward them.

"Mother, I'm starving. Have we anything to eat?" Steven asked as he took his mother by the arm and led her toward the house.

Meanwhile, Bell slid an arm around Harriet's shoulders and turned her toward the back lawn. "Miss Walters, I want your opinion of a tree," he said.

"A tree? What tree? What are you talking about, sir?" she asked as the gentleman led her along the side of the house.

When they reached the back lawn, Bell pointed to a tree, his arm still draped around Harriet's shoulders. "There, that's the one. Don't you think that it has the most peculiar shape?"

"I don't understand you, sir. It looks perfectly normal to me," she retorted.

Bell pointed past Harriet's face. "That part in the middle. Do you not see the shape of a fox in the branches?"

"There? I don't see it," she said, squinting at the tree.

"Neither do I," he said before drawing her into his arms and kissing her. Harriet froze in his embrace and staggered a little when he released her. He took a step back to study her face.

"I must confess that there's nothing wrong with the tree, Harriet. I just wanted to kiss you," he said, his perfect dimples showing.

"Oh," was all she replied. Harriet's mind was a blank, and she could think of nothing to say. This couldn't be happening to her. She must be dreaming.

"As a matter of fact, I'm going to do it again," he said, advancing on her. Bell held her longer this time, kissing her hungrily. She did not respond to his touch, and her gaze dropped to the ground when he released her.

Bell stroked the side of her face with one hand. "Is something wrong, Harriet?" he asked.

"I've never been kissed before, Mr. Bell."

"Never? What a sin. How did you like it?"

Her eyes rose to meet his. "I liked it very much," she said, her hands encircling his neck.

Chapter Thirty-One

The remainder of the afternoon passed in a blur for Harriet. She continued kissing Bell until she felt dizzy and thought she had better stop. He escorted her back to the house and kissed the palm of her hand before leaving her without a word. She went upstairs to her room and lay down with a cold compress pressed over her eyes. She felt so many things: excitement, confusion, and guilt. It was wrong to kiss a man to whom she was not engaged; to kiss Mr. Bell so passionately must be a sin! But if that were true, why had she enjoyed it so much? What harm had it done her?

Such conflicting emotions were exhausting, and Harriet fell asleep. When she woke, the early evening sun was slanting through her windows, and it was time to dress for dinner. Harriet chose a light, Grecian-style gown which flattered her shapely arms and shoulders. Her fingers trembled as she loosely arranged her thick hair, and chose a white rose from the vase upon her dressing table to tuck into her curls.

Harriet felt nervous as she went downstairs, wondering how Mr. Bell would react on seeing her again. What if he did something scandalous in front of the others? As it turned out, however, he did not treat her any differently at all. He smiled, teased her a little, and conversed as easily with her as he did with everyone else. However, when the men rejoined the ladies in the drawing room after dinner, he waylaid her by the French doors and pulled her outside. They walked along the side of the house until coming upon a niche hidden from the moonlight, and he pressed her gently against the wall. Taking her face between his hands, he kissed her fervently before breaking from her mouth to trail kisses across her eyes and cheeks. He paused for a moment and looked away, his breathing ragged. She hid her face against his shoulder, trying not to tremble.

"I couldn't wait any longer to get you to myself, dearest girl. I thought that I would go mad during that interminable meal. How clever of you to slip away to the doors." He bent to kiss her ear and the hollow of her neck. Harriet giggled nervously as his lips tickled her shoulder.

"You don't say anything, my darling," Bell said. "What are you thinking? It's too dark – I can't see your face. Come for a walk in the moonlight with me." He took her hand and drew her out onto the gravelled drive beside the house.

Harriet gazed up into the diamond sky, the scent of roses and jasmine mingling in a breeze that cooled her burning face. The night made her feel bold and a little wild. She raised Bell's hand to her lips, and then pressed it against her cheek.

"I don't feel myself tonight, Augustus. I feel feverish, in fact. Perhaps I have lost my head?"

Bell chuckled and swung her off her feet, sweeping her around in a circle before setting her down again. She clung to him for a moment to catch her breath.

"That sounds just about right, my little angel," he said.

Harriet was thrilled. All her life, she had felt big and clumsy, but with Bell enfolding her in his arms, she felt small and protected. She looked up into his black eyes and saw a spark. Did they reflect the moonlight, or was it passion that she saw blazing there?

"Augustus, my darling," she sighed, standing on tiptoe to reach his mouth. She clung to him, and they heard footsteps approaching on the gravel. Breaking free of his arms, Harriet patted her hair and tried to slow her breathing.

Harold and Abigail strolled toward them, laughing and talking. When the couples were face-to-face, Abigail smiled and linked her arm with Harriet's. Harriet hoped that she appeared calm as she smiled back at her friend.

"Isn't it a wonderful evening, Miss Walters?" Abigail asked. "Harold and I came out to enjoy the night air. I see that you and Mr. Bell had the same idea.

"Yes, it's a perfect night," Bell said.

Abigail turned to consider him. "Harold and I were studying the constellations, but we are both such city dwellers that we had difficulty in identifying them. Do you know the night sky, sir?"

"I used to know it very well when I was a boy, but no longer, I fear."

Harold said, "What about billiards, Bell? The other gentlemen are playing, and they have been asking after you. Shall we join them?"

Bell took a long look at Harriet before replying, "Billiards is more in my area of expertise."

"Excellent," Harold said. "Lead the way, sir." He paced back to the house beside Bell while Harriet and Abigail followed behind. When the couples reached the house, the gentlemen bowed and left for the billiards room, leaving the ladies in the hallway.

Abigail said, "Diane has already gone to bed. I think I'll turn in, too. What about you, Miss Walters?"

"I think I will go up. It's been a very active day," she replied, avoiding Abigail's eyes.

"Yes, plenty of fresh air and exercise. After you." Abigail drew back for her friend to pass.

As Harriet climbed the stairs, she wondered how much Abigail guessed of her situation. Reaching her doorway, she decided to find out.

"I wonder if you would mind stepping in for a moment, Miss Pope? I would appreciate your help in unfastening the back of my gown." She kept her back to the wall to obscure the fact that her gown had no fastenings at all.

"Certainly, Miss Walters," Abigail said. Harriet entered her room and lit the candles while her friend shut the door.

Abigail wasted no time in saying, "I was surprised to see you alone with Mr. Bell this evening. I do hope that you know what you're doing, Miss Walters. Mr. Bell has quite a wild reputation."

A sharp retort to mind her own business came to mind, but Harriet bit back the words. Instead she replied, "I'm afraid I don't at all know what I'm doing, Miss Pope."

"I think it's time we progressed to first names, don't you, Harriet?"

"Yes," Harriet said with a smile.

"So, what of Mr. Bell?"

Harriet met Abigail's eyes. "We were becoming better acquainted when things progressed very quickly today. I let him kiss me – several times – and I kissed him back, too. Oh, Abigail, it was so thrilling!"

"Yes, I have found kissing Harold thrilling as well."

"It's very daring of us. Is it wrong, do you think?"

Abigail paused to consider her response. "I don't see how 'wrong' plays into it. It feels very natural to me. Of course, Harold and I are committed to each other."

"Do you mean that you're engaged?" Harriet asked in surprise. The young couple had known each other but a few weeks.

"Not formally," Abigail replied.

Harriet sat down upon the bed. "Tell me what you mean," she said, patting the mattress beside her.

Abigail sat down. "Harold and I cannot afford to marry until he finishes his education. I suggested that Father could help us, but Harold is too proud to take his money, and he won't ask his own father for help, since his father already spends all his spare money on Harold's education. We shall have to wait for two years before we can marry, but we'll put the time to good use. Harold is directing my medical studies so that I'll be prepared when he is ready to begin his career. We're thinking of starting a country practice."

"What will you do in the practice?"

Abigail put her head upon the pillow and crossed her ankles. "I shall assist with surgical procedures – Harold says that my stitching is neater than his – help him examine female patients, assist with child birth, clean wounds, set broken bones – all sorts of things. I shall have to start slowly until my credibility is established, but that is why we want to work in some backward little corner where expectations will not be high and people will appreciate what help we can give them. Most of our clients will be farmers and labourers, I assume."

"Why, it sounds like your plan for missionary work."

"Yes, except that we shall not leave England. We may go to Scotland – Harold's people are from there – or maybe to one of the islands. It will be inexpensive to hire a woman to do the cooking and cleaning, so I will not have to bother with it. I shall be useful, Harriet. I very much look forward to my new life with Harold. It will be exciting." Abigail's eyes sparkled as she turned her head to smile at her friend.

"It certainly sounds like it. I envy you, Abigail. You have your life all planned."

"Which brings the conversation back to you, Harriet. Have you and Mr. Bell made any plans?"

"Oh, no. Nothing at all. That is, he has not said anything to me about marriage, and I have no expectations of him."

"If you do not mind me being so personal, then what are you doing with him?"

Harriet shook her head. "I hardly know. It just happened. But no one has ever kissed me before, or even acted as if he wanted to." She thought about Mr. Ash and the way he had kissed her hand, and quickly amended her words. "That is, no one has ever kissed my mouth before."

"I understand. No one had ever kissed me or seemed likely to before Harold. But, do you like Mr. Bell?"

"Like him? Yes, I do. Being with him is so freeing. When we're together, I feel that I can do anything without shocking him. He feels confined by London society, and has encouraged me to be freer. He has helped me to see life in a new light."

Abigail nodded. "I've said before how alike we are in our unconventionality, Harriet. Maybe you can find happiness with Mr. Bell."

"Maybe. I really don't know. Diane said that Mr. Bell would be a good flirtation for me. Perhaps that's all this is."

Abigail rolled off the bed and stood up. "I would ignore any advice Diane has to offer, Harriet. She never has anyone else's interests at heart, other than her son's, perhaps. You should follow your own mind, I always say. But, it's getting late and I'm tired. I've enjoyed our talk very much. It's nice to share things with another female, sometimes." She leaned down and kissed Harriet on the cheek, causing Harriet to look up in surprise. "Sleep well." Abigail turned to go, but Harriet stopped her.

"Just a minute, Abigail, if you don't mind." Her friend waited for her to continue. "Since we have been sharing matters of the heart with each other, I wonder if you would answer something that has long puzzled me."

"What is it?" Abigail asked, leaning against the wall.

"Your relationship with Steven. I don't understand why you seemed so reluctant to let him escort us to the Warners' ball."

Abigail did an extraordinary thing; her face coloured and she looked embarrassed. "Oh, that. It was nothing, just a childish infatuation I once had for him. Of course, I could never let it amount to anything. It would have ruined my plans to practise medicine. Romance is one thing, but medicine is for life."

"I see," Harriet said slowly.

"Well, if that's all, I wish you a good night, Harriet."

"Good night, and thank you, Abigail," Harriet said as the young woman left the room. When the door closed, she shook her head at her friend's words. Abigail was a very determined person, but Harriet wondered how well she knew her own heart. For that matter, Harriet wondered how well she knew her own heart, but a good night's sleep would help her to see more clearly in the morning. She washed her face, blew out the candles, and went to bed.

Chapter Thirty-Two

Harriet woke feeling refreshed and ready for anything the next day. She went down to breakfast and discovered Bell, Diane, and Steven together. Diane met her eye with a smug smile, and Harriet wondered what Augustus had been telling her. She flushed, and took a place at the table, busying herself with her plate.

Bell said, "You're not up with the birds today, Harriet."

Harriet's flush deepened as she wondered if the other two would notice Augustus' use of her first name. "No, Mr. Bell. I must have been overly tired last night," she said.

Bell smiled and winked. Harriet sighed. Discretion was going to be very difficult if Augustus was going to be so transparent. The gentleman snorted, as if reading her mind, and Diane looked up from stirring sugar into her coffee.

"What is so amusing, Augustus?"

"Nothing – a private joke between Harriet and myself." Harriet noticed Steven watching her.

"Would you care to go for a walk this morning, Harriet?" Bell asked.

"Yes, thank you," she said, "but first there is a letter that I must address in time to catch the morning post."

"We have envelopes in the tray on the library table, Harriet," Diane said. "Feel free to help yourself."

"Thank you, I will. I'll just go upstairs and fetch the letter now." Harriet returned downstairs directly afterward and headed for the library. The door was ajar and the room was dark. She walked to the table and was reaching for an envelope when Bell said, "There you are, my dear."

Harriet whirled and caught sight of the gentleman on the sofa. "Oh, Augustus! You startled me."

"Feeling a little nervy this morning, darling?" He got up and rounded the table to kiss her hand. "Actually, I am feeling a little nervy myself."

"Really? I wouldn't have thought that you had a nerve in your body."

"I have something very important to ask you, my darling, and I'm not sure of your answer. My happiness lies entirely within your power."

"Whatever are you talking about, Augustus?"

"Come with me to the sofa," he said, leading her there. They sat, and he took her hand. "My dearest Harriet, I am not a callow youth. I'm sure that you have heard rumours about me. Perhaps people have even warned you against me?"

"To be perfectly truthful, Augustus . . . ."

"Of course. No doubt these people had your best interests at heart. I have been self-centred and careless in my personal affairs, even wicked by some people's standards. But I have never cared about other people's standards, Harriet. You've seen that, haven't you?"

"Yes, I have. To be truthful, I thought that your behaviour was outrageous when I first met you."

Bell smiled. "No doubt you would have. You were such a shy little thing that I confess I enjoyed shocking you. But I believe that our thinking has grown closer over the past few weeks. Do you not agree that society seeks to enslave us with meaningless conventions?"

Harriet hesitated. "I am conservative by nature, Augustus, because I have never wanted to draw attention to myself. But since knowing you, I have come to believe that I should not sacrifice my happiness to satisfy other people's standards. I have tasted freedom, and I do not want to give it up."

"Exactly what I meant, my darling. I have seen you blossom into a woman who thinks for herself and acknowledges her true feelings. I admire you greatly, and with the recent expression of our physical attraction, these feelings have grown into love. I want to start life afresh, to escape London and all its temptations and begin again somewhere new with you. I want to marry you, my love. Will you have me?" Bell slipped from the couch to kneel before her. He took both her hands and gazed into her eyes. Harriet stared back, surprised by this sudden offer.

"I – I don't know what to say, Augustus. I didn't dream that you felt this way about me so soon."

"Bless your heart, you are too modest, my dear. You are a beautiful, beguiling creature. You should have men falling at your feet." He pulled her to him and kissed her. Harriet gently pushed him away and stood up.

"Beautiful, Augustus?" She went to stand beside the window. Her own reflection gazed back at her: a long-faced woman with a wide mouth and brown eyes. Her eyes were her best feature; they were large with golden flecks. The hair had been tamed and the ruddy complexion calmed. Today she might be considered handsome, but never beautiful.

Bell came to stand behind her and she saw his reflection beside hers. He was certainly handsome. "Yes, you are beautiful, Harriet." He turned her to him. "I can see that my proposal has taken you by surprise, my darling. Think upon it, and give me your answer tomorrow, if you will. But never doubt my heart, dearest." He kissed her again, and she let her body soften against him. She looked up into his eyes.

"Tomorrow, Augustus. I will give you my answer tomorrow."

As she left the library, Harriet's mind was in a whirl. She did what she always did whenever she needed to think; Harriet went for a long walk.

The day was warm and windy with an overcast sky, but Harriet took no notice of the world around her. The first matter she had to consider was whether or not she could rely upon Augustus' declaration of love. Harriet did not want to throw this opportunity away; heaven knows, she might never receive another marriage proposal again. She had to think this one through very carefully.

She had once harboured hopes of a permanent relationship with Mr. Ash, but nothing had happened between them before her departure for London. It was possible that she had read more into his actions than he had intended, and that he felt only friendship for her.

She put thoughts of the schoolmaster aside. She could not rely upon him.

Marrying Augustus might be dangerous, however, given his reputation with women. Even if he did truly love her, would he remain faithful? She had lived in London long enough to know that some women turned a blind eye to their husband's dalliances, but she wasn't sure that she could bear the humiliation herself. If she and Augustus had children, would they be enough to compensate for his infidelity? Perhaps so. Having a family of her own, a possibility that she had dismissed long ago, was certainly an inducement.

Another danger to consider was Augustus' gambling habit. He had told her himself that gambling was the only thing that still excited him. If she married him, Augustus would have control of her inheritance. What if he squandered it all away?

On the other hand, Augustus had talked about wanting to leave London and its temptations to start fresh somewhere else. Maybe if they moved to a small city or even to the country after they married, he would show some restraint? But Augustus had also spoken of emigrating to India or to the colonies. If he chose to leave England, could she bear to leave family and friends behind? Abigail spoke of life as a great adventure, but Harriet wasn't sure that she would like an adventure as great as that.

Well, there were definitely dangers to marrying Augustus, but there were advantages, too. He was kind, and he was certainly affectionate. He was also handsome, tall, and strong, and she felt a thrill whenever he held her in his arms and kissed her. She also found his company exciting, and she liked that she could share her private thoughts with him. He had talked about being "free," and she had enjoyed the things that they had done together: a wild horseback ride in the rain, waltzing, wading in a brook. She had felt independence and exhilaration in these small acts, and agreed with him that some of the laws imposed by society were needlessly restrictive. But once they were married and had children, would his opinion change? Would he expect obedience and conventional behaviour from the mother of his children? What could she do to safeguard her freedom?

The more that she thought, the more Harriet wondered exactly what she wanted from life. She had never really considered this before. Life had always just happened to her. She had done what her parents had expected, and after the move to Rexton, she had bowed to her aunt's will. That was only right; she had been beholden to Aunt Edna for her livelihood, and compliance had been a fair exchange. Mrs. Evans' will had changed all that, but Harriet had been so occupied with the pleasures of her London visit that she hadn't made any decisions about the future, except to defer making them.

Would she be better off remaining independent and not marrying Augustus at all? The thought frightened her. It would take a great deal of strength to make all her of own decisions, and to forge a life alone. She could travel, but would she enjoy doing it alone? She could live with her mother in Mrs. Evans' house and still stay close to her aunt, but one day they would be gone and she would be alone again. Which was she was more willing to risk – freedom, or loneliness?

Harriet climbed to the crest of a hill and groaned when she realized how close the house was. Rather than helping her to make a decision, the walk had left her with even more questions. She decided to slip inside the house and remain in her room until it was time to come down for dinner. Perhaps her emotions on seeing Augustus again would help her to know the right answer.

But when Harriet saw him again just before dinner, she didn't feel any more enlightened than she had before. Augustus sought her out and sat beside her at the table. He was amusing and attentive, and acted pleased to be with her. Perhaps he truly believed that she was different from all other women, and that she alone could make him happy. Shouldn't she be satisfied with that? If only she could rid herself of the niggling doubt that she would not be happy with him.

Harriet hid her turmoil behind bright smiles and silly chatter. She was proud of how well she was masking her emotions until she noticed the colonel frowning at her. When the gentlemen rejoined the ladies after brandy, she turned to find Colonel York standing beside her.

"Colonel," she said, "Mr. Bell was just telling me a story about his horse."

"Yes," he replied, "I overheard him. Very entertaining. But I wonder if you would care to take a turn on the drive with me, Miss Walters?" The colonel's expression was solemn, and she wondered if something had upset him.

"Of course. Please excuse me, Mr. Bell."

"Certainly, my dear," he said. "Just don't keep her away too long, sir."

"I'm afraid that I can't promise you that, Bell," the colonel replied. "Miss Walters?" She followed him outside through the drawing room doors.

It was a fine evening for a walk, the air warm and dry with a filmy white cloud enveloping the moon. The gentleman paused to remove a cigar from his pocket and lit it, the spicy aroma of tobacco wafting toward Harriet as he puffed.

"Shall we?" he asked. They strolled toward the front of the house, not speaking until they had reached it. Colonel York was the first to break their silence.

"Miss Walters, I make it a point not to interfere in other people's business," he said. "It's too easy to make enemies by offending someone with good intentions, and I would not like to lose your friendship. Your company means too much to me."

He paused, and Harriet said, "Of course, Colonel. I feel the same way about you."

"Well, I'm about to break my own rule, my dear. I saw something through the library window this morning that deeply disturbed me."

"Let me guess, sir. You saw Mr. Bell kissing me?"

The gentleman nodded. "Yes. I didn't mean to spy on you, Miss Walters, but I was sitting on the lawn reading the papers when I happened to glance up at the window."

Harriet patted his arm. "It's all right, colonel. Mr. Bell was proposing marriage to me."

"Ah. I see," the colonel said, looking into her eyes.

"So you needn't worry about me. All is well." She took his arm and they continued past the house.

"You accepted him?"

Harriet paused. "After careful consideration, I have decided to accept Mr. Bell." There. She had made a decision and voiced it aloud to Colonel York. Now she would not go back on it.

"Miss Walters, I'm sorry to hear you say that."

She turned to face him, but it was hard to see his features in the dim light. "Why? Is it because you do not like him? I have noticed a certain reticence in your manner whenever you are in his company."

"It's true that I do not like the man, Miss Walters. He is somewhat of a buffoon, in my opinion. I'm sorry if my words offend you, but I will speak bluntly when it affects your future happiness."

Harriet stiffened. She could not counter the colonel's assessment of Augustus' behaviour, but he was unacquainted with her intended's better side. "I'm sorry that you do not care for him, sir, but you are entitled to your opinion," she said.

The colonel laid his hand upon her arm. "You are offended, my dear. Please, let me finish. If it were only distaste for his manners that concerned me, I would not presume to interfere where my opinion would be unwelcome. But it is more than that, I fear."

Harriet's heart began to beat more rapidly. "What else is there?" she asked.

"As you know, I breed race horses. I attend most of the matches in the southern circuit, and I know quite a few people in the racing world. I have encountered Bell at the races on more than one occasion, and I am well acquainted with his reputation. He owes a very large gambling debt to a gentleman who races horses. The debt is of long standing, and the gentleman has only held off calling the law on Bell out of deference to Bell's father. The gentleman is an old friend of his."

Harriet felt as if she were standing on the edge of a very tall precipice. "I know that he gambles and has a reputation for losing large sums, Colonel, but gossip often exaggerates the truth."

"The story is true, Miss Walters. I heard if from the gentleman to whom the money is owed. I am sorry, but it would be best to know everything about Bell before you commit yourself to him."

"Is it such a large sum, colonel?" she whispered.

"It will ruin him. I don't see how it can be paid without selling part of the family estate, which I've heard his father refuses to do. My friend is in quite a conundrum about it. I fear that Bell's only course is to marry a wealthy woman. When I heard that Mabel left you shares in her husband's bank, I was afraid that Bell might try to take advantage of you, and now he has."

"I see," Harriet said.

"I'm very sorry, Miss Walters."

"Well, there had to be a reason for Mr. Bell's proposal. To be perfectly honest, I wondered when Augustus offered himself to me."

Colonel York seized Harriet's hand. "Don't talk such nonsense. Bell is a scoundrel, and he doesn't deserve you."

Harriet took a deep breath. "I don't have any illusions about myself anymore, colonel. I'm quite aware that my person alone is not likely to attract a husband. I also do not belittle myself. I would make a good wife, although I would certainly not describe myself as 'beguiling.'"

"I don't know what to say to you, Miss Walters. If it weren't that I am old enough to be your father, I would make an offer for you myself."

Harriet leaned forward to kiss his cheek. "Thank you, Colonel. You are a dear man and a good friend. And I thank you for the information about Mr. Bell's financial situation, but I ask you not to repeat the story to anyone else, for my sake. I may still accept him."

The gentleman sputtered, "Good heavens – no! You mustn't do such a thing, Miss Walters."

"Come now, Colonel, calm yourself. You're right. Mr. Bell is a scoundrel, but he also has some attractive qualities. He realizes that I have the means to save him, so he asked me to marry him and make a fresh start away from London. Perhaps we could build something fine together somewhere else. I would certainly try. But I intend to confront him with your revelation, and see if we can come to an honest agreement between us. Marriages are often built upon financial considerations, although I believe there to be some real affection between us as well."

"Miss Walters, please promise me that you will wait before you speak to him. Sleep on it, at the very least. Come morning you might decide to send him away with a box on the ears, as he truly deserves."

Harriet laughed. "Yes, I will agree to that. Augustus is not expecting a decision until tomorrow anyway, and it is growing too late for a confrontation tonight. Thank you for your advice." She smiled, but the colonel shook his head.

"I certainly hope that you know what you are doing, my dear," was his final remark. Harriet smiled to herself as they went inside. That was the second time today that someone had said that to her, and at last she felt as if she did.

Chapter Thirty-Three

When Harriet and the colonel returned to the drawing room, they found Diane and Steven playing cards alone.

"Has everyone else gone to bed?" Harriet asked.

"Edward is working in the library, Augustus has gone up, and Abigail and Mr. Gwinn are wandering about somewhere," Diane said. "Steven and I are not ready to turn in yet. Would you care to join us?"

"No thank you, Diane. Colonel York and I were just saying how tired we are. I think I'll make an early evening of it."

Colonel York hid a false yawn behind his hand. "Let me escort you upstairs, Miss Walters. I am quite ready for bed myself." They bid Diane and Steven good night and went upstairs. The colonel paused on his threshold to glance across the hallway at her.

"Privately, Miss Walters, I hope that you will wake tomorrow with a change of heart. Sleep well, my dear."

Harriet smiled. "I am very proud to have such a stalwart friend. Thank you, and don't worry about me. Good night, Colonel." She waved and closed the bedroom door behind her.

One of the maids had left a candle burning on the table just inside the door. Harriet lit a candelabra and turned toward the room. She started, and almost lost her grip on the candelabra. Augustus lay half-naked upon her pillows, his only garment a pair of pantaloons. The rest of his clothing was tossed on a chair next to the bed.

"I was wondering how much longer the colonel was going to keep you," he said, holding out his arms to her.

Harriet hurried forward. "Augustus, what are you doing here?" she hissed.

"Waiting for you to make me a very happy man." He grinned and patted the mattress beside him. "Come here, my love."

"I certainly will not," she said, backing away. "Augustus, remove yourself from my bed."

He sprang up and stalked toward her. "It occurred to me that there was one more inducement I could give you for accepting my marriage proposal, my dear," he said in a husky voice.

"Stop, Augustus," Harriet said, backing away from him until she bumped into the wall, knocking a picture to the floor. Augustus took the candelabra from her and deposited it on the table. Placing his hands upon her shoulders, he ran them lightly down her arms. Harriet stared at the impressive musculature of his shoulders and chest revealed so starkly before her eyes.

He pressed against her, pinning her to the wall. Kissing her on the throat, he whispered, "I know how much you've enjoyed my kisses, Harriet. There is so much more pleasure that I can give you. Let me show you now, my darling." He bent to kiss her mouth, and she thrust her knee sharply into his groin. Bell folded in half, his hands grasping his knees, his mouth gasping for breath. Harriet darted away from him.

"You're right, Augustus, that just gave me quite a lot of pleasure," she said. He couldn't move, so she took a step closer.

"Did you think seducing me or getting me with child would bind me to you? That is very devious of you."

He struggled for breath. "No, Harriet. Not like that. I love you."

Harriet bent to look into his eyes. "Maybe you have feelings for me, Augustus – you certainly need my inheritance – but there is a difference between freedom and irresponsibility. I'm glad that you came here tonight. You have helped me to decide. You are not an honourable man, and I will not have you."

There was pounding on her door. "Miss Walters, is something amiss?" Colonel York shouted. Harriet hurried to open the door.

"Colonel, I'm very happy to see you. Come in, please," she said.

He pushed past her into the room, his eyes fixed upon Bell's heaving form. "The blackguard," he muttered.

"Would you do me a great favour and remove Mr. Bell and his things from my room, please?" she said in distaste.

"I would be delighted to," he replied, advancing upon Bell. "Please wait in the corridor, my dear," he said over his shoulder.

"I shall. Goodbye, Mr. Bell," Harriet said, shutting the door behind her. Out in the hallway, she heard voices and a thud. Three minutes later, both men emerged, Bell fully dressed now. The colonel had twisted his arm behind him and was marching him down the hallway. Harriet watched as they disappeared around the bend toward Bell's room. Moments later, the colonel reappeared.

"Has he hurt you, Miss Walters?" he asked with concern.

"I'm quite all right, Colonel, and very much in your debt," she said, taking his hand.

"Not at all," he said, beginning to calm down. "The flat-out gall of the wretch is hard to credit." After a pause, he added, "Actually, things turned out well in the end. I wish that you could have been spared that disgusting scene, but I'm glad that you learned the villain's true colours before it was too late."

"I'm curious. I heard you talking to him inside my room. What did you say, Colonel?"

"I suggested that he leave the house first thing in the morning so as not to inflict his presence upon you a minute longer than necessary. It's a shame I can't insist he leave tonight, but it would be inconsiderate to wake up a groomsman at this hour."

"I see," Harriet said thoughtfully. "Actually, Colonel, I feel quite ready to leave myself. I've been away from home too long, and there is nothing to hold me here any longer."

"I understand, my dear, but how will you get there? You came to London in Diane's carriage, and you don't know how she might react. Diane might still side with that slug." He paused before adding, "If you will allow me, Miss Walters, I would be happy to escort you home. This whole incident has left a bad taste in my mouth, and I have no desire to remain here, either."

Harriet smiled. "Colonel York, you are the best man I've ever known. I shouldn't impose upon you like this, but the situation is rather dire. I'll pack my things tonight so that I am ready to leave first thing in the morning." Harriet hesitated, the smile fading from her face. "But perhaps I should go downstairs and explain the situation to Diane before she goes to bed? That would be the right thing to do. She's been my hostess for months, and I can't just leave without an explanation."

"Would you like me to come with you, my dear?"

"No thank you, kind sir. I will face Diane alone. No doubt you have your own packing to do."

The colonel patted her shoulder. "Stiff upper lip and off to battle then, Miss Walters. I shall see you in the morning. You're doing the right thing, you know."

"I know, Colonel. I'll see you in the morning."

Harriet went downstairs to the drawing room in search of Diane. She found her still at cards with Steven. Her encounter with Augustus and its aftermath seemed to have taken an eternity, but it had really only lasted several minutes.

Diane looked up. "I thought that you had gone to bed, Harriet. Is there something you require?"

"No thank you," Harriet said, walking up to the table. "I came back because I have something to tell you. I will be leaving first thing in the morning. Colonel York is taking me home."

Diane leaned back in her chair to stare at her. "This is all very sudden, my dear. Has something happened?"

Harriet took a deep breath. "It's a private matter, but there has been an unfortunate incident between myself and Mr. Bell, and I wish to depart as quickly as possible."

Diane shook her head. "That fool. I told him not to be so hasty."

"Mother, what's going on?" Steven asked.

Harriet was shocked. "Did you know that Augustus was going to try to seduce me tonight, Diane?" she demanded. Steven choked and stared from Harriet to his mother.

Diane gazed calmly back at Harriet. "No, not exactly. He told me that he had proposed marriage, and was concerned that you might not accept him. He did mention something about trying to convince you by any means available. Are you sure that you're doing the right thing, Harriet? Augustus is rather reckless, but you can overlook that, can't you?"

"Overlook it? The cur just forced himself on me. Would you advise me to accept such a man?" Harriet demanded.

"Don't be too hard on Augustus. He's in a desperate situation. He would marry you and quite possibly make you a very happy woman. Don't be such a prude, dear."

Harriet stared down at the cold, calculating expression in Diane's beautiful eyes. "Tell me, Diane, when you were recommending Augustus to me, did you know about his ruinous gambling debt?"

Diane shrugged. "Of course. What else would have induced me to think of you as a suitable match for him? With the bank shares Mother left you, it seemed like a reasonable solution."

"Mother, you didn't," Steven said, rising to his feet.

Diane looked at him. "Why not, Steven? I could stomach Mother giving Harriet the house in Rexton – there is scarcely any property attached to it – but to give her half of the bank shares was outrageous." Diane rose to her feet and leaned across the table toward her son. "That was Papa's bank, the business he poured his life into. She should never have left the shares outside of the family. It was wrong, and that is why Mother didn't tell me about it before it was too late." Diane's face was white except for an angry red spot in each cheek. "Those shares are your legacy, Steven, and that woman should never have taken them from you," she said, pointing at Harriet.

Harriet stared back at her, her colour high and her eyes flashing. Wordlessly, she turned and left the room.

"Harriet, wait! I'm so sorry," Steven called.

Diane shrieked, "Don't you dare go after her, Steven!"

Edward threw open the door to the library just as Harriet stormed past. "What's wrong, Miss Walters? Why is Diane shouting?" he asked, but she swept past him and ran up the staircase. When she reached her room, Harriet slammed the door and locked it before breaking into tears.

Harriet and the colonel descended the stairs at first light, their luggage already loaded into his carriage. None of the family was present to say goodbye. Symonds waited for them in the foyer with a large wicker basket, however.

"Good morning, Colonel York, Miss Walters. I was instructed to have a breakfast prepared for you to take upon your journey." He bowed and presented the basket to the colonel.

"Thank you Symonds. Please convey my thanks to Mrs. Fitzwilliam," he said.

"Mrs. Fitzwilliam didn't leave the instructions, sir. My wishes for a pleasant journey." The butler opened the front door, and Colonel York and Harriet brushed past him.

"I wonder who arranged breakfast for us?" the colonel asked as they descended the stairs to the driveway.

"I did," Steven said, stepping forward from beside the horses. "I am so sorry, Harriet. Mother has used you abominably. I know that Grandmother held you in high esteem and would never have stood for your mistreatment. I hope that you will still consider me your friend, at least."

Harriet took his proffered hand. "Of course we are still friends. I'm very glad to have known you, Steven, and if ever you wish to visit your grandmother's home in Rexton, you will be welcome."

"Thank you," he said, shaking her hand. He shook hands with the colonel, too, who placed the basket in the carriage.

"I wonder if you would do me a small service, Steven," Harriet said. "I've written a note to Abigail. Would you see that she gets it? I've not had the opportunity to say goodbye to her, and I would hate to leave her without a word."

"Of course," Steven said, taking the note and slipping it into his pocket.

"Please tell her that I look forward to a letter once she returns home. I would like to hear from you as well, although I will understand if it is impossible for you to write."

"Of course I will write, Harriet, although I am not the best correspondent. Mother cannot track my letters from Oxford."

"Well then, I would love to know how you and Mr. Gwinn are getting on. I expect great things from both of you." She smiled at Steven, turned to the carriage, and the colonel handed her in.

"Have a good journey. I hope to see you again in London some time, sir," Steven said.

The colonel tipped his hat. "I'm sure that our paths will cross again, young man. The best of luck to you." Colonel York jiggled the reins, and the carriage made a circle at the end of the drive before trotting past Steven.

"Goodbye," Harriet called, turning to wave over her shoulder. Steven waved back, and then they had passed the house and were down the lane.

On their way through the park, the colonel said, "What an eventful few days it has been, Miss Walters."

Harriet gazed straight ahead, her face composed. "It was an eventful few months for me. What a lot has happened since I left Rexton back in April."

"Do you regret coming to London, my dear?"

"Oh no, Colonel. I've always wanted to see London, and someday, in better circumstances, I shall return. I met many good people there – Steven, Abigail, Mr. Gwinn – and you, of course." She smiled. "But I've had enough society and parties and intrigue to last me a good long time. We're going home to Rexton, Colonel, where I will show you Mrs. Evans' home and introduce you to Mother and Aunt Edna. You will stay and have a good long visit with us, won't you?"

He grinned at her. "I would enjoy a long visit with you and your family, Miss Walters. My nerves have taken a beating these past few days, and I deserve a holiday."

"You shall have one, sir," she said, relaxing back into her seat and looking forward to home.

Chapter Thirty-Four

"Hello, Grace, I'm back," Harriet said when the maid opened the door and gawked at her. "This is Colonel York. Where are Mother and Aunt Edna?"

"They're in the sitting room, Miss."

"Thank you. We'll show ourselves in."

Harriet took the colonel's arm and rushed him down the hallway. "Mother! Aunt Edna! I'm home," she called on the way. The door to the sitting room burst open, and Mrs. Walters flew out.

"Harriet, what a surprise!" she squealed. She clasped her daughter in her arms and rocked her back and forth ecstatically.

"I can't get out, Edwina. You're blocking the way," Aunt Edna protested, poking her sister in the back. "Make room. I want to see Harriet, too."

Mrs. Walters stepped back and Aunt Edna embraced Harriet. Looking over her niece's shoulder, she noticed Colonel York loitering in the hallway.

"But who is this gentleman? Where are your manners, girl? Introduce him to your mother and me."

Harriet turned to take the gentleman's arm. "Of course. My apologies. This is Colonel York, an old friend of Mrs. Evans' and a dear friend of mine. He drove me home from the Fitzwilliams' estate in Hampshire." The colonel bowed while Aunt Edna nodded and turned back to Harriet.

"You did not write to say that you were coming. We didn't expect to see you until the end of the month. What happened to bring you home early?"

Mrs. Walters, who was peering over her sister's shoulder at the colonel, gently pushed Aunt Edna out of the doorway. "How kind of you to bring my daughter home, Colonel York. Do come into the sitting room and let us offer you a cold drink. It's warm today. Grace!"

"Yes, ma'am?" said the maid, who had been hovering in the hallway.

"Please bring us some chilled orgeat lemonade and apple cake."

"Yes, ma'am."

Harriet spent the remainder of the afternoon telling her family about her London adventures. She spoke so long that Grace finally interrupted to inquire if Cook should hold dinner.

Aunt Edna glanced at the mantle clock. "Goodness gracious, look at the time. I had no idea that it was so late. Harriet, you've talked the day away."

"It was fascinating listening to you, Harriet. I feel as if I've been to London myself," her mother declared.

"Now you don't ever need to go," her sister said.

"I don't suppose I ever shall." Mrs. Walters smiled at Colonel York. "I have never ventured far from home, sir."

He smiled back. "No reason to, Mrs. Walters. You seem to have everything you need right here."

"You'll have to judge that for yourself when Harriet takes you for a tour of the village tomorrow," the lady replied.

"Grace," Aunt Edna said, "Colonel York will be staying with us. Tell Cook to hold dinner for half an hour, and then take him upstairs to his room. Have George carry up the luggage. He's put away the colonel's horses, hasn't he?"

"He has, ma'am," Grace said before hurrying away.

Harriet and her mother exchanged glances; Aunt Edna never delayed her dinner.

"Thank you, Mrs. Slater. It's kind of you to let me impose upon you with no advance warning," the gentleman said.

"We're happy to have you, Colonel. I look forward to sharing stories about Mabel with you. She mentioned you and your wife on several occasions."

"I would enjoy that," he said with a bow.

Harriet offered to show the colonel to his room. After they had left, Edna looked at her sister. "Well, well, Edwina, there's more story here than Harriet has told us."

Mrs. Walters rose to join her sister on the couch. "I agree. I don't believe that Harriet would leave Diane's company so precipitately simply out of fear of overstaying her welcome."

"See what you can learn from her in her room tonight, and if it isn't much, we'll work on the colonel tomorrow. We'll get to the bottom of this yet."

During dinner, Harriet inquired after her sister and her family and heard that all were well. "Helen writes that the twins have not been practising their piano lessons as industriously as they should, and that I may find them sadly regressed on my return," Mrs. Walters said.

"I'm sure that you'll soon have them set right, if you return to Helen's," Harriet replied.

"What do you mean, dear?"

"Only that we have not made any plans, Mother – you, Aunt Edna, and I. There is no need to go back to Helen's house unless you want to."

"Edna and I wondered what you planned to do after your return. We weren't even certain that you were returning. You seemed to be enjoying yourself so much in your letters.

"Oh, there was never any danger of me remaining in London. I'm a country girl at heart, after all. But you haven't told me how everyone is in Rexton?"

Aunt Edna and Mrs. Walters spent the next half hour relating the village news, including the dressmaker's holiday in France.

"And how is Mrs. Higgins?" Harriet asked.

"Not at all well, I fear. She fell earlier this summer, and hasn't been able to leave her cottage," her mother said. "She was bed-ridden until last week."

"The poor dear!" Harriet exclaimed. "I shall visit her tomorrow, after I've taken the colonel on our tour."

"Don't let me detain you from visiting your friend, Miss Walters. Our tour can wait until the afternoon. Actually, I think I would enjoy a lazy morning tomorrow."

"That sounds like a good plan," Harriet said. "I'm very tired myself tonight. Perhaps I shouldn't have had that glass of Madeira after dinner. I'm finding it difficult to keep my eyes open." Rising, the two travellers wished the ladies a good evening and went upstairs to bed.

"Drat," Edna said, suddenly frowning.

"What is it?"

"We didn't get any information out of Harriet about that 'Bell' man. You're growing forgetful, Edwina."

"Oh, Edna," her sister sighed.

Chapter Thirty-Five

Harriet left before breakfast the next morning to visit Mrs. Higgins. When she arrived at the cottage, she was pleasantly surprised at how tidy it looked. The tall grasses bordering the front walk had been cut, the roses were tied back, and the shutters had a fresh coat of white paint. After admiring the improvements, she walked up the path and knocked loudly on the front door.

"Just a moment. I'm coming," the widow called. After a few minutes' delay, the door opened and Mrs. Higgins appeared, leaning on a cane. "Oh, Miss Walters, you're back. I'm so glad to see you," she said, giving the young woman a hug. "Come in, come in."

"Cook sent you some seed cake. Shall I carry it into the kitchen for you?" Harriet asked.

"How kind of her. Yes please, dear. You just go on ahead and I'll follow. I'm not very fast on my feet these days."

"Yes, Mother told me about your fall. I do hope that you're feeling better?"

"I wrenched my back and my knee. My son moved my bed downstairs to the dining room so I could manage better. Everyone's been looking after me, including your mother. The doctor said that I can walk with the cane for a few hours each day, but after that I must rest and put my feet up. I've never been so lazy in all my life."

"I'm glad that you're able to walk now. No doubt you'll be as good as new in a few more weeks."

Mrs. Higgins hobbled over to the stove to fetch the tea kettle. "I'll just make us a pot of tea," she said.

"No, please, let me," Harriet said, hurrying over to lift the tea pot down from its shelf. The widow settled on a cushioned chair beside the kitchen table and sighed.

"There, that's better. Dr. Mackenzie thinks it will take some time for my back to mend. As a matter of fact, he doesn't think I should live alone in my cottage anymore. He's afraid it will be too much for me."

"I'm so sorry to hear that, Mrs. Higgins," Harriet said, steeping the tea. She unwrapped the seed cake, cut two large slices, and placed them on plates. "What will you do?"

"I'm afraid it's time to sell the cottage and move on, my dear," the widow said, glancing around the kitchen. "My nephew – that's Henry, Oliver's father – has a big house. He's got a bedroom on the ground floor that they can spare, and he's asked me to come live with them. My own two sons would take me, but I can't manage the stairs in their houses. Besides, Henry is like a son to me. I helped raise him after his mother died." Mrs. Higgins shook her head. "It will be hard, leaving here. It's the only home I've ever known, beside my parents' house. I'd like to get a little money for the place to help with things. I don't want to be a burden to anyone. It may not be a fancy house, but it's snug and sound. Of course, it's a little bit out of the way, but the walk is easy enough. We used to ride in a cart when we still had the horses. I've still got the cart in one of the sheds. Well, the good Lord will provide. And I'm grateful to your Mr. Ash for helping me to keep up the place. He's been really good to me with all his help."

Harriet had been pouring out the tea when Mrs. Higgins let that comment slip. "Mr. Ash? What do you mean he's been helping you with the place, Mrs. Higgins? Isn't he in Bath on holiday?"

Mrs. Higgins put down her cup and stared at Harriet. "In Bath? No, he couldn't go because of his sister's trouble. I'm surprised that you didn't know, Miss Walters."

"No, I haven't heard from him since I left for London. What trouble did his sister have?"

"Well, it was actually his sister's husband that had the trouble. He's a sailor, you know, and he got sick in some foreign place. He came home, but the sickness went into his lungs. The doctor said he should get away to some place hot and dry, so he and his wife went to Spain. They couldn't afford the trip, so Mr. Ash and his parents gave them the money. The children stayed behind with their grandparents. The headmaster has been letting Mr. Ash lodge at the school this summer. But didn't your mother tell you, Miss Walters? I told her about Mr. Ash."

"No, Mrs. Higgins," Harriet said, taking a sip of her tea, "it must have slipped Mother's mind. But I've only been home since yesterday, and there was so much to talk about."

"Yes, I'm sure that's what it was. I had a dead apple tree in the garden, so he and the school's groundskeeper took it down for me. Mr. Ash is coming by in the morning to chop up the pieces for fire wood. It's too bad he has to do it when it's so warm, but he wants to tidy up the mess. Last time he was here, I was still in bed, and my son's wife, Ellie, left them some sandwiches and ale for after all their hard work. Now that I'm up again, I'd like to make him something special to thank him for his labour. I was thinking of a meat pie, but it's hard to make when I have to use a cane."

Harriet heard herself say, "Would you like me to help you?"

The widow smiled. "Well, that's very kind of you. I didn't want to ask, but I'd be glad of your help. I was wondering how I was going to grind up the beef and the pork. That's a two-handed job, that is. If you don't mind coming by early tomorrow morning, a meat pie takes a bit of time to make, and I don't like to fire up the stove in the worst heat of the day."

"Of course, Mrs. Higgins. I could come by eight o' clock, if that will suit?"

"That would suit me fine, my love," she said, reaching across the table to pat Harriet's hand. "It will be like old times having you and Mr. Ash sharing a meal together in this house."

Harriet fumed on the brisk walk home. She suspected her aunt of deliberately omitting the information about Mr. Ash, and of persuading her mother to remain silent as well.

The two sisters had finished their breakfast and were drinking tea on a crumb-scattered cloth when Harriet arrived.

"Has Colonel York come down yet?" she asked, joining them at the table.

"No, dear, we haven't seen him yet," her mother said. "He must be enjoying his lie-in."

"Just as well. There's something I'd like to discuss in private with the two of you," Harriet said, pouring herself a cup of tea. "I've just returned from Mrs. Higgins' house. She told me that Mr. Ash has been helping her to tidy up her gardens this summer." The young woman looked up in time to catch her aunt shaking her head at her mother.

"I was surprised to hear that Mr. Ash didn't go to Bath this summer, Aunt. No doubt you'll remember his plans to study the Roman excavations there. Apparently, his brother-in-law had some health problems, and Mr. Ash used his holiday money to help pay for a rest cure in Spain."

"I think I remember you mentioning something about that, Edwina," Aunt Edna said.

"Yes, that's right. Of course, I don't know Mr. Ash personally."

"Was that any reason to ignore him when I asked for news of the village yesterday, Mother? Aunt?"

Aunt Edna banged her cup down on its saucer. "I'll thank you to keep a civil tongue when you speak to me, Miss. We were doing it for your own good. Do you know what that young man has sunk to? He's working as a gardener at the school."

"A gardener? What are you talking about, Aunt?"

"I'm telling you, Harriet, the school has employed him as a gardener. I saw him on the street the other day, and he was brown as a nut. You don't imagine that I would encourage a friendship between you and a gardener, now, would you?"

"There must be some mistake. Mrs. Higgins told me that he is boarding at the school this summer. Perhaps he's just helping out in their gardens."

"Or maybe they discovered something about him that makes him unfit to continue as a teacher." The elderly lady shook her head.

"Aunt Edna, you're impossible. That is purely malicious conjecture. Mr. Ash is a fine man and he has been a good friend to us. I shall not ignore him, and if you do not care to entertain him in this house, then I shall entertain him at Mrs. Evans.'" Harriet and her aunt glared at each other while her mother hurried to intervene.

"Now Edna – Harriet – let's not fight. You've only been home a day, dear. Besides, we don't want the colonel to come downstairs and find us bickering." Mrs. Walters turned to her sister, who folded her arms across her chest and stared out the window. "Edna, I know you think that Mr. Ash is unworthy of Harriet's friendship, but he sounds like an honourable young man, and you have to admit that he has done a favour or two for both you and Harriet." Aunt Edna shrugged. "There. Don't worry, Harriet, we shall be happy to entertain your schoolmaster here, should he call."

Harriet nodded. "Thank you. As a matter of fact, I'm returning to Mrs. Higgins' cottage first thing in the morning to help her make a meat pie for Mr. Ash's dinner. He's chopping firewood for her tomorrow."

Aunt Edna turned to stare at her niece. "You're going to cook, Harriet? Whatever will you do next – polish her silver?" Harriet sighed.

"Come, now, Edna," Mrs. Walters said. "Mrs. Higgins has just finished bed rest, and she's not very strong yet. I'm sure that she doesn't have much money laid by, and Mr. Ash has been helping her prepare the house for sale. What else can the poor widow do to show her appreciation? Harriet is just being neighbourly."

Harriet added, "You can blame yourself for my friendship with Mrs. Higgins, Aunt. You're the one who wanted me to visit the parish widows."

"Visit them. Not cook for them."

Colonel York cleared his throat loudly from the hallway before entering the room.

"Good morning, Colonel, and what a fine morning it is," Mrs. Walters said with a cheery smile. "Won't you take a seat and have some breakfast?"

Aunt Edna rang the bell, and Grace appeared in the doorway. "Grace, the colonel is ready for his breakfast now. Bring some fresh toast and hot tea."

"Right away, ma'am," the maid said, scurrying away.

"Thank you, Mrs. Slater. I've got quite an appetite this morning."

Harriet was still trying to calm herself after her spat with Aunt Edna. "Are you looking forward to our tour, sir?" she asked.

"Most definitely, Miss Walters. That, and to getting some exercise. I'm a bit stiff yet from the drive."

"Perfect. We shall leave right after breakfast."

They left the house an hour later. Harriet took the colonel to the lending library and to the village stores, where the gentleman bought some sweets for his hostesses. They left the main street to stroll through the park, emerging beside St. Michael's Church. Rounding the corner and walking another three blocks, they arrived at Mrs. Evans' house.

"What a handsome building," the gentleman said, looking through the iron fence at the house.

"Yes. It looks rather grand from the street, but inside you'll find it's very comfortable and homely. Shall we go in?"

Rogers opened the front door for them. "I received your note informing of your return, Miss Walters. We are glad that you are back from London. I trust that you will find everything just as it was, as you instructed."

"Thank you for taking care of the house, Rogers. It can't have been very lively for you and the other servants these past few months. I promise that I will make a decision about the house before the end of summer."

"Very good, Miss," the butler said with a bow.

"I'll show the colonel around the house myself."

"As you wish," the butler said, "although I am not certain that you have seen the entire house for yourself yet. If you require my help, please ring and I should be happy to be of assistance." He nodded and departed, leaving Harriet and Colonel York to wander about the first floor. They admired the morning room and the dining room, but it was the sitting room that caught the colonel's fancy.

"Isn't this just like Mabel," he said, looking around the sunny room with its over-stuffed furniture and cheery colours.

"Yes. I almost expected to see her reading the papers on the sofa when we came in." Harriet pointed out some of the objects that Mrs. Evans had acquired on her travels, and then they climbed the staircase to the second floor. Harriet had seen Mrs. Evans' room, but the others were unfamiliar to her. One of the bedrooms had definitely belonged to a gentleman; the wallpaper was a masculine tan-and-cream stripe, and the furniture was a rich mahogany wood. A green-shaded lamp sat on a table beside a leather armchair in convenient proximity to a bookcase. Colonel York chose a leather-bound book from one of the shelves.

"This was definitely Richard's room," he said, flipping through the pages. "He loved poetry. Not what you would expect from a banker, but he was a man of many dimensions." The colonel replaced the volume on the shelf.

"I wish I had known him."

"Yes, you would have liked each other."

They left the room and went next door to Mrs. Evans.' The colonel poked his head through the door while Harriet went inside.

"I always thought that this was the prettiest room in the house," she said. She picked up a pillow from the bed. "All of the embroidery is Mrs. Evans' work." Her gaze wandered to the portrait of her friend and Diane over the mantle. "Come in and have a look at this picture, Colonel," she invited.

They stood together before the painting. "That's an excellent likeness of Mabel as a young woman," he said. "She was a real beauty. Not that it was just her beauty that attracted people. You could see the kindness inside her, too."

Harriet looked from the mother to the little girl. "Diane looked so angelic there."

The gentleman snorted. "I didn't know her when she was that age. She and Mabel spent a lot of time here in those days. Her parents thought it was healthier than raising a child in London. They were so worried about Diane's health in the early years." He sighed. "Maybe they spoiled her too much?"

Harriet turned to him. "Who can say, Colonel? It's hard to believe that someone as generous and honest as Mrs. Evans could have raised a daughter like Diane. Mrs. Evans loved her, though."

"Yes, but she left you this house and half her bank shares, Miss Walters. Mabel might have loved Diane, but she was no fool." Harriet nodded. After a moment, she said, "Shall we go?"

They finished touring the house, discovering a nursery, a sewing room, and a classroom on the third floor. Returning downstairs, Colonel York paused at the front door.

"Mabel made a big house feel really homely and welcoming. I think that you would be happy living here, should you decide to stay in Rexton."

"I don't know where else I would call home," she said. They investigated the spacious stable and garden before heading home.

Chapter Thirty-Six

Even though Harriet rose at dawn the next day, Mrs. Higgins had already prepared the pastry for the meat pie by the time that she arrived. "I've got a pot of tea brewing, Miss Walters," the widow said, laying out a wedge of cheese and some bread for Harriet's breakfast.

Harriet poured herself a cup and sat down at the table where Mrs. Higgins was rolling out the pastry. "I'm sorry that I didn't get here sooner, Mrs. Higgins. You must have been up with the larks this morning."

"I've been making pastry for so long that I can practically whip up a batch in my sleep, my love. Now, we'll just move this out of the way and get you started with grinding the meat." Harriet nodded, chewing as quickly as she could and gulping down her tea.

Harriet was wearing one of her old Willoway gowns, a light, plain dress with short sleeves that bared her arms for work. Her hair was pinned into a loose knot on the top of her head, as much to keep it out of the way as to cool her neck. She tied a towel around her waist and was ready to help. Harriet soon mastered the workings of the grinder and minced up all of the meat. When that was done, she peeled and chopped onions and potatoes.

"I like to add a little apple to the filling for a touch of sweetness," Mrs. Higgins said, slicing the fruit finely and adding it to the other ingredients. She added herbs, salt and pepper, and mixed everything together with her hands. Pouring the filling onto a pastry circle, she capped it with another, pinched the pastry seams together, and tied it all into a clean cloth.

"Now, Miss Walters, if you would fill my big soup pot half full of water, the pie needs to simmer for three hours."

"Right away," Harriet said, fetching the pot and taking it to the pump in the yard. She primed the pump half a dozen times before the water began to flow. The pot was a third full when she heard a voice behind her say, "Miss Walters, what are you doing here?"

Harriet's heart raced; she knew whose voice it was. She looked up and saw Mr. Ash staring at her in amazement. Her aunt had been right; his skin was tanned a light brown and there were golden streaks in his hair. He was dressed for manual labour in a pair of boots, pants, and a rough, collarless shirt. Harriet straightened, her face flushed and her damp hair hanging in tendrils.

"I'm so glad to see you again," she said, wiping a damp hand on her skirt and extending it to him. Ash took her hand and shook it, his face breaking into a wide smile. Harriet could feel the calluses on his fingers. "I came to help Mrs. Higgins make your dinner."

"I beg your pardon?"

"When I visited Mrs. Higgins yesterday, she told me that she wanted to make something special for your dinner to thank you for your help today, but she didn't feel up to doing it alone. I volunteered to help."

"That was extremely kind of you. But when did you get back from London?"

"Just the day before yesterday. Actually, I wasn't in London at the end. I was staying at the Fitzwilliams' farm in Hampshire. A friend of mine, Colonel York, brought me home in his carriage. He's visiting with us at Aunt Edna's house."

The smile vanished from Ash's face, and he released Harriet's hand. "I see. This Colonel York was another house guest of the Fitzwilliams?"

"Yes. He was a good friend of Mrs. Evans, too, and has taken a fatherly interest in me." Harriet expected Ash to look happier with this explanation, but his demeanour was still cool.

"I see," he said again.

"Mrs. Higgins told me of your kindness in helping her."

"Yes – well – my plans didn't work out this summer. I was visiting my family in Bristol when Mrs. Higgins had her accident. When I came to see how she was doing on my return, I noticed that she needed a little help with tidying up the grounds around her house."

"I noticed the improvements right away. I had no idea that a history master could be so handy." This brought a smile to the young man's face.

"It's true. I've been picking up new skills from the school's groundskeeper, Mr. Buxton. Mr. Harris was kind enough to give me my board for the summer in exchange for helping out around the grounds. Buxton is in his seventies, and some of the heavier work is getting beyond him."

"That would explain my aunt's impression that you had become a professional gardener," Harriet said with an impish grin. Ash frowned.

"Miss Walters, what's become of my soup pot?" Mrs. Higgins called from the kitchen window.

"Coming, Mrs. Higgins."

"Let me help you with that," Ash said, reaching for the pump handle.

"No need, sir. It's almost full enough." Harriet bent back to the pump and soon had the water at the desired level. "There, all done," she said, heaving up the pot and heading for the kitchen door before he could offer to carry it.

Ash's expression was quizzical as he followed her to the door. "You're joking about the gardening, aren't you Miss Walters? Hello, Mrs. Higgins. How are you feeling today?"

"Quite jolly with all this company, my love. Would you like a cup of tea? Have you had your breakfast?"

"Yes, thank you. I wouldn't mind a second cup, though."

"I'll get it, Mrs. Higgins. You should rest," Harriet said. Ash's eyes followed her as she moved about the kitchen.

"Miss Walters has told me all about her trip to London. She had a wonderful time."

"Yes, indeed," Harriet said. "I visited the British Museum, Hampton Court, Westminster Abbey – oh, so many places. I went to my first opera, and to the theatre, too. It was all very grand and exciting."

"I'd be interested to hear the details. Tell me, what other new friends did you make while you were there?"

Harriet smiled to herself, glad to think that Mr. Ash might be feeling the pains of jealousy. "The Fitzwilliams introduced me to quite a few important gentlemen and their wives – just as you predicted, sir – although none became any more than acquaintances. And there was one particular friend of Diane's who was interesting, Augustus Bell. Mr. Bell had some fascinating ideas about how modern society enslaves us with false standards of decorum. We had several conversations about that."

"Did you really?" Ash muttered. "And did he convince you of his doctrine?"

Harriet grew serious. "To some extent. Mr. Bell taught me the value of saying what I feel no matter what people's expectations are of me. Because of him, I stopped worrying about appearing foolish or inadequate in public, and discovered the importance of making my own decisions. It was a liberating experience."

Ash studied her. "It sounds as if he made quite an impression on you, Miss Walters."

Harriet smiled, the playfulness returning to her eyes. "He did, until I discovered what a scoundrel he was. But that story will have to wait until another time."

Mrs. Higgins sighed. "I wish that I were young again. London sounds like a magical place. I've never been more than fifteen miles from Rexton."

Harriet bent to hug her friend. "But London is also full of foolish ladies and gentlemen, Mrs. Higgins, who care more about their appearance and their amusements than anything else. It's very dirty, with smoky air and refuse in the streets and in the river, and very expensive. There are a few rich people who enjoy its advantages, but many more people who live in squalor. For all its attractions, I'm glad to come home to Rexton again."

"And we're glad you're back, aren't we, Mr. Ash?" the widow said, returning Harriet's embrace.

"Of course," Ash replied, watching them.

Chapter Thirty-Seven

Harriet spent several hours with her friends that day. Ash carried an armchair outside into the shade so that Mrs. Higgins could join them in comfort. She laughed when she saw the awkward way the gentleman chopped wood, and called out suggestions to improve his technique. Ash grinned and promised to do better. Harriet raked up the mess of twigs from the felling and dismembering of the tree, and tied the sticks into bundles. She picked up the blocks of wood as Ash cut them, and stacked them neatly by the kitchen door. When the schoolmaster stopped to rest on the grass beside Mrs. Higgins, Harriet fetched glasses of cool buttermilk for everyone. Ash caught her eye as he took the glass; she could see him remembering other occasions when she had offered him buttermilk.

When the firewood was chopped and stacked, Mrs. Higgins hobbled back inside while Harriet and Ash spent another hour weeding the vegetable garden. They passed the time talking about Harriet's trip, Ash listening quietly to everything she said. When the weeding was finished and Harriet had gathered fresh beans and dill for a salad, they rejoined Mrs. Higgins in the kitchen. The meat pie was cooked and resting on a covered plate, the delicious scent making Harriet ravenous.

Ash hurried back outside to wash at the pump while Harriet laid the table. She glanced out the window while fetching cutlery from beside the sink, and saw him drying himself with a towel. Harriet could not help but notice that, while Ash was longer and leaner than Augustus, his musculature showed evidence of hard physical labour.

Mrs. Higgins came to stand beside her. "He doesn't have an ounce to spare on him, but what he's got is put together right," she said, patting Harriet upon the shoulder. "We talked about you while you were gone, you know. He asked if I had heard from you."

"There isn't someone else in his life, is there?" Harriet asked. That would account for his restraint.

"Another woman? Of course not. I can tell that young man is sweet on you, my love." She turned back toward the window and called, "Are you going to be much longer, Mr. Ash? We don't want the meat pie getting cold."

"Coming, Mrs. Higgins," he shouted, looking up to see the two women watching from the window. Ash pulled the shirt over his head and smoothed his hair with his fingers.

Mrs. Higgins carried the beans to the table while Harriet brought a plate of pickles and a bowl of sweet relish. Ash strode through the kitchen door, his cheeks slightly flushed, and took a seat beside the widow. The table looked very festive with Mrs. Higgins' wedding china and a bouquet of flowers that Harriet had picked from the garden. Harriet carried over the meat pie and placed it ceremoniously before their hostess.

"There – doesn't that look good?" Mrs. Higgins asked as Ash lowered his face to inhale the meaty fragrance. She sliced into the rich pastry, steam rising from the slit, and dished generous helpings onto their plates. They passed serving dishes back and forth before pausing to say grace.

"Thank you, dear Lord, for the food which you provide, and for the friendship and help of these good young people," Mrs. Higgins said. "May they reap the true happiness they deserve for their kindness."

"Amen," Harriet and Ash replied. They fell onto the food, and Ash moaned in pleasure at his first bite.

"Mrs. Higgins," he said, "I will chop firewood for you every day of my life if you will cook for me."

"Thank you, my love. It's a real pleasure to cook for people who enjoy their food. But now that Miss Walters knows the recipe, you can chop wood for her instead." Mrs. Higgins winked at him.

"Mmm hmm," he responded, glancing at Harriet before looking away.

When the meal was finished, Ash settled Mrs. Higgins in the parlour while Harriet cleaned up the kitchen. She joined them when she was finished and sat down on the sofa beside him. Ash jumped up and said that it was time for him to be getting back to the school.

"I assume Mrs. Slater's carriage will be coming for you, Miss Walters," he said.

"No, sir. It's a beautiful day, so I walked." When the young man remained silent, she shrugged and added, "It's not very far."

Mrs. Higgins looked at the gentleman and frowned. "I'm sure that Miss Walters hasn't had nearly enough time to tell you about her trip, Mr. Ash. She could tell you the rest on the walk home."

The schoolmaster looked at Harriet and blinked. Harriet sputtered, "That's not necessary, sir. You must be tired, and I would not want to take you out of your way."

"Goodness, it's not much more than a stretch of the legs for a strong young man like you," the widow said.

"Of course, Mrs. Higgins," he replied. Turning to Harriet, he said, "Miss Walters, you promised to tell me what it was about your Mr. Bell that made him a scoundrel. Will you indulge me with the story on the way home?"

"Perhaps I shall tell you part of it," she replied with a smile. They spent a few more minutes ensuring that Mrs. Higgins had everything that she required before gathering up their things. Harriet bent to kiss the widow's cheek, and Mrs. Higgins whispered, "He's just shy, my love. Try to be more encouraging." Harriet rolled her eyes and bade her friend goodbye.

"I'll look in on you again in a few days, Mrs. Higgins," Ash said while Harriet exited into the hallway.

"What's wrong with you, my lad? In my day, men weren't so slow in their courting," she said in a fierce whisper. The schoolmaster stepped back in surprise. "Get on with you before Miss Walters grows tired of waiting," she said, shooing him into the hallway. In a louder voice, she said, "Have a nice walk, you two." Harriet and Ash waved as they passed the parlour window and strolled down the lane together.

The walk home began very quietly. Ash did not offer Harriet his arm as he had done on previous occasions, but kept some distance between them. Harriet could not account for the change in her friend's manner, but decided that she would try to draw him out.

Harriet knew that the schoolmaster shared her love of architecture, so she began by speaking of the cathedrals she had seen during her travels. Her admiration and passion for these magnificent structures invoked a similar response in him. Soon Ash was sharing recollections from his visit to London, and they compared impressions.

Harriet changed the subject to Ash's cancelled plans to visit Bath that summer. He was reticent at first, but became more effusive when speaking of his sister's unflagging fortitude in nursing her husband through a long and difficult illness, and of the grateful tears she had shed on learning of the trip to Spain. Ash spoke with rueful humour of the turbulent days when his nieces and nephews first came to stay with his parents, and of his admiration for their patience. Harriet reciprocated by telling him of her sister's unruly brood, and how her own patience was taxed whenever she visited them.

The walk became more enjoyable as Ash forgot to be aloof with her. Harriet revelled in the comfort she felt in his company, an ease that she had never experienced with the exciting and provocative Mr. Bell. They had walked up the sidewalk to Harriet's front door before Ash seemed to recall what he was doing. He looked at her, and Harriet watched the warmth drain from his eyes while his expression became guarded again.

Dismayed by this regression, Harriet blurted out, "Mr. Ash, I have not enjoyed myself so much in months."

Ash's eyebrows rose and he smiled. "After all the glories you experienced in London, Miss Walters?"

"How can they compare with the glory of Mrs. Higgins' meat pie and sweet relish?" she said. Ash laughed, and Harriet felt encouraged enough to take his arm. He stiffened, and Harriet removed her hand and clasped it with its fellow at her waist, glancing in embarrassment at the ground.

"Miss Walters," he said, trying to catch her eye, "I know that you will be occupied with your London visitor, and that we may not see each other again for a time. After that, you may decide to return with him to London, or perhaps even travel abroad? I just want to say how much I've enjoyed our friendship, and that I wish you all the best in your new life, whatever that may be." He waited until she looked up before bowing and turning to leave.

"Mr. Ash," Harriet called after him in an anxious voice, "I have no intention of leaving Rexton."

"You don't?" he said, turning back again.

Harriet met his eyes. "I have no plans to go anywhere. Why did it sound as if you were saying good-bye to me just now?"

As they stared at each other, Colonel York and Mrs. Walters drove up the street and parked before the house. They laughed, and then the colonel jumped down to assist Mrs. Walters from the carriage. They were strolling up the sidewalk before Mrs. Walters noticed Harriet and Ash.

"Why Harriet, who is this?" she said with a smile.

"Mother – Colonel York – this is Mr. Joseph Ash," Harriet said. "We have just returned from Mrs. Higgins' house."

"Of course," Mrs. Walters said, her smile growing brighter. "I've heard all about you, sir. Mrs. Higgins told me how helpful you've been since her accident."

Colonel York bowed to the schoolmaster, who returned the gesture. "I've just brought your mother home from her parish visits, Harriet," the colonel said.

"Yes, Colonel York has been most kind. He thought it too warm for me to walk today, and insisted on driving me in his carriage. He has very patiently sat through three visits." Mrs. Walters and the colonel exchanged a smile. "Now, Mr. Ash, won't you come inside and join us in a cool drink? I'm sure that you and Harriet must be warm from your walk home."

"That's very kind of you, but I am hardly fit for company in my current state," Ash said, looking down at his soiled work clothes.

"Nonsense, we are quite casual in this household," Mrs. Walters replied.

Harriet thought of her aunt and smiled at this bold-faced lie. "Where is Aunt Edna, Mother?" she said aloud.

"She said that she was going to take a nap, dear."

"Your invitation is very gracious, Mrs. Walters," Ash said, "but perhaps another time?"

"I understand, sir. You would probably like a rest yourself. How would dinner tomorrow night suit instead?"

"Tomorrow night?" Ash stammered. He looked at Harriet, who tucked her hand into his arm.

"Mr. Ash, my sister and my daughter have all had the pleasure of your company. I would like the opportunity to get to know you as well," Mrs. Walters said.

Harriet smiled at her mother's tenacity, and turned back to Mr. Ash. His eyes sought hers before saying, "That's very kind. I would be happy to accept, Mrs. Walters."

"Wonderful. I'm afraid that we dine early in my sister's house. Would six o'clock be convenient?"

"That would suit me, ma'am."

"Shall I come for you in my carriage?" the colonel asked. Harriet beamed at him, and he winked.

"Please don't bother, sir. I wouldn't want to inconvenience you," Ash hastened to say.

"Why, it's no trouble at all, young man. My animals are getting fat from a lack of exercise. As a matter of fact, you might oblige me by letting me drive you home today. I'm new to Rexton, and you could show me where to fetch you tomorrow, if you would be so kind?"

Ash nodded. "You're very generous, Colonel."

"Not at all. It will give us a chance to talk. I understand that you're the history master at the boys' school?" He clapped Ash on the shoulder and steered him toward the carriage. Harriet watched them leave, and then her mother linked arms and turned her toward the house.

"Did you have a nice day, Harriet?" she asked.

"I have now, Mother. Thank you so much," Harriet replied, kissing her upon the cheek.

"I'm glad, dearest. I look forward to getting to know your young friend. I hear such conflicting reports from my sister and Mrs. Higgins that I don't know what to believe. Of course, if he is a friend of yours, I'm sure that he's a good person."

"He is, Mother. He's a very good person."

"I thought as much. Now, let us tell Edna that Mr. Ash is coming to dine tomorrow."

Chapter Thirty-Eight

Dinner was rather difficult that evening as everyone tried to ignore Aunt Edna's palpable disapproval of the morrow's young guest. She either stared at her plate, grinding her food between her teeth, or glared at Mrs. Walters and Harriet. Mrs. Walters chose to ignore her sister and chatted with Colonel York instead, while Harriet was lost in her own thoughts. She was both thrilled and terrified to think of Mr. Ash dining with them tomorrow. What would everyone say and do?

After dinner, Harriet pleaded fatigue and went upstairs to retire. Colonel York caught up with her at the top of the stairs, however.

"Forgot my cigars in my other coat," he said, walking beside her down the hallway.

Harriet abandoned all pretence of indifference to grab his arm. "What do you think of Mr. Ash?" she asked.

"I liked him, my dear," the gentleman said with a smile, "not that we talked for very long. He's a quiet man, but what he says is sound. I asked him a few questions about his profession, but he soon turned the conversation to your London visit."

"What did he want to know?"

"In a roundabout way, whether you had any suitors. I take it that you mentioned Mr. Bell to him?"

"I did, yes."

"Well, he wanted to know if Bell had been courting you. I told him that he should ask you that."

"Thank you, you are very wise," she said, embracing him. The colonel patted her back.

"I'm glad that I did the right thing, my dear. Relationships between men and women can be so tricky."

"You certainly did. My association with Mr. Bell has to be explained in just the right light. Not that anything improper occurred."

"No, you made sure of that." He grinned and chucked her softly under the chin. "Are you looking forward to tomorrow evening?"

Harriet grimaced. "I'm looking forward to a closer association between you, mother, and Mr. Ash, and I'm hoping that Aunt Edna will be in a more reasonable frame of mind by then."

The gentleman stopped with Harriet before her door. "She can be rather fierce, your aunt."

Harriet nodded. "Yes, but I'm determined not to let her bully me or Mr. Ash."

"Good for you, Miss Walters. Stand your ground. Don't worry, your mother and I will intervene if she draws blood."

"Thank you, Colonel. Just don't get caught in the cross-fire," Harriet said with a wry grin. The gentleman smiled, saluted, and went back downstairs.

Harriet went into her room and closed the door. She collapsed against it and looked across the room at the window. The evening had turned rainy, and a soft drizzle filmed the glass. She opened the window, and drew up a chair to sit beside it. Leaning on the sill, she sniffed the delightful fragrance of damp earth and wet greenery. The scent reminded her of Willoway and of the many times she had looked out her bedroom window over the countryside. She loved living in the country; the smells, the wide open spaces, and the freedom of going for long walks without ever seeing a soul. City life had its advantages, too – going to the theatre, visiting galleries and museums, admiring the jewels and gowns of elegant ladies – but she felt at peace in the country. If only she could live in both worlds!

Harriet shook her head. The old Harriet would sigh and wish for things that she couldn't have, but the new Harriet had resources and made her own decisions. She had organized the move from Willoway all by herself; surely she could figure out what to do with her future. She decided to begin by devising a list of the things she did and did not want.

Harriet retrieved a sheet of paper and a pencil from her writing desk and returned to the window sill. At the top of the page, she wrote, "Mrs. Evans's house." Harriet thought hard about that item. She loved the house because it reminded her of her friend, but it would always feel like Mrs. Evans' house, and not her own. Besides, if she wanted the peace of the country and the excitement of the city, life in Rexton fitted with neither. She should be practical and sell the house, but if her mother wanted to make a home with her, where would they live?

She wrote "Mother" next on the sheet. Was her mother happy living with Aunt Edna, or did she want to return to Helen and her family? Would she prefer living with Harriet? What her mother needed was a permanent home surrounded by people who loved her, plus a regular income so that she need not worry about money ever again. It would be better if her mother had control over that income; she would feel more secure if she did not have to rely upon an allowance. Harriet put down her pencil. She had to consult her mother. The sun was low in the sky, but hadn't set yet. She would see if her mother was in her room.

She crossed the hall and knocked on the door. "Come in," Mrs. Walters answered. Harriet went in. Her mother sat beside her bed, repairing a tear in a chemise.

"Harriet, I thought that you were asleep," she said, putting down her sewing.

"No, Mother. I've been busy thinking, in fact. It's time I made some plans, but I can't do that without consulting you first. Harriet knelt on the floor and rested her elbows on her mother's chair. "What do you want to do, Mother? Where do you want to live?"

Mrs. Walters stroked her daughter's hair. "I've been thinking about that a lot lately, dearest. Perhaps it's time I went back to Helen."

"Were you happy there, Mother?"

Mrs. Walters shrugged. "To be truthful, dear, it's a little chaotic with all the children running about. Helen is a very indulgent mother. I did feel that I was making progress with the twins, however."

"What about Rexton, dear? Do you like living here?"

"Rexton is home to me, too, Harriet. My home before I married your father, that is."

"What about living with Aunt Edna?"

Mrs. Walters smiled. "There's a trick to living with your aunt. You have to know when to be deaf. I've been comfortable here, although it can be very quiet with just two old women rattling around the house."

"Would you rather that we set up housekeeping together, Mother? Some cozy place in the country, maybe? You see, I've decided that I don't want to live in Mrs. Evans' house. I'm thinking of selling it."

Mrs. Walters studied Harriet's face. "Do you really think that you would be happy living with me in the country?"

"To be truthful, Mother, I would also like to travel, but you would be welcome to come with me."

Mrs. Walters shook her head. "I'm too much of a homebody to want to travel."

"Which means that you would be home by yourself if I went away." Harriet sat back on her heels and took a deep breath. "Mother, I'd like to transfer a third of my bank shares to you for the duration of your life, returning to me on your – when you're gone. I don't want you to worry anymore. So, once you have the bank shares, where would you like to live?"

Her mother put a hand over her heart and sat back in her chair. "My, Harriet, that's very generous of you. I'm sure I won't need that much money to live on."

"But I want you to have too much money, Mother. Too much money would make you feel secure."

Mrs. Walters was silent as she thought. "Well, I suppose that I would prefer to stay here with Edna, if she'll have me. It would make a difference if I were able to help with the expenses."

"You mean that she wouldn't be able to boss you around as much?"

Her mother smiled. "You've lived with Edna, Harriet. You know what she's like. But she's family, and I love her. Being on a more equal footing would help. But . . . ."

"What is it, dear?" Harriet asked, taking her mother's hand.

"I do wish that I could do something for the twins. They show such promise, and they get lost in that mob of brothers and sisters."

Harriet smiled. "Why not ask them here?"

"What?"

Harriet stood up and began pacing the floor. "They're certainly old enough to leave home. They'll be young women in a few years. You talked about how quiet it is with just you and Aunt Edna in the house. Wouldn't it be livelier with the girls here? They are responsible and well-behaved – they've been looking after their younger brothers and sisters for years. Aunt Edna grew accustomed to having me in the house quickly enough. Why not ask her? But I should wait until after you've talked to her about staying, Mother. Aunt Edna needs time to adjust to change."

"Harriet, you've given me a lot to think about."

"Well, one thing is settled. I shall see Mrs. Evans' solicitor first thing tomorrow morning, and have the bank shares transferred to you. Meanwhile, you can talk to Aunt Edna about living with her. Does that suit you?"

"Why not? It won't be such a big change, after all. I'm already living here. I like your plan, my dear. I'll just have to talk Edna into seeing things our way."

"I'm so glad," Harriet said, bending to hug her mother. "It hasn't been easy for you, losing father and Willoway. You deserve some happiness in your life again."

Mrs. Walters stroked her hair. "You're a good daughter, Harriet, and a kind woman. Thank you, dearest."

Harriet kissed her and straightened. "I'm going back to my room now. I have more planning to do. Sweet dreams."

"Sweet dreams, Harriet, although I don't believe that I'll sleep a wink with all I've got to think about." Harriet smiled and left the room.

Chapter Thirty-Nine

Harriet left the house directly after breakfast the next morning to see Mr. Burton. She waited while he prepared the legal papers so that she could sign them right away. After that, she visited Mrs. Higgins for several hours before returning home.

She found her mother and Aunt Edna in the sitting room, with Colonel York pretending to read the papers while listening in on their conversation.

"I think that would work, Edwina," Aunt Edna was saying. "I will review the household accounts and come up with a sum. You can pay me annually or semi-annually, depending on how often the bank shares pay out." Her aunt looked up. "Hello Harriet. Your mother and I have been discussing her suggestion that we set up house together permanently. I think that it might work, but you're foolish for transferring the bank shares to her."

Harriet sat on the arm of the sofa and kissed her aunt's cheek. "Never mind, doing so makes me happy. But let's talk about other things. I have a couple of announcements that I'd like you all to hear." Colonel York put down his papers and listened openly this time.

"Whatever else have you been up to, Niece?"

"Just this. I'm going to sell Mrs. Evans' house and buy Mrs. Higgins' cottage. I'm going to live in the cottage as soon as I've made some improvements to it."

Her aunt stared at her. "Are you quite mad, Harriet? Sell Mabel's beautiful house and move into a puny workman's cottage?" Her teeth snapped audibly together.

Harriet sat down on the sofa between her mother and her aunt, taking each of their hands. Aunt Edna tried to snatch her own back again, but Harriet wouldn't let it go.

"Please listen, Aunt. I love Mrs. Evans' house, but it's too grand for me. I want to live in a simple house in the country, when I'm not away travelling. Mrs. Higgins' house is in a perfect location – just far enough outside the village to be in the country, but close enough to walk into the village. A cart comes with the house. I shall use that for short jaunts, and buy a carriage for longer trips, such as visiting Helen. I'll need to buy a pair of horses. You can advise me on that, can you not, Colonel?"

"I'd be happy to, Miss Walters."

Harriet shot him a grateful smile before turning back to her aunt. "I'm not saying that Mrs. Higgins' house is perfect, Aunt Edna. I should like running water in the kitchen and a bathroom beside my chamber. I plan to install servants' quarters behind the kitchen, and enlarge the bedroom I'll use for myself. But when it is all finished, I shall have the perfect house.

Aunt Edna humphed and folded her arms over her chest. "You mean to live there alone, Harriet?"

"Yes, except for a servant or two. I shall hire a groomsman, but he can live out, at least for now. The barn needs a second floor added on for living quarters."

"That's wise, Harriet. You don't want to undertake too much at first," Mrs. Walters said. "Perhaps Mrs. Higgins' neighbour's eldest son would do? I think his name is Tom."

"Don't encourage her, Edwina. Harriet can't live out there alone."

"Of course I can. You've lived alone in your house all these years. And I'll still be close enough to visit you and mother whenever we like."

"It sounds ideal," said Mrs. Walters. "I'm so pleased for you, dear."

"It won't be easy finding someone to buy Mabel's place," Aunt Edna grumped. "No one around here has enough money."

"What about Mrs. Hensley? She's been doing well with her dressmaker's shop," Mrs. Walters suggested.

"Nonsense, Edwina, she has the lease to pay on her store. She can't manage both."

Colonel York cleared his throat. "Actually, ladies, I've been considering the house for myself, if Miss Walters didn't want it."

All three women stared at him. "Really, Colonel?" Harriet asked.

"I've been thinking of the stable. It's larger than the one I have at home, and there's good pasture beside it. It's getting more and more expensive to keep my horses in London, and I've been thinking about finding someplace less extravagant. That, and I like Mabel's house. It's old-fashioned and well-built. It may be a bit large for me, but I will want to invite some of my racing friends down from London from time-to-time. Besides, the staff is already in place."

"I'd sell it to you at an excellent price," Harriet said with a laugh. "Wouldn't it be wonderful having us all together in Rexton?"

"Has everyone gone mad?" Aunt Edna howled.

"Excuse me, Harriet," her mother said, pushing her over to sit beside her sister. "Now, Edna, this is the answer to all of your worries. You were concerned that Harriet would be so taken with London that she wouldn't come back, and now she'll be settling down right here in Rexton."

"Were you, Aunt?" Harriet said, touched that the old lady had missed her.

"Hush," Aunt Edna said, glaring at her niece before returning her attention to her sister.

"And you were worried that Harriet would sell Mabel's house, and that strangers would make all kinds of dreadful changes to it."

"I like it just the way it is, Mrs. Slater," the colonel added.

"Also, you won't have to worry about where the money is coming from to replace the roof on your house, now that I'll be sharing the expenses."

"That's true. I hated to ask my daughters for help."

"You see, Aunt Edna," Harriet said, reaching around her mother to squeeze her aunt's hand, "everything is going to turn out better than you had imagined."

"Well, I'll have to think about it. I shall rest in my room before dinner. Don't forget that Mr. Ash of yours is coming. He just about went clear out of my mind with everything that's happening around here."

"I won't forget, Aunt Edna. I have plans for Mr. Ash, too," Harriet boldly said.

Aunt Edna shook her head. "I didn't know what I was agreeing to when I took you into my house, Harriet Walters. To think of all that has happened to me in just one short year."

"I know, Aunt. Isn't it exhilarating?"

"Humph," the old lady said as she stamped out of the room.

Chapter Forty

Mr. Ash, looking very presentable in his best waistcoat and Sunday pair of shoes, struggled to follow the dinner conversation that evening. Everyone was speaking at once and interrupting each other. Aunt Edna was negotiating her share of the colonel's hazelnut harvest that autumn. Mrs. Walters was begging Harriet to expand the servants' quarters in the cottage from two bedrooms to three in case she wished to hire more staff in the future. Harriet was trying to convince Aunt Edna that she was perfectly capable of looking after a few chickens, while Aunt Edna insisted that no lady should ever clean out a hen house.

The schoolmaster was agreeing with Mrs. Walters that apple blossom wallpaper would look lovely and fresh in the parlour when he noticed that everyone else had stopped talking. Looking up from his raspberry custard tart, he saw the colonel smiling at Harriet, and Mrs. Slater staring at him.

"I beg your pardon, Mr. Ash. Our conversation has been rather scattered this evening," Harriet's mother said. "Would you care for some more wine?"

"Better not, young man, you don't have much of a head for drink, as I recall," Aunt Edna interjected.

"Aunt!"

"You and Mabel may have hid it from everyone else, but don't think that I didn't notice, Harriet. Not that it was his fault. My cider is pretty potent, and shouldn't be forced in imprudent amounts on people with empty stomachs. Bear that in mind this fall, Colonel," she added, wagging a finger at the gentleman.

"Is that so, Mrs. Slater? Perhaps you'll try some of my home-made currant wine, then? It's very tasty, and it has some kick."

Aunt Edna smiled. "Once I've pressed some cider, we'll have a little dinner party."

The gentleman raised his glass. "Last man – or woman – standing wins."

Aunt Edna laughed out loud. "You might make a good neighbour at that, sir. Well, if we're all finished, shall we rise, ladies?"

"If you don't mind, Mr. Ash, it's a fine evening and I'd rather go for an after-dinner walk than sit here drinking port and smoking cigars with you," the colonel said.

"Fine with me, sir," Ash replied. "I'm not really fond of either."

"I hope you don't mind, Colonel, but I would like to kidnap Mr. Ash for a walk with me," Harriet said. The young man stiffened and stared at her from across the table.

"Not at all," the colonel replied. "The gentleman is all yours."

"Would that be agreeable to you, sir?"

"A walk would be enjoyable. Lead on, Miss Walters."

Harriet and Ash began by following the gravel path through the formal garden, Harriet pointing out one or two of her favourite blooms while Ash remained mostly silent. As they emerged from the box hedge, the young woman indicated the miniature temple on the crest of the hill.

"It has a wonderful view, particularly at this time of day when the sun gives the garden a lovely golden sheen. Would you care to see it?

"It sounds idyllic," he said, indicating that she should precede him.

They followed the bridge over the brook and arrived at the temple. Harriet passed through the portico to sit on the wrought-iron bench. Ash paused on the threshold, looking around the plain interior before taking a seat on the bench beside her. Rays of warm sunlight puddled on the floor just inside the doorway, but did not penetrate into the cool interior. Ash gazed out over the landscape while Harriet studied his profile. He turned and looked into her eyes.

"Miss Walters, I think that you have brought me here for a purpose. What do you want with me?" he asked in a cool voice.

Harriet was startled by the directness of his question. "You come right to the point," she said. He said nothing. "Very well, sir, there is something that I wish to discuss with you." He nodded. "As you heard tonight, I have made some important decisions recently."

"Yes," he interrupted. "I was amazed to hear that you are buying Mrs. Higgins' property. Why?"

Harriet explained her desire to live in the country without being too far away from her mother and her aunt, as well as her need for independence. "I could not continue to live in my aunt's home under her thumb, although she is dear to me."

"I can understand your desire to have your own household, Miss Walters. What did Mrs. Higgins say to your offer?"

"She was doubtful, at first. Like my aunt, she did not think the cottage an appropriate place for an unmarried young lady to live alone. She also feared that my offer came out of a desire to do her a kindness rather than serving my best interests. I was able to convince her that her cottage would make the perfect home for me. In the end, she was pleased that her house was going to someone who would treasure it. Her family will help her to pack her belongings, and she will move in with her nephew at week's end. She cried a little to think that she was actually leaving her home. I invited her to visit anytime she liked, but she declined. 'It wouldn't be wise, Miss Walters,' she said. 'Better to make a clean break of it and move on. But you must come and visit me and Oliver at my nephew's house,' and I promised her that I would."

Ash nodded. "I congratulate you. Everything has worked out magically well. You have found the perfect home, your mother is taking up residence with your aunt, you have secured a worthy owner for Mrs. Evans' house, and you are keeping the colonel close by. But you have still not answered my question. What do you want with me?"

Harriet rose from the bench, took a deep breath, and blurted out, "I want you to marry me."

Ash stared at her, his mouth dropping open. "What on earth for?" he asked.

"Because you have so much to offer, Mr. Ash."

The young man laughed. "You must be jesting. I have nothing to offer you, or any other woman. I have no home, my salary is inappreciable, my possessions are of no monetary value, and any inheritance I receive from my parents will have only sentimental value. All that I possess you see sitting here before you on this bench."

Harriet sat beside him and reached for his arm. "You do not see it from my point of view, sir."

"Pray, enlighten me then."

"When I marry, my inheritance will become my husband's property. Now, I might have gone to London seeking a man of fortune to combine his resources with my own, making us both appreciably wealthier, but what would my life have been? I would have had to assume a place in society, spending my days visiting other well-to-do wives, going to dinner parties, perhaps taking up a charity, and breeding. Remember the story I told you about my friend, Abigail Pope?"

"The young woman who studies medicine?"

"That's right. Abigail's great ambition is to put her medical knowledge to good use. She was willing to marry a missionary and leave her family for an uncivilized country to achieve that goal. Fortunately, she met Harold Gwinn, who will allow her to become his assistant when he opens his medical practice. And they love each other. It is a brilliant, providential match."

"So, you want me to be your 'Harold Gwinn,' Miss Walters? Tell me, what are your ambitions?"

Harriet stared at him. "I want to explore the world around me. I want to learn. I want to speak with educated people – men of ideas – not just parish widows or society people who care only for their own advancement or amusements. I want to study history. I want to travel and learn about other cultures. I want adventure and a big life, not a life dictated by society. And, when I am not travelling, I want to live in the country surrounded by nature and sunshine and peace. I want freedom, Mr. Ash."

The young man's eyes grew large as he listened to her speech. "And you think that I will somehow provide you with all of that?"

"Yes, I do. Tell me – if you had not so selflessly given up your savings to your sister this summer – what would you have done with your holidays?"

"Gone to Bath to examine the Roman ruins."

"Exactly. And what would you do if you had a thousand pounds to spend any way you chose?"

Ash's eyes shone. "I would go to Rome, Miss Walters. I would see the Coliseum, the Pantheon, and the Forum. I would study the ancient civilization that melded with our own eighteen centuries ago."

"Yes. And if you were in Italy, would you stop to visit other cities, such as Florence and Venice?"

"Of course. Who would not want to see all that architecture and art and history – to absorb them like a sponge – to wallow in them, in fact?"

Harriet nodded, her body tense with excitement. She took his hands. "We could do those things together, Joseph. We could have those adventures. We could share Mrs. Evans' inheritance and have the lives we both dream of."

Ash ran his hands threw his hair and jumped up, pacing in the same space that Harriet had just vacated. "My teaching . . . ?"

"You could continue teaching if you wanted. That was one of my considerations in buying Mrs. Higgins' cottage – its proximity to the school."

Ash stared at her.

"You could teach during the school year, and we could travel in the summer. What a wondrous life we could have! While you are teaching, I could read and study. You could direct my education in British and Roman history. And we could have dinner parties for the other teachers. I would particularly like to know the headmaster's wife. She sounds so likable. And I would like to know Mr. Harris better, too. He always has such a twinkle in his eye. I think that he must have a devilish sense of humour."

Ash smiled. "Oh, he does, Harriet. They are very likable people. They've been good to me, too. I would enjoy entertaining them in my own home."

Harriet held out her hand and he took it, joining her on the bench again. "What do you think, Joseph? Doesn't it sound like the perfect life?"

He beamed back at her. "It does. It sounds wonderful." Then the smile transformed itself into a frown. "But, Harriet, you don't need me to have that wonderful life. You are an independent woman of means. You could achieve all of that on your own."

Harriet blushed and glanced down at her hands. "I could, Joseph, but I don't want to be alone anymore. I want someone to share my life with. More than that, I want someone who wants to share his life with me. Someone who finds me attractive, someone who could want me in that way." Her voice faltered, and her eyes glistened with tears. She closed them, and turned her face away in embarrassment.

She felt Joseph's calloused hand cup one side of her face and turn it back toward him. She sighed and opened her eyes. His other hand rose to brush the hair away from her face, coming to rest on her shoulder. She felt too vulnerable to look into his eyes, afraid that she would find pity there. He drew her to him, resting his face against hers. Tentatively, she reached her hands around his back, trembling. His face turned, and he kissed her on the cheek, the eyes, and then tenderly on the mouth. Harriet was very still, her eyes closed, waiting. The breath caught in his throat, and he kissed her more fervently, pressing her body hard against his. Harriet gasped and returned his kiss.

An hour later, the evening sky was a dusky blue with the last tinges of the pink and purple sunset fading from it. It was dark inside the temple. Harriet sat on Ash's lap, clasped in his arms, their heads touching as they talked. Ash looked up and sighed.

"We must go, my love. If we don't get back soon, your aunt will come looking for us. If she found us like this, I fear that she would have me horsewhipped."

Harriet laughed, laying her head on Ash's shoulder and snuggling against his chest. He groaned. "No, don't start all that again or we'll never leave. Of course, if things get out of hand, you know what to do with scoundrels." Harriet pulled a face and punched him lightly on the shoulder. "Ouch," he complained, "the abuse starts already."

Harriet laughed, gave him a quick kiss, and hopped off his lap. She stretched her back to ease muscles cramped in one position for too long. Ash rubbed his legs to improve their circulation.

Harriet grinned mischievously and held out her hand. "Come, Joseph, let's go in and tell them that we've set the wedding day. I can't wait to see Aunt Edna's face when we tell her that we're getting married in just three weeks. Long enough to read the bans, and then off for a quick honeymoon in Bath!"

Chapter Forty-One

When Harriet and Ash returned to announce their wedding plans, they found the two ladies and the colonel worrying about their whereabouts. Their announcement set the house into an uproar, and it was full on two o'clock in the morning before Colonel York rescued the exhausted schoolmaster and delivered him home in his carriage.

Mrs. Walters and Harriet weathered Aunt Edna's emotional storm over the next two days by never being at home, but after that the aunt could not resist getting caught up in the wedding preparations and the cottage's renovation plans. Mrs. Higgins left her home at the end of the week as planned, and then the five were always either at the cottage or at Aunt Edna's house.

Harriet, Ash, and the colonel did have a day's respite spent visiting a racing acquaintance of the colonel's to purchase a carriage and a pair of horses. The middle-aged gentleman wanted to sell his curricle in favour of something speedier, and Colonel York bargained him down to a very good price.

The curricle, looking very festive decked out in bows and ribbons, carried Harriet and the colonel to St. Michael's Church on her wedding day. Harriet looked radiant in her wedding gown with her father's seed pearl necklace around her throat, while Joseph looked handsome in the new wedding suit his parents had purchased for him. Ash's sister and her husband were not able to return from Spain in time for the wedding, but the bridegroom's family was represented by his parents and his four little nieces and nephews. Harriet's brother-in-law gave her away, while Helen had an extra handkerchief ready for Mrs. Walters' happy tears. Even Aunt Edna's eyes were suspiciously shiny during the ceremony. Mrs. Higgins and Oliver sat in the pew behind Harriet's mother. Aunt Edna insisted that the wedding meal be served in her home, and

Harriet compromised by paying for the refreshments. Mr. Ash, Senior, his wife, and their grandchildren stayed at Aunt Edna's house for the festivities, while Helen, Sinclair, and their nine children were accommodated in Mrs. Evans' larger home, affording the bride and bridegroom's families an opportunity to get to know each other. Harriet escaped the bedlam by sleeping in her cottage the night before the wedding, and she and Ash spent a blissful wedding night there before departing for Bath the next day.

Weeks later when the school term was already a month old, Harriet and Ash invited the headmaster and his wife to a small dinner party to celebrate the completion of the renovations. Mrs. Walters, Aunt Edna, and Colonel York had overseen the changes to the cottage during the couple's wedding trip. As a wedding present, Aunt Edna allowed Harriet to poach Sara, the kitchen maid, to be her new cook, and Cook had been ferried over to the cottage to assist the nervous girl with the dinner party preparations. Susan, another recent hire, served at table.

"I think that Sara did very well tonight, don't you, Joseph?" Harriet said, crawling into bed beside her husband after their guests had departed.

"Yes, everything was very good," he replied, opening his arms to snuggle his new wife against his chest.

"Susan had one difficult moment when she spilled wine while serving Mrs. Harris, but she managed to finish the rest of the meal without any other mishaps."

"I didn't notice, my love," Ash replied, his chin grazing the top of Harriet's head as he yawned.

"I didn't think so. You were busy talking with Mr. Harris at the time. Mrs. Harris simply blotted the spill with her napkin without even interrupting the conversation. She is just as kind as I imagined her to be, and she shares the headmaster's sense of humour, too."

"Yes, they are very good people," Ash murmured. Harriet glanced up into his face. Joseph's eyes had already closed.

"Darling, there is something I've been longing to discuss with you all day, but we haven't been alone together since breakfast."

"Hmm?"

Harriet rolled onto her back and reached for the bed-side table. "Rogers sent a note after you left this morning, asking me to drop by Mrs. Evans' house. He said that there was a packet he wished to give to me before the colonel takes possession of the house next Monday." Harriet reached into the table drawer and pulled out a diamond necklace, the gems sparkling brilliantly in the candle light. She held the necklace at arm's length, turning it this way and that to catch the fire in the central pendant.

"This is one of two necklaces that Mrs. Evans always kept in her drawing room safe, the other being the pearl necklace that I gave to Diane. Rogers said that this necklace was Mrs. Evans' favourite, but she was never comfortable wearing it. Mr. Evans had exquisite taste, don't you think?"

Harriet glanced at her husband, who was fast asleep. She returned the necklace to the drawer and blew out the candle. Rolling over, she cradled against his side. Harriet's hair spilling over his bare chest must have tickled Ash, for he reached up to scratch before draping an arm over her shoulders.

"Never mind, darling," Harriet whispered. "I'll keep it as a surprise for the morning." She kissed his shoulder and burrowed down to sleep.

~ The End ~

Always a voracious reader, Cathy Spencer cut her teeth on Sir Arthur Conan Doyle, Agatha Christie, Jane Austen, and Charlotte Brontë. She is married to a singer/actor/university teacher. He didn't actually say, "Marry me and see Canada" when he proposed, but that's practically what happened. They have lived on the west coast in Vancouver, on the east coast in St. John's, in Calgary, and are currently living in Hamilton, Ontario.

Cathy has written a cozy mystery with an amateur sleuth set in the Rocky Mountain Foothills of Alberta. It's the first in the Anna Nolan series, entitled *Framed for Murder*. She's currently working on the sequel, *Town Haunts*. She's also written another historical romance set in England after the Napoleonic wars entitled *The Marriage Market*, plus two collections of short stories.

Connect with Cathy Spencer
Facebook: https://www.facebook.com/CathySpencerAuthor
Blog: http://cmspencer.blogspot.ca/